Copyright © 2024 J Benjamin Sanders Jr

All rights reserved.

No part of this book may be reproduced in any form or by any electronic or mechanical means, including information storage and retrieval systems, without written permission from the author, except for the use of brief quotations in a book review.

Edited by Twyla Beth Lambert

Cover Design by ambient studios

Print ISBN 978-1-957529-15-8

Ebook ISBN 978-1-957529-16-5

LCCN 2024931805

This book is a work of fiction. Names, characters, businesses, places, events, locales, and incidents are either the products of the author's imagination or used in a fictitious manner. Any resemblance to actual persons, living or dead, or actual events, is purely coincidental. Brand names are the property of the respective companies; author and publisher hold no claim.

MEXICANOS HUSTLE

J BENJAMIN SANDERS, JR

publisher's note

Although not fantasy, nor science fiction, this book takes place
in a different world. Language and attitudes contained herein
are reflective of the time in which the story is set and do not
align with contemporary sensibilities.

This book is dedicated to my wife, Rosemary Gouger, the Goddess in my life who sustains me. The Dallas Fort Worth Writer's Workshop who schooled me. My sons Brian and Robert, who I wish could have been here to share in the dream. And lastly, the real Glenn Owen Helka, who, in 1968, served beside me in India Company, Third Battalion, Fifth Marines in Vietnam. He, like so many young men, never made it back home.

one

LYING FLAT ON HIS BACK, Glenn Helka stared up at the dizzily swirly lights beneath the steel ceiling. There were a lot more up there than he remembered when he climbed into the ring. He heard a train roaring past, its heavy iron wheels rumbling over the track, ready to grind him to a pulp if he didn't get his ass in gear. He would have, too, if he hadn't been hit by the thing. He saw it coming, big and black. No matter how hard he tried to get out of its way, he couldn't move fast enough. Then he heard the counting.

"Four."

Glenn rolled over onto his side, managing to get to his knees. His hair hung down in front of his eyes, but it didn't matter—the sweat and a right hook had already blinded him.

"Five."

Taking a deep breath, he reached out to grab the ropes, using them to help him climb to his feet. He leaned back, blinking hard. The roar of the train turned into the roar of the crowd. He stared at the man across the ring, but he was no more than a blur.

"Six."

Glenn shoved his mouthpiece back in, swallowing blood that lay on his tongue like a copper penny. Something hot ran down over his lips and dripped off his chin. He tried to breathe in, but his nose had been filled with mud. He could no longer smell the stale cigarette smoke, the rosin, or the broken dreams.

"Seven."

He wondered if Paco might throw in the towel. Part of him wanted his friend to do it. Part of him wanted the fight to go on. Rolling his shoulders, he stepped away from the ropes.

"Eight. You good?"

Glenn nodded. "Yeah, I'm good."

"Tell me your name."

"Glenn Helka."

"What day is it?"

"Thursday."

"How many fingers?" The referee lifted his hand with his thumb and middle finger folded over, making the okay sign.

"Three."

"Okay. Give me your gloves." The referee wiped them on his shirt before he backed away, shooting out his right hand like a knife. "Box."

Julio moved in, his shoulders rolling, head bobbing, tasting his opponent's blood. Glenn saw his predatory smile behind the massive mouthpiece. Julio was already counting his purse, hoping for a quick end, but Glenn had other thoughts. Hunching low, Glenn crossed the ring to meet him. He caught Julio's straight right but missed the uppercut until it met his chin and he met the canvas.

The only thing that saved Glenn was the bell. Paco dragged him to his stool like a piece of fresh roadkill. Glenn leaned back with his arms slung over the ropes. Sweat poured off his naked chest, leaving the thick hair matted and curling. Behind him, the crowd sounded like a whisper in an echo chamber. Either everyone had caught laryngitis at the same time, or his ears had quit working. It wasn't them inside the ring getting their hat handed to them—the old-timey, polite way of saying Glenn was getting his ass kicked.

Paco cracked an ammonia capsule under his nose. Glenn couldn't smell it, but burning fumes hitting his eyes managed to get a few of Glenn's synapses working. Still, he felt like a V8 firing on four cylinders. He began to think he had been out of the game for too long. Maybe he shouldn't have watched that second Ali-Frazier fight at Seamus's bar last month. It probably gave him delusions of grandeur, like the old fire horse who didn't know when to retire and went chasing after the firetruck only to find himself in the way, with nothing to do until they hauled him off to the glue factory.

"*Jefe*. I knew this was a bad idea. It's a stupid way to bring in a bond jumper. That guy is bigger, faster, and a lot younger than you."

"You left out he hits harder, probably goes to church regularly, and is nice to dogs. Hell, the judges could award him the fight on points for being an upstanding citizen and the way he treats his mama." Breathing deep, he turned his head and spit blood onto the edge of the ring.

"I think you should be more worried about him knocking you out than losing on points. I'm throwing in the towel."

"Don't. I still have a chance." Glenn shook his head, forcing himself to concentrate through the thick sludge that currently served as a thought process. The sponge slammed into his back. The cold water hit his overheated body, releasing a gasp of pleasure. Glenn tried to breathe deep through his nose, but the air couldn't get through the swelling.

Glenn looked across the ring at his opponent, slumped on his stool as if he had the fight in the bag, his cut man working on the slice over his left eye. In the center, a pretty, braless ring girl pranced around on a pair of stiletto heels so high her ankles wobbled when she walked. Even Glenn noticed how the stilt-like shoes made her ass do interesting things. She wore a midriff-baring t-shirt and shorts two sizes too small. The girl flashed a toothy smile while holding a large sign with the number four over her head. It got a roar of approval from the crowd, filled with catcalls and indecent propositions that would make a Tijuana whore blush with shame. "At least we know where he is. If I get a knockout, he won't give us any trouble when we slap the cuffs on. Plus, we can add the purse to the rest of the bounty. Call it a bonus."

"From what I'm seeing, that's a big if. You sure doing all this is worth it?"

The bowtie-wearing referee in a sweat-stained shirt came over. He pointed at Paco and growled. "Clear the ring."

Paco shoved Glenn's mouthpiece in, grabbed the bucket, and scuttled backward. He wrapped his hand around the stool leg, then waited for his man to stand before he dragged it out. The crowd roared when the bell sounded, anticipating bloodletting mayhem. Glenn raised his gloved hands and advanced toward the center of the ring, rolling his shoulders and pawing the air with his left. His focus was intense enough to suppress all the sounds except for his—and his opponent's—raspy breathing.

Julio Martinez, who fought under the name of Butcher Boy Vasquez, met him there. Blood still trickled down the side of his face from the cut caused by one of Glenn's savage right hooks. Glenn read the anger in the other man's eyes and the confidence. After all, the promoter had promised the man an easy fight with a no-name opponent.

"You going down, *puta*," Julio said. He threw a crushing left hook toward Glenn's ribs. Or it would have been crushing if it landed. Glenn leaned over and caught the punch on his elbow, but missed blocking the hard right that met his jaw, knocking it sideways hard enough to send his mouthpiece spinning through the air. It did several slow cartwheels, throwing off blood and spit. Glenn lost sight of it when he toppled backward like an East Texas pine at a beaver convention. He touched ass first, then his shoulders, and his head last. That's when the lights went out.

The next thing Glenn knew, he was staring up at a company of angels circling over his head, ready to escort his soul up to the Pearly Gates where Saint Peter would most likely review his life and *tsk* with disappointment. The angels soon faded, and he tried to focus but saw two of everything. Two referees held up the hand of a couple of Julios who danced around on the balls of their feet. Paco pulled him upright—the ammonia smell slapping him in the face again—reminding him of an ignored pail full of piss-soaked diapers.

"You have him on the ropes now," Paco snarled.

"Screw you. So, he got in a lucky punch."

"Yeah. The fight's over. You got the loser's purse." Paco helped Glenn to stand well enough to watch Julio come across the ring to shake hands and give the winner's speech, but the buzzing in Glenn's ears made it hard to hear. He probably said something about what a good fighter Glenn was and how Julio got lucky. They both knew it was bullshit, but polite bullshit, since Glenn got his ass beat but good.

Glenn thanked the referee, then climbed through the ropes to join Paco on the way to the locker room.

"Go by the office and pick up the money, but hurry. We gotta catch Julio before he can leave." Glenn stripped off his gloves and grabbed a towel to rub across his face, wiping away the Vaseline, blood, and sweat. He skipped the shower, doing a quick change of clothes and stuffing his fighting gear in a bag. Paco showed up while Glenn was bent over tying his shoe and waved a twenty at him.

"Should have known that bastard would cheap out on us." Glenn grabbed his jacket, tossing his bag to Paco, who he grabbed it in midair. They hurried out the side door that led to the parking lot. Out there, Glenn tasted the tarry flavor of sunbaked asphalt mingled with traces of alcohol from broken whiskey bottles and piss where most of the local derelicts found it more convenient to empty their bladders.

Relieved when he saw no sign of Julio, he waited against the wall covered with peeling posters of bygone fights after sending Paco on to fetch the car.

Glenn didn't have long to wait. The door swung back and a grinning Julio stepped through, his teeth flashing like neon lights in a bar window. The fighter was walking on air, swaggering like his farts smelled like vanilla and lilacs.

Digging his right hand into his jacket pocket, Glenn pushed off the wall and called out. "Hey, Butcher Boy."

"Yeah, man?" Julio looked confused for a second until he recognized his handiwork on Glenn's face.

"That was one hell of a fight. I didn't get to give you a proper handshake back in the ring. Thought I would hang around, hoping I could catch you before you took off, to congratulate you on one helluva fight."

"I appreciate that, man." Julio stuck out his paw. Glenn pulled his out of his pocket and threw a quick uppercut that landed on the point of the fighter's chin. It popped like a can of beer run over by a semi. Julio's eyes rolled up, and he fell like someone stole all his bones. Then Glenn kicked him in the balls for the hell of it.

Grinning, Glenn slipped his brass knuckles back into his pocket and reached for his cuffs.

Monica Hamilton drove into the small border town of McHenry, Texas, passing anyone who got in her way. She nearly forced some slow-moving vehicles off the road into a ditch, passing them with a hand shoved against the horn like she was Gabriel calling out the army of God's angels. Her boat of a gray Buick got about eight miles to the gallon, which Monica thought was hell on anyone's pocketbook ever since the Arabs decided to cut off the oil supply to the world so they could drive up the price to more than eighty cents a gallon. Who in their right mind thought that was a good idea? She zoomed past the city sign—considering the speed limit a suggestion—where several local civic organizations' placards had been hung to advertise how urbane those in charge considered their tiny metropolis to be. She thought that soon they would be as snooty as those assholes in Highland Park, the hoity-toity enclave on the outskirts of Dallas where she'd lived for the past twenty years. Here, she flew past signs for the Veterans of Foreign Wars, Rotary Club, Freemasons, and several others she failed to read in passing. Most of the homes on the north side of town were cheap, frame houses with clapboard or aluminum siding. Decorated with minimal effort and little imagination, they didn't impress her. Not that she found anything wrong with small Texas towns. They just weren't her thing. It wasn't because they never seemed to have a decent restaurant, but the shopping was always the pits. No Tiche or Neiman-Marcus to be found nearer than Houston.

Monica had picked the car up in Brownsville after she flew back from the Mexican resort town of Jalpa, desperate to find some way she could get her son, Darren, home. So far, she hadn't had much luck.

She looked past the unremarkable neighborhood to see the steeply sloped spires of the courthouse peeking over the rooftops like a magician's castle. The perfect marker to guide her downtown. Monica checked in her rearview mirror at a stop sign, saw nobody behind her, then glanced down at the crumpled and coffee-stained card to check the address for Helka Investigations one last time. It's not that she had trouble with street names, but the numbers often slipped her mind.

Family shops filled the downtown square except for the Woolworth's—big whoop on that one—and maybe the Rexall. Monica pulled in front of the only hotel, the Paraíso. It wasn't much to look at with its worn art deco façade. A shabby reminder of what the town had once been or pretended to be. Monica figured for one night she could deal with the pretentiousness before she had to drive back to Brownsville and catch a flight to Love Field.

The inside didn't look much better than the outside. It showed the wear and tear of years, no doubt from back when Black Jack Pershing was chasing bandits back into Mexico and he needed a place to prop up his boots. Monica bet, if she looked closely enough, she could still find some of his horse shit on the furniture. She carried her bags to the check-in desk, dropped them, and slapped the service bell. A man in a cheap suit stepped out of a tiny office, flashing a weary smile in her direction.

"May I help you?"

"A room for the night. I assume you take Diners Club." It came out more of a challenge than a question, but the clerk seemed to be up to it.

"Of course. We don't get many people who stop here that use it, but we accept it." He slid the register across for Monica to fill out.

"I want your best room." She grabbed the pen, wrote out the requested information, then pushed it back.

"Will you require anything else?"

"A hot bath. A bartender who knows how to make a decent martini. Also, a restaurant that serves something other than Tex-Mex or chicken fried steaks. Not necessarily in that order, although it would be nice to have the martini first."

The clerk passed her a key. "Three-twenty, we recently had it remodeled. The hotel bar is across the lobby. I'm afraid we don't have an inhouse kitchen, but we can order something in..." He glanced down at the register. "Mrs. Hamilton."

"I also need to find a private detective by the name of Glenn Helka. I have a job for him."

two

GLENN AND PACO dropped Julio off at the jail, leading him in while he was still unsteady on his feet, his face slack, and his eyes unfocused. Glenn's face had turned near black where Julio had punched him. It made him look like he was coming home from a minstrel show, still wearing half his makeup.

After getting his papers signed, Glenn dropped Paco off and headed for his home away from the office. The single-wide trailer house sat on a bare lot on the edge of McHenry, with no neighbor closer than a mile. Some folks had taken to calling them "mobile homes" to make them sound classier, like you can call a house made of tin and cardboard that came on wheels "classy." Except there wasn't much mobile about a twelve by sixty-foot metal building with no tires. The thing rested atop stacks of cinder blocks, secured with straps of steel to keep it from being blown all the way to the Panhandle in case a tornado or hurricane decided to drop in. To Glenn's mind, that was the only time it would be mobile.

A long time ago, the thing had been painted beige and white. Over time, it had faded to a Pepto Bismol pink with tints of dirty gray. He had a cooling unit plugged into every window to help him survive the South Texas summers. A doghouse sat to one side—only he didn't have a dog. Alongside that sat a carport above a faded cherry-red '52 Ford pickup, polka dotted with smears of pink putty and with no engine. The pickup sat up on cinder blocks, leaving the bare wheel hubs exposed. He pulled up next to the steps, realizing he forgot to leave the stoop light on. No one with a lick of sense would ever describe it as a porch, even under the most generous terms. There was barely enough room for him to teeter on the top step while he dug for the key.

Glenn grabbed his gear and stepped inside. The place smelled like a grease pit at a gas station. He tossed his bag on the sofa and headed for the refrigerator where he grabbed a bottle of Shiner. Taking a seat at the kitchen table, he stared at the Ford's engine spread out in parts, a shit-load of assembly still required, the result of one of those promises he made to himself to rebuild it in his spare time. It had been nearly three years now, and the pieces required more dusting than oiling.

"When this next job is done." He took a healthy swig, belched, then pointed the neck of the bottle at the motor. "I promise."

There was no sign his ex-wife, Alice, had ever lived there except for a few pictures he hadn't gotten around to dealing with. Unless someone took the time to look in the spare bedroom where he had tossed all her stuff before he locked the door—clothing, makeup, and whatever she left behind after she had the divorce papers served. Glenn would sooner set fire to it, burn the whole place down, than look in there again.

Instead, he grabbed another Shiner. He stepped outside where he flopped down in a seat beside the cut-down oil drum filled with wood scraps. He grabbed a fistful of newspaper and stuffed it between the wood. Pulling out his Zippo, he fired it off. Ignoring his body's complaints, he sank back to drink his Shiner while gazing up at the stars. He reflected on his stupidity, climbing into the ring like that, thinking he could still throw leather like he was a teenager. Tasting blood, the cold beer felt good against his sore gums. The only sound beyond the crackle of the burning wood were crickets, coyotes, and maybe the whisper of the wind if you strained really hard to listen. A place where a man could, if he had a mind to, do some heavy thinking. Or put on a quiet drunk if thinking became too much of a burden.

His beer was half gone when he saw the lights, two angry-looking beams bouncing along the highway, sweeping around the curves in the road like they were on a snipe hunt. They neared his place before they slowed down and pulled in. The tires rolled smoothly over the dust and crunched over the gravel he used to fill the potholes in a vain attempt to keep the ground level. It stopped with its lights staring straight at him for a few seconds, bright as an accusing angel, before fading to an orange blink. The driver's door creaked open. The interior light was out, leaving the driver in the dark. A soft voice said, "My God, Glenn Helka. You sure look like shit."

three

ONE OF THE first things Monica did after reaching her room was to have room service send up three martinis. She knocked the first one back straight away. The second she drank a little slower while she stripped down to her birthday suit and ran the tub full of water. It was one of those old-fashioned clawfoot tubs big enough to do laps in. She sat on the toilet and rubbed her feet. Wearing even low heels was becoming uncomfortable. Driving made them hurt even more. She ran her hands over her belly rolls, slid them up to heft her titties, and rubbed underneath where her bra had been too tight and left red marks on her skin.

"Might as well breathe, girls. You're free for the night. Enjoy it while you can." Grabbing the last martini, she stepped into the tub and sat down. Monica let her body sink until her feet touched the end. The only parts of her body sticking out of the water were her head and nipples. The nipples stuck up like the noses of two inquisitive otters. Her head, brown hair cut short and feathered, lay back at the proper angle for her to pick up her drink and sip without spilling. She let the heat seep into her sore muscles while she considered how her trip to Mexico had gone. Not like she had expected. It couldn't have gone worse than if she'd planned to elope with her first cousin.

Two day earlier, she'd found herself on an old two-seat Cessna on her way down to Jalpa, staring out the window at the wall of mountains when the pilot's voice came through her headphones. "We are here, *Señora* Hamilton,"

It had been a rough, nearly two-hour flight from the Ruiz airport at Zacatecas. Add that to the two and a half hours it had taken to get from Dallas to Houston, plus another six to get to Zacatecas, it had left her feeling she'd been wrung out and put away wet. Then, finally in Jalpa, she'd had no more tears to spare. Her eyes had burned and she'd dreaded looking in the mirror, knowing she must be a sight, her makeup no doubt a soggy mask that would embarrass a clown. She hadn't had much time to pack after the call came about Darren. She'd tossed a change of clothes into a bag, figuring if she forgot anything, she would be able to buy what she needed at the hotel. It had already been late in the day. The sun had reached the peaks of the Sierra Morones Mountains, and the shadows had spread across the valley like an oil stain, painting the town of brightly colored buildings nestled between the two ranges a darker hue. The plane had tilted almost up on its side, then swung in a slow wide arc. Since the city had no airport, the pilot had had to search for a flat place to land. From what she could see, he hadn't had many places to choose from. Her contact had explained that the only safe place was a long, narrow field on the south side of town. He had agreed to meet her there.

The pilot had lined up the plane, easing the nose down when he spotted the impromptu strip. Monica's stomach had clawed at her throat while they descended. Flying had never been her strong suit. She didn't understand how a heavy plane could stay up in the air, but she sure as hell understood how it could fall to the ground.

"Hold on. This will be a bumpy landing," the pilot had warned before the wheels touched. It had hit hard enough for her head to snap back and her headphones to slip down. Gasping, she'd thought the seatbelt might cut her in two when the plane hit again. After a minute, the ride had smoothed out. They had rolled to a stop, and she'd silently sworn she would never do that again.

"We are here," the pilot had said, stating the obvious when he killed the engine, but Monica hadn't minded. Glad to be back on the ground again, she would have about killed for a decent martini, maybe maim for one, but would certainly have killed for two since, amenity-wise, the small plane left a lot to be desired. Like bitter coffee in a thermos bad.

"Thank you, Armando." Monica had slipped off the headphones and passed them to the pilot. She'd run her fingers through her brown hair, no doubt a mess.

"Your ride, I think she is here." He'd nodded forward. She had looked through the window to see an old Ford station wagon coming across the field, throwing up a cloud of dust as it bounced over the rough spots. Its antenna whipped back and forth through the air like a silver rapier ready to cut down anything that got in its way. The car had skewed to a shuddering stop beside the small plane, causing the antenna to do a final parry before settling down. A thin man with a Cesar Romero mustache and wearing an ill-fitting suit had unfolded himself from behind the wheel and waved.

"*Hola, Señora* Hamilton." He'd flashed a grin laced with gold, pulling out a handkerchief to mop his face while coming around to open her door.

"*Señor* Alejandra Manuel Rodriquez Esteban, attorney at law, at your service." He had extended a hand to help her step down. The air had seemed thinner there, heavy with the turpentine scent of juniper. It had mingled with the sweet and subtle smell of the early blooming prickly pear that grew in scattered patches on the hillsides.

"Thanks, Mister Esteban. I hope you have made all the proper arrangements. I'm anxious to return home as soon as possible. After they have released Darren." Monica had stood on the dusty ground beside the plane, trying to get her land legs back. She had rubbed her back, enjoying the cool breeze that came down from the mountains. For March, the day had felt quite warm. The air had been dry enough to suck the sweat from her blouse.

The attorney had grinned. "Please. Alejandro, *por favor*. Let me extend my condolences."

"That's very gracious of you. Now, about Darren."

"*Sí,* your son." He'd clenched his jaws, then stretched his mouth in a grotesque frown, looking like a man trying to figure out how to deliver bad news. "Well, it's the *policía*. There have been some complications in processing the paperwork. To release him from the hospital. There are certain requisites yet to be fulfilled to speed up the process."

"I see. I assume you're talking about a bribe. How much?" Monica had anticipated the problem and brought extra cash. That's the way Mexico worked, but that didn't make the idea any more palatable. Already sore and stiff from the long, rough trip, she hadn't been in any mood to nitpick.

"Not so much." He'd shrugged, his eyes everywhere but on her.

"How much?"

"A thousand *Americano*."

She had clenched her teeth until her jaws hurt. "Those thieving sons of bitches."

"*Por favor, señora*. Please let me drive you into town. Perhaps there is a way for the Honorable Captain Hernando de Lopez-Gutierrez to help you resolve this dilemma." Alejandro had opened the passenger door and waited.

Anxious to see Darren, Monica had held her tongue as she climbed in. She'd stared out the window on the drive into town, hardly noticing the green fields sprouting with whatever crop drove the local economy. They had entered the town, with its houses painted in bright colors dotting the European-style roads thanks to the French invasion some time back in the eighteen hundreds. Alejandro had continued along the street until they reached the local police station.

Alejandro had parked in front of the station, then fumbled out a handkerchief to wipe his face. "We are here. We must talk to the captain. He needs you to sign several more forms. You must offer him the money, but do it in a way that will not be deemed an insult. For a thief, our good captain is quite a stickler for following the proper decorum." He'd run a nervous hand over his oiled and slicked back hair. "I beg you, *señora*, do not do or say anything that could upset the captain, or he will make it harder for you to get your son released so you can take him home."

"You're the lawyer. I promise to hold my tongue until I can get Darren out of here. Like they say back home, you don't let a stranger salt your melon for you. Now let's get this over with." Monica had climbed out and crossed the walk to the front door. Alejandro had beat her there, holding it open so she passed through without slowing.

She'd followed the lawyer to a closed door. He had knocked, waiting until a deep voice called out for them to enter. Inside, she'd stared at the walls decorated with framed photographs, certificates, and police patches. A man sat behind a desk wearing a dark brown and khaki uniform, the twin silver bars of his rank pinned to his collar. Monica had studied him, aware that he had to be the soulless bastard keeping her son from her.

"*Señora* Hamilton?" He'd motioned for her to take a seat.

"Captain Gutierrez." She had taken one seat. Alejandro had taken the other. "I understand you have some papers that require my signature."

Hernando Gutierrez had sighed, his head giving a weary nod, and then he'd shrugged, acting as if he bore the weight of the world on his shoulders. His demeanor said he would do all he could to accommodate the American *señora*, even though they both knew it was only so much bullshit. "It is so. Government regulations must be followed, even in times such as these." He had opened a file and pushed it across his desk, cocking his eyebrow in the manner of an unasked question.

"Of course, Captain." Monica had opened her purse to extract an envelope, placing it beside the file. "I believe you'll find all the documents in order."

The money had vanished, she'd signed the papers to his satisfaction, and they had gone back into a file. Captain Hernando de Lopez-Gutierrez had stood, set his cap on his head, and grabbed the hem of his jacket to pull it smooth. "*Gracias, Señora* Hamilton. Everything seems to be in order. I will send the forms to the hospital so they can release your son. Would you care to see his body?"

four

THE ALARM ERUPTED, sounding like an angry hornet. Glenn eased up, reached across, then slammed his hand down hard enough to shift his bed into another time zone. One that would allow him to get another hour of sleep. That dream ended when someone behind him started poking him hard enough to bruise his bruises. He took the hint and rolled up until he sat on the edge of his bed, resting there a moment with his hands on his knees and his head hanging down, trying to ignore the after-fight twinges and pains all fighters get, telling them they needed to consider finding another lifestyle.

A lot of people who served in the military get in the habit of becoming an early riser, jumping out of the rack before the sun can crack the horizon, ready to face the day after an icy shower while looking forward to a full breakfast. Glenn never got the hang of that. The little buzzer that rattled him from his sleep was lucky he didn't shoot the bastard. He arched his back, twisted sideways to take the strain off his tender ribs, and winced.

"Hurt?" A soft hand touched his back, then reached up until it slipped over his shoulder.

"Yeah. Butcher Boy Vasquez didn't hold back. I guess he wanted to make sure I got his message."

The bed shifted behind him. Two arms wrapped around, one hand slipped between his thighs to cup his crotch, and a sharp chin rested on his shoulder. He felt her nipples pressing against him, still swollen from last night's abuse. "What message would that be?"

"That I'm a naughty little boy who doesn't play well with others. Some people don't like that. They want to make you pay the price."

"Is that how you got all of these?" Her soft hands ran over his bruised flesh.

"Yeah, from a fight I had while busting a bond jumper."

"What about these?" Her head dropped until she could kiss the puckered scars across his back.

Glenn stiffened. "Stop it, Beth. You know I don't like to talk about that."

Beth fell back on the bed laughing. "I thought you liked the girl-friend experience."

"Not if it's going to cost me extra."

"Party pooper, you know I never charge you extra. I'm going to take quick a shower." The bed shifted again when Beth rolled off the other side and walked naked into his bathroom. He missed the warmth of her body pressed against his. Even feeling as beat up as he did, he took the time to admire the way her dimpled ass swayed and the way her long, bottle-blonde hair tumbled down to tickle her shoulder blades.

"Bring me the aspirin when you come back. I have a headache from hell." Glenn did his best to ignore the little man trying to beat his way through his skull from the inside.

"You shouldn't have drunk so much last night." She stuck her head out, tossing him the bottle.

"I only had two beers. Besides, it's not the alcohol. It's the abuse." He dumped out a handful of pills, washing them down with the dregs of the warm, flat Shiner sitting on his nightstand next to the empty foil rubber package.

"Lubricated for your pleasure, my ass," Glenn said softly. Fucking with a rubber was better than no fucking, which he would have been doing without one. The not fucking part. Beth had her rules—no rubber, no pussy. Glenn closed his eyes and scrunched his neck, waiting for the pain to subside.

Beth didn't hog the shower. Five minutes later she came out, sans makeup. She reached back to twist her hair into a ponytail, securing it with an elastic. Beth scoured the room for her clothes. Neither had been too particular about how they undressed when they came in last night after he called up at Lilly's house of... well, basically it was a house of whores, but that wouldn't look right on the marquee. Something like that would raise the hackles of all the church ladies in the neighborhood. Beth found her panties in the corner and scooped them up. She checked them over before frowning and shoving them in her purse. "We could have stayed at Lilly's. That would have saved me the drive out here."

"You know I prefer to do it in my bed."

"For god's sakes." Beth rolled her eyes as she slipped her bra on. "You can say fuck. It won't bother me. If it bothers you, you could always say screw." Doing the snap, she palmed the cups to adjust her tits. Not that she had an abundance, but she had enough.

Once she finished tightening the belt on her jeans, Beth slung her purse over her shoulder then stood there, hip shot to one side, hand resting on her waist.

"My wallet's on the dresser."

She nodded, picked it up, pulled out a twenty and a five. Beth showed him before she dropped the money into her purse. She turned to leave, paused a second, then turned back to cross the room, using her knee to pry his legs apart. Sliding between, she leaned down and kissed him. It was more than a friend's kiss but less than a lover's. "Same time next week?"

"Better wait for me to call you. I'm headed out of town for a few days. Not sure when I'll get back."

"Your loss, lover. You know what happens when you don't fuck regularly—that shit backs up and gives you an awful disposition. I mean, even worse than usual." She sashayed across the room, flashing him an over-the-shoulder grin before she vanished. He sat there until he heard the front door click, followed by her car starting and a spray of gravel from her spinning wheels.

"Damn it, Glenn. You're getting too old for this kind of life." He made his way to the shower, hoping the hot water would wash away some of the sins and pain. Mostly the pain. He felt like he could live with the sins when it came down to it.

He considered making his bed, but gave it up as a lost cause, even as the Marine in him said to do it. His battered and bruised body said fuck it, it would only be messed up again later. After he dressed, he peeked into the refrigerator. He saw nothing but bottles lined up like soldiers, Cokes on the left, Shiners on the right, with a no man's land between them. He had once put some leftover Mexican food in there. It didn't make it.

Glenn decided he needed coffee, lots of java juice to kickstart both body and mind. He knew the best place to get it. He drove into McHenry proper, parking outside his office for a few minutes, dreading the walk up the stairs. Helka Investigations—that's what the sign on the door to his office said—was located above the McHenry Electronics store, whose motto was, *Life too hard? We make it easier with electricity.* Like it was some sort of challenge. Hell, Ben Franklin did it with a kite and a key.

That's how he made his living, investigating. How he ended up in the asshole of the world called McHenry, Texas, on the Mexican border? Well, first of all, it's home. His daddy, Burt Helka, still lived there. The old man still needed him to be around. He had been pushed into his present career by his friend Charlie Gaines, who figured if he was going to be a pain in the ass, he might as well be earning money to do it. The office might not be much, but it was his as long as he could pay the rent, which was not always a given.

Inside the small office, he found his gal Friday, Paloma, behind her desk, sorting the mail. Overhead, a slow-moving ceiling fan barely stirred the stale air, and the dust motes seemed to be winning. Today, she looked comfortable in a thin cotton blouse and short skirt, her long, raven hair tied back in a ponytail, a style that seemed to be all the rage. Paloma looked up with a frown when he opened the door and stepped in.

"*Gato mojado*! What the hell did you get into?"

Touching the cuts and bruises on his face, he grinned. Then realized grinning had been a bad idea. It hurt like hell. "Picked up a little tip money while busting a bond skipper."

Paloma tilted her head toward his inner office. "Okay. Company."

"Paying or demanding?"

"A single woman. She doesn't look much like a bill collector. So, paying? Want a coffee?"

"Better wait until I find out what she wants, Doll. We might need something stronger."

Glenn found the woman sitting in his spare office chair, dressed in a neat gray suit, purse in her lap gripped tightly with both hands like she feared it would make a break for the door and only she could wrestle it into compliance. A pillbox hat rested on her short-styled brown hair, dropping a fishnet veil over her eyes. He sat down, staring as he gave her the once-over. A good-looking woman who appeared to be on the low side of forty. Her makeup applied with a deft touch that tried to hide the little sag to the jowls as well as the dark smudges and bags under her eyes. And a pair of two-toed crow marks at the eye's corners. She tried to smile, but her heart wasn't in it. All in all, she looked like somebody had beat her puppy, stuffed it into a tow sack, and tossed it off a bridge. "Mister Helka?"

He nodded. "Yes, ma'am."

"Your sign says you open for business at eight o'clock."

"More like *-ish*, depending on the kind of night I have. Now, what can I do for you?" Glenn pulled out his pack of Luckies, snapped the pack until one popped out, then grabbed it with his teeth.

"Well, if appearances mean anything, it looks like you had a bad one. Can I have one of those?"

"Sure." He extended the pack. She drew one out and leaned forward until she reached his lighter. She leaned back, letting a plume of smoke slip from her lips with a contented sigh.

"My name is Monica Hamilton. I need help. It's my son. I need him brought back from Mexico."

Sucking on his own cancer stick, Glenn let the smoke slip deep into his lungs and do its thing. Something about the first cigarette of the day took the edge off, gave one a sense of being alive... before the hacking set in. "Is he in some sort of trouble? In jail, or mixed up with the wrong people?"

"No, nothing like that." Tears welled, threatening to spill. Glenn shoved a box of tissues across his desk, watching as she plucked out a fistful. She dabbed at her eyes and released a shuddering sigh. "He's dead, Mister Helka. I need someone to bring him home."

"Escorting bodies is a little out of my area of expertise. Aren't there people who specialize in that sort of thing?"

"Yes. But there have been some problems. He died while on spring break—an accident. I have been dealing with the local authorities. But every time I believe we have things resolved, another issue crops up. I even went down there myself, but they still haven't released Darren. I don't know how much longer I can go on." She almost lost it then. It started with rising tears, trembling lips, leaking nose. Monica grabbed another fistful of tissues, blew her nose, and dabbed her eyes.

When she looked up, except for the red eyes, all traces of her momentary lapse were gone. She wore a look of anger for exposing herself so readily. Glenn felt she was one snapped nerve away from shooting someone. Lucky for him, that someone was on the other side of the border.

Glenn pulled a bottle of Kentucky Bonded from his bottom drawer, splashed a couple of fingers into a clean glass, and shoved it over. She stubbed out her cigarette, took a sip. She coughed when the whiskey hit her throat but recovered nicely. "Thank you."

"Let me guess. To them, you're nothing but a rich *Americano* who they want to grease the skids to get things moving. How much so far?"

"The first payment went to the police. A thousand dollars. Five hundred to the coroner. Another five hundred to the mortician. Then the local government officials demanded more money for the paperwork I need to submit so they can transport the body. So far, it's cost me three thousand dollars. That includes money that went to a local lawyer. He's telling me it could take another ten thousand and weeks before I can get my son home, maybe more."

Glenn poured himself a drink and knocked it back, savoring the burn. "So, you want me to be on hand when they release your son?"

"No, Mister Helka. I want you to steal Darren's body so he can be brought home."

five

GLENN STUDIED HER CAREFULLY, not sure he heard correctly. He had done what he considered some low things to earn his money since he opened up his business, but he had never resorted to snatching a body before, which made him question the trajectory of his career that he would even consider doing such a thing. He also saw the steel-like determination beneath the woman's pain. Not the usual female client who faked helplessness because they figured it would allow them to wind some poor stupid schmuck around their finger. This woman looked ready to fight, like a wolf mother protecting her dead cub. He found himself wanting to help this woman because of her grit. Also, the money would be a consideration; money was always a consideration.

"You do realize Mexico has its own way of conducting business? Me being an American wouldn't cut much ice with them. If I'm caught breaking their laws, they would as soon throw me into one of their prisons as look at me. The only way to get out of one of those hellholes is to buy your way out. As you can see, I'm not exactly rolling in it."

"I'm not an idiot, Mister Helka. Despite my handicap of being a woman."

"What does your husband think of this crazy idea?"

"I have been a widow for six years now. Even if I wasn't, it wouldn't make a damn bit of difference. I am prepared to pay you five thousand dollars to bring my son to me. Half now, half when he's delivered to the Eternal Slumber Funeral Home here in McHenry. I've already made arrangements for them to receive the body and get it ready to make the trip to Dallas." She opened her purse, removed a thick envelope, and placed it on his desk. "Inside you'll find the information you need to reach my contact in Jalpa. He's a local lawyer who has been well paid to help me with the problem. I expect him to assist you, as well."

"Five thousand to steal your son, then bring him home?" He waited a moment until she nodded.

Glenn stared at the envelope, his hand itching to count the money, but he didn't reach for it. He was on the precipice between a bad idea and good deed. That much money could dig him out of his hole, plus keep him going for a couple of months. "Plus, expenses."

He was pushing it. To be honest he was banking on her desperation. She glared, tight-lipped, but gave him another nod. "I have a room over at the Paraíso until tomorrow. Then I have to go back to Dallas for a few days to handle some pressing business. By the time I get back, I expect you'll have the job completed."

"One last question. Why me, lady?"

She stood, still clutching her purse like it was her favorite lap dog and she didn't want it to get its feet dirty. "To be honest? Everyone else from here to Brownsville turned me down. If you'd have turned me down, I'd have kept on driving until I reached El Paso."

He watched her march toward the door, then listened to the timpani of her heels on the stairs. Damn, that was an ego deflator. Glenn tried not to take it personal as he gripped the bottle to pour himself another drink, nursing the raw whiskey. Staring at the envelope, he thought, *barrel scrapings*, like in *from the bottom of*. That's what Mrs. Monica Hamilton considered him. But he took the job anyway. Five thousand dollars was five thousand dollars. In the sacred year of our Lord nineteen and seventy-four, that came to more than half a year's wages for most people, no matter who it came from.

"*Jefe*. She hired you, yes?" Paloma stood, arms crossed, shoulder against the door frame.

Paloma was smart, efficient, but also pretty. Not beautiful, but pretty, with doe eyes, pointed chin, pouty lips, a nose a little too wide, and skin the color of a new born fawn.

He drained the glass, then set it aside. "You know I don't know any Mexican, Doll. So, I don't know why you keep using it."

"You're a liar. You know, it wouldn't hurt you to learn more. Besides, it's not Mexican. It's Spanish for boss. Now do you have a job, or not? Because we need more cash coming in than these bond jumpers are giving you. I've been putting off some of the bills, but we're getting second and third notices. If things don't change soon, we'll be doing company business from the sidewalk."

He tapped the envelope. "I have a job. This is our first payment. Want to take it to the bank?"

Paloma picked up the envelope and thumbed through it. "*Madre de Dios*, what does she want you to do? Is it legal?"

"The job calls for me to make a little trip across the border," Glenn said, then explained the situation, wondering if he had made the right choice. If he got in trouble in Mexico, he had little hope of finagling his way out of it, not with the laws stacked against non-citizens. Unless you had a shit load of money, which he didn't.

"Poor woman, to lose her child. How did it happen?"

He cocked an eyebrow, causing Paloma to blush. "I didn't ask."

"You can be such an idiot, sometimes. One thing for sure, you can't go down there alone." She stood there, waiting for him to respond, her look saying she was ready to rip him a new asshole if he said no to her going. But he did something she didn't expect. He almost showed a little common sense, but not in the way she wanted.

"I suppose I could take Paco with me. He knows the lingo. Enough to get by anyway."

"Ha. If you want to order something in a cheap *taqueria*, maybe, or cuss someone out."

Despite how he might tease her, Glenn realized Paloma had the kind of voice that transcended language, and the words would roll off her tongue like warm honey. Only he hated to admit it, afraid it might give her ideas that would get her in trouble, and she had enough of that trying to raise her little brother on her own.

"Who would you suggest then?" Glenn poured another three

fingers of the Kentucky nectar into his glass, already anticipating her answer. He almost enjoyed teasing her.

"You could take me. After all, I was born there."

"Not a good idea, Doll."

"Why not? Don't give me that bullshit about it being too dangerous. All you have to do is bring back a body."

"Wrong. We're *stealing* a body and *smuggling* it across the border. Something most civilized societies frown upon to the point of personal aggravation."

She walked across the room and leaned close, her palms flat on his desk. In that position, she filled her blouse enough to strain against the thin cotton material. Glenn could make out the stitching on her cheap bra and almost read her laundry mark. Plus, a trickle of sweat slipped down her neck to vanish into that dark valley between those soft peaks that held so much promise. An untouchable promise, because no matter how much he liked to tease her, Paloma was strictly hands-off. "Then you need someone who can negotiate with the smugglers. Someone who can get you across without getting caught or shot. They know the best routes to avoid the border patrols. Also, someone who can protect you from getting your butt kicked. Again."

Glenn licked his lips and dropped his eyes until he stared down into his glass, giving the impression he was considering her idea but really stalling for time. "I need muscle. Moving a body won't be easy. Hell, a funeral takes six grown men, so you won't be much help in that department."

"Oh, *Señor* Glenn," she laughed. "Muscle is cheap, but brains aren't. You'll be taking me along for my brains."

"No promises, Doll. But I'll think about it."

"If you do, you won't be sorry."

"I already half am."

"No, you're not." She straightened up and tugged her blouse, giving him the chance to look away and remove the temptation, at least for the moment. "Sheriff Gaines left a message for you. He wants you to come see him."

"What does he want?"

Paloma shrugged and turned on her heels to return to her desk in the front office. Glenn finished his drink, thought about it, but decided to put the bottle away. He noticed Charlie didn't say call. He said to stop by, which meant he had something on his mind he wanted to keep private. They got along well enough since they had the glorious green crotch in common. Charlie did his time in the ice hell of Korea, while Glenn did his in the sweltering jungles of Vietnam. Until LBJ and his fair-haired boy, Westmoreland, shit in the fan. That blew it all across southeast Asia, leaving him and the other jarheads standing nearly neck deep. Then Nixon fucked it up so bad people were climbing onto buildings to reach helicopters minutes before the NVA got there to plant their flag up Uncle Sam's ass. Sighing, he stood and made for the door. "Be back after I find out what he wants."

"Sure, *jefe*. I'll hold down the fort."

Glenn headed down the stairs until he reached the sidewalk, where he ignored his car and turned toward the county courthouse. He decided to walk the couple of blocks to the sheriff's office, hoping to loosen up his still tight muscles. Like most small towns, almost everything important lay within walking distance in McHenry, which made walking faster than driving. Then there was the time saved not having to find a place to park your rolling oven.

He stepped out of the sun, leaving the heat outside of the sheriff's office, taking a moment to let his eyes adjust. Sheila sat at the front desk in the otherwise empty office, a khaki uniform-wearing chubby redhead with pale, freckled skin. In South Texas, a sunstroke waiting to happen.

"The boss in?"

She paused her typing to look him over. "What the hell happened to you?"

He rubbed his face. "Fight Night at the Sunset Center."

"Yeah, I heard about that particular bit of stupidity. Also heard your prisoner was a little damaged when you brought him in. Better watch yourself if one of them decides to complain."

"I should worry about someone resisting arrest? Not likely."

Sheila laughed. She had a nice laugh, even if it did go with a cruel streak. "I heard all y'all jarheads weren't the smartest people in the world. You seemed to be going out of your way to prove it."

"Don't let your boss hear you say that. Might hurt his feelings some."

"I doubt it," she snorted. "He's a different breed of jarhead. Go on back."

Glenn stepped past her into the inner sanctum of the sheriff's department, leaving the whispering fans and the typewriter clatter behind. He knocked on the frame of the open door. Charlie looked up and shook his head. Pushing his chair back, he laced his fingers over his belly. "You know, there are two things I hate in this world, chucks and flies, and the more I see of chucks, the better I like flies. A chuck that's a Bohunk is even worse. A Bohunk that's been dumb enough to get his ass busted up in a fight is even worser. What the hell you been doing?"

"Yeah, I pretty much feel the same way about splibs. A splib that wears a badge and likes to throw his weight around is even worse, and I don't think worser is a word. I was out chasing a bond jumper who took it personal that I was trying to arrest him. You needed to see me?"

"Not the way I heard it." Charlie Gaines was a rarity in Texas, so rare he was probably one of a kind. A Black sheriff. He had held the office since the early sixties because nobody else wanted the job bad enough to try to take it. Not in Hidalgo County, not since the last sheriff ended up in federal prison. He motioned for Glenn to take a seat. "You sure look like shit."

"Been getting that a lot lately." Leaning back, Glenn stretched his legs and folded his hands over his no longer flat belly. "What's on your mind?"

"How's your daddy doing these days?"

"Forgetful. He can also be mean as hell on a bad day. It's the only thing he's got to look forward to since the accident. The bad part is when he forgets and goes through the house looking for mama. I thank God almost every day that he has Fatima around to help keep an eye on him. But you didn't call me over here to talk about my daddy."

"No, I didn't." Charlie leaned forward and planted his arms on his desk. "Sylvia's been asking about you. She still has that friend, Tina, she wants you to meet."

"Dammit, Charlie. You know I ain't worth a shit for blind dates.

Every one I've been on has been a disaster of titanic proportions, nearly biblical. Including floods, famines, and lost wallets."

"That's because you're your own worst enemy. It doesn't have to be that way."

"I'll think about it. But that's not why you wanted to see me, either."

"You're right about that. Seen Miguel Garcia recently?"

"Paloma's brother?" He shook his head. "No, why?"

"Seems he's gotten himself mixed up with a bad crowd. Alonzo Ortega and his crew. I don't have anything definite. That's why I'm talking to you instead of her. I would hate to see that boy break his sister's heart, which he will if he keeps traveling down the path he's on."

"What have you heard, Charlie?"

"Ortega has that pawnshop over on Fifth. Deputy Harris saw Miguel going in with an armload of stuff. A few minutes later, he came out counting a fistful of greenbacks. We know Ortega deals with stolen goods, but we've never been able to hang anything on him. I also believe he's smuggling marijuana from across the border and selling it all over the county. Be a shame if we ended up busting Miguel for handling stolen goods but couldn't do the same for Ortega for dealing."

"Yeah, it would. I'll have a talk with him. Then I'll let you know what I find out." Glenn stared at the toe of his shoes for a minute and sighed. "You know, Charlie, there's a time I could have ended up like that. I remember being young, thinking I was so smart, but I was stupid. The Corps saved me from that, or at least I believe it did. Too bad he can't go that route, at least not for a while. He's too young."

"Well, you better find some way to keep him out of trouble. The Corps wasn't the only thing that saved your ass. You might want to think on that."

Glenn left soon after that, wondering how the hell he could save Paloma's little brother and keep him alive. Or keep his scrawny brown ass out of prison. But first, he had to take care of his business with Hugo Shadrack.

six

STEPPING out of the cool confines of the sheriff's office, Glenn stood on the stone-cut steps in the sticky afternoon where the sun beat down, sucking the water from you like a vampire sucks blood. He tilted his head back to let the heat of the early spring sun lave him with its warming fingers. It felt good against his bruises, like a lizard sunning itself on a flat rock. The heat eased the pain of his bruised face. It also made him feel a touch of regret. Paloma would gladly tell him it had more to do with the years he toted around, and not so much his decision to step back into the ring to try to relive his glory days, which were never as glorious as one remembered. He limped across the manicured lawn of the courthouse, ignoring the *Do Not Walk on the Grass* sign, passing close enough to the bird shit-covered statue of General Sam to say howdy before offering him a drink—that is, if the general happened to be in a drinking mood. Which was mostly never since he was made of bronze.

The walk didn't loosen him up like he thought it would, so he made his way back to his Fairlane, gently squeezing in behind the wheel. The vinyl seat covers were hot enough to sear a brisket or melt your ass to the seat.

Hugo's place was located in the more affordable part of town, mainly where several storefronts had gone bust and maintenance had become a lost cause. It sat in a strip shopping center on Third Avenue, several blocks behind the courthouse, still within walking distance for the destitute and desperate, but not the near lame. Glenn dodged the potholes dotting the parking lot. It was like playing bumper cars at the county fair, and he was fighting to keep from getting whiplash.

Making it across the parking lot in one piece, Glenn pulled up in front of Hugo Shadrack's Bail Bonds Service, its red neon window light buzzing like a swarm of angry hornets. He reached down to grab the paper on Julio Martinez. One last check ensured he had everything in order before he climbed out of his car. He stopped a moment, leaning back against the fender to burn a Lucky, fortifying himself with a heady dose of nicotine while looking the place over. Like most bondsmen, Hugo's place was a dump. The windows were plastered over with peeling and faded handbills advertising his services. *In jail? We bail. Notary. Cash only.* The neon phone numbers were bright red, reaching two feet high. Lettering advertised 24-hour service, not that anybody in McHenry needed 24-hour service or that Hugo was actually available as advertised. He said it gave the casual thieves and murderers a sense of comfort, thinking he would be there for them.

Feeling somewhat better but still stiff, he tossed the butt into one of the many water-filled potholes on his way to the door. Some were deep enough to go diving in, the perfect place to search for a sunken treasure. Inside, the air was stale with cigar smoke and dust, like one of those Egyptian tombs where mummies would leer while they lumbered after half-naked women, like their dicks hadn't rotted off or turned into bug food a couple of thousand years ago.

Penny Barnes, Hugo's fifty-plus-year-old secretary, no bigger than a sparrow, sat behind a desk piled with folders nearly as high as her beehive hairdo. A cigarette hung from the corner of her mouth, mostly ash, and glued in place with her dark red lipstick. She glanced up, letting go with a surprised cackle when she got a good look at his face. "You let yourself get on the wrong side of one of your jumpers again?"

"Is everybody I run into today going to criticize my looks?"

"When you come in looking like something the dog dug out of the litter box, then yes." Her voice had a buzzsaw quality, left by her three-pack-a-day habit, no doubt. Penny always had one on deck, waiting for the current stub to get so short it would blister her lips before she used it to fire off the next one.

"Is that sonofabitch Helka out there?" Hugo screamed from his office. He was hidden behind the dirty windows covered with dusty Venetian blinds and a row of file cabinets stacked with yellowed papers that nobody had bothered to look at since Harry Truman had been in office.

"Yeah. It's me, Hugo." Glenn gave Penny a wave before he vanished through Hugo's door. The man sat behind his desk like a fat bullfrog on a lily pad, chewing and puffing on a thick cigar. A few errant strands topped his sweat-sheened bald head that sat right atop his shoulders. Half glasses perched on the tip of his pointed nose as he looked expectantly at Glenn who said, "I have the receipt for Martinez. He's safe in the county lockup until Harris County sends someone down to pick him up."

Hugo stuck out a fat-fingered hand for Glenn to hand the paperwork over. Glenn then dropped into one of the unmatched office chairs, giving the office of wood-paneled walls the once over. From the overflowing shelves, the out-of-date pin-up calendars of naked women holding tools like they were ready to rebuild a V8 engine and not get their titties covered with grease, nothing ever seemed to change. Hugo scanned the receipt to make sure all the i's were dotted and the t's were crossed. The good news was the clerk had been smart enough to spell their own name right. "Penny, cut this asshole a check for five bills. Then call Houston to let Lovey know we got her man."

Hugo's chair groaned like an overloaded mule when he sat back. He took his cigar from his lopsided mouth and leaned over to spit into the wastebasket, leaving the trash well covered with brown juice stains. "These skippers are killing me. Having to pay out fifteen percent of the money they put up to get their asses into court to stand in front of a judge. I'm telling you, it's no way to run a business."

"Sounds like you need to find yourself a better class of thieves and murderers."

"Don't be a smart ass. My bad luck is your good luck. I could be handing those papers off to someone else, you know. Let them do the dirty work. Then maybe I could save myself a little money."

"You could. But you know there's no one in this part of the state near as good as I am at tracking these people down."

"Don't I know it." Hugo sat up and pawed through a stack of papers. "I have another skipper here I need to have picked up. Lubbock says he robbed a couple of banks. I believe his bond was twenty-five thousand, which means he put up twenty-five hundred. Fifteen percent would come out to—shit, you figure it out, and don't forget my two percent."

"Sorry, can't do it right now. I have another job that's taking me to Mexico for a couple of days. It pays me better than tracking down a bank robber. One who's probably armed to the teeth and ain't too shy about proving it." Glenn shrugged when Hugo looked up to glare over his glasses.

"You turning me down, you ungrateful sonofabitch?"

"Sounds like it."

"Well, shit. I didn't expect that." Hugo slumped back in his chair, tapping a pencil against the edge of the desk. He didn't look very happy as he stared across his desk with small piggish eyes. "Tell you what. This asshole ain't going nowhere. Give me a call when you get back. Then you can decide what we can fucking do about him. Now, get the hell out of here, I got me some work to do. Penny! Where the hell is that goddamn Johnson file?"

On his way out, Glenn signed for his check. He thanked Penny and made a whistling exit, grinning when she complained in that raw husky voice about his noise pollution. Neither stopped until he passed through the door, the whistling or the complaining.

Before he did anything else about Miguel's situation, Glenn needed to stop by his office, even though he wasn't looking forward to climbing those stairs. They weren't so bad when he wasn't all bruised up, but it seemed lately that every beating added a half-dozen years to his joints. Then once you factored in the longer healing times, it almost wasn't worth it. He longed for the days when he could go out to tie one on and feel right as rain the next morning. Now it seemed, if he stubbed his pinky toe, it would lay him up for a week.

Walking back to the office, the heat had risen a bit. His sweat left a Rorschach stain on his back and made wet sunbursts under his armpits. He made the climb, listening to his battered ribs complaining with every deep breath, only to find Paloma wasn't in. Most likely she was still at the bank making sure his money was safe from his spendthrift habits and his business had been saved by holding off his creditors for the moment. Now, how to deal with the problem of Alonzo Ortega? To Glenn's mind, the simplest solution was almost always the best solution—be stronger and more brutal than your adversary. If they have a knife, you'd better have a gun. If they have a gun, you'd better have a bigger gun. And if they have a bigger gun, you damn well had better have an exit strategy. He swapped his .38 for a pair of .45s, his pride and joys. A matched set of .45 caliber Colt M1911s in a custom shoulder rig—one had a C on its hand grips, the other had an S, which stood for Chesty and Smedley, the most decorated Marines to ever serve our glorious country. An undeclared gift, courtesy of an oblivious Green Machine after Glenn left the Vietnam War behind. Instead of turning them in, he'd stuck them deep into his duffle bag so he could smuggle them home. He'd checked the magazines and made sure the safeties were in place. All it would have taken was one stupid mistake to end up shooting himself in the armpit.

On his way out of the office, Glenn stopped to snatch up a picture of Miguel that Paloma kept on her desk. It showed a cute kid in a baseball uniform, down on one knee, grinning, clutching a bat ready to swing. The image turned Glenn's thoughts back to all those evenings he spent with Paloma watching the kid play on the dusty ball fields while wolfing down overcooked hot dogs on stale or soggy buns covered in canned chili and canned cheese, washing it down with flat Cokes in those small paper cups. That was before Miguel got too old for baseball and became such a persistent pain in the ass for his sister. Tucking the picture away, he headed down the stairs, still moving gently. That's when he almost ran over Paloma, her arms filled with shopping bags.

She stared at his shoulder rig until he slipped his coat on. "Where are you going, *jefe*?"

He eyed the armload of grocery bags, stuffed to the point of bursting. "Business, Doll. What the hell did you do? Buy out the whole goddamn Woolworth's?"

"Office supplies, and my lunch. I had no idea when you would get back. When you get together with Charlie, you both usually lose track of time. You start one of your sessions, talking about the old days when you won the war single-handedly."

"Never said I won it single-handedly. Just saying, without the Marines being there, we would have lost it a whole lot sooner. Right now, I've got to go out and talk to a man about a lame horse. Plus, I left a check from Hugo on your desk. Take care of it, will you?"

"You think all I have to do is run back to the bank every time you get a nickel? Now help me carry this stuff in."

Giving him no choice, she shoved the bags into Glenn's arms. He turned around and carried them up to the office, dropping them on Paloma's desk. Peeking inside, he eyed the cans of Maxwell House. The big kind. "I hope you left some money in the account. You know, for things like paying the rent and other bills."

"Don't be an ass. The way you bring in money, we have to stock up when we can."

He ignored the insult. "While I'm out, give Paco a call. Tell him we have another case."

"But, what about...?"

Glenn raised his hand to cut her off. "No matter what I decide about you, I still need Paco. We'll talk about the rest later."

He turned away, half expecting her to throw something at his back, but all he heard was some muttering under her breath while she wrestled with the bags. Since Paloma was such a good Catholic girl who never swore in anger, Glenn thought he must be mistaken. He gave her the benefit of the doubt when he thought he heard the words *fucking sonofabitch*.

He stopped at the top of the stairs. "I heard that. It wasn't nice."

She raised her voice, switching to Spanish.

"That wasn't nice, either, even if I don't know what it means." He hurried down the stairs while laughing and stepped out into the harsh afternoon light. The South Texas sun was bright enough to burn out an ordinary man's eyes unless you were born to it or had a good pair of Foster Grants. The streets were all but empty with only a few slow-moving cars drifting down the sunbaked streets, the half-melted tar sucking at their wheels and sounded like tape being ripped off a roll. There were several that had been pointed nose-first into the curb in front of the local shops, the drivers smart enough to seek shade or a place with conditioned air. It was the kind of afternoon made for siestas, or cooking eggs on the sidewalk. Or at least staying behind doors until the heat began to dissipate. Unless you were someone like Glenn who didn't have that option.

Sliding into his car, the heat-soaked vinyl seared his flesh even through his clothes. He reached up to pull his shades from the visor and slipped them on, which made the world feel ten degrees cooler. That was the trouble with parking downtown, shade was a lost hope. Not even the sturdy post oaks could stand up to the heat. Even with the A/C turned all the way down, it blew like a sirocco for the first few minutes, causing sweat to trickle from his hairline. It ran down the side of his face and slipped under his collar while he backed out and headed down the street.

It took Glenn a few minutes to reach the pawnshop, slowing down when he passed the store. The windows blocked the view inside, filled with guns, musical instruments, and jewelry displays. Ortega's pawnshop seemed to the place to go if you were looking for a trombone, sousaphone, or a lid of grass sold under the counter. He then scanned the streets until he spotted a couple of Charlie's men a block away—windows down, elbows hanging out, faces shiny with sweat. And eyes hidden behind sunglasses while they watched the pawnshop. He passed on by, reached the corner, then circled the block, before pulling up in front. He sat there for a moment to stare at the neon come-ons to hock the family jewels, promising the few extra bucks would help them live the life of Riley.

Glenn climbed out, turned his back to the storefront, and raised his arms over his head to stretch. Let his coat fall open long enough to expose his shoulder rig to the deputies if they were paying attention. He buttoned his jacket, shrugged, and crossed through the door that set a bell to jingling over his head.

He stopped a moment while his eyes adjusted to the dim interior. The slow-turning, dust-laden ceiling fans creaked, blades sagging like the heat done tuckered them out while they did their best to stir the stale air. The store was thick with the musty smell of old clothes and oiled metal. On the border, the oiled metal smell could either be tools, guns, or both. Beneath that, Glenn noted the stringent smell of raw marijuana, a scent most wouldn't notice, but if they did, wouldn't recognize it.

A lone man stood behind the counter. Glenn assumed him to be Ortega, a man who liked his jewelry. He was short, stocky, with a round face, slicked-back hair, and tattooed arms hidden beneath his long sleeves. Or they would have been if he hadn't rolled up his cuffs. The heat made people do stupid things. Glenn nodded as he headed for the glass counter where the pawnshop kept their collection of pistols. He leaned down close enough to get a good look as he checked them out, waiting for the man to join him.

"See something you like, *señor*?" The clerk set his ring-laden hands on the glass, seeming not to care about the smudges.

"I was told to ask for Alonzo Ortega, that he would make me a good deal."

The clerk studied him for a moment, his dark eyes cold as a truck-load of Sweetwater rattlers. "I know you, seen you around town. You're that bounty hunter over on Main, with the upstairs office. Looks like you had a rough day."

"Yeah, that's me." He rubbed his hand over his bruised face. "I've had better. I prefer to be called a private investigator."

The clerk shrugged. "I'm Alonzo."

Glenn continued to check out the display case full of pistols until one caught his eye. "Let me see that Colt Python."

Alonzo pulled out a key, unlocked the case, and slid the door back. Bending down, he grabbed the chromed pistol with black grips and set it on the top. He motioned that Glenn was free to examine it.

Glenn picked it up, hefted the heavy weapon in his palm, and spun the cylinder, listening to the clicks. It sounded as smooth as a rachet. Holding it to his ear, he pulled the trigger to dry-fire it several times, listening to the action. Satisfied, Glenn opened the cylinder and stuck his thumb beneath, angling it so he was able to check the barrel with the light reflected from his thumbnail. It looked to be clean, smooth, with no sign of rust. Except for a little lint clinging to the oiled metal. "Do you have some .357 loads handy?"

Reaching inside the case, Alonzo set half a box of cartridges on the counter, pulling five out. Glenn smiled and let him have the gun. "You load it. I can sometimes be a little clumsy. Don't want either of us chasing cartridges across the floor."

Alonzo shrugged. Dropping the rounds into the cylinder, he snapped it closed. He looked a little nervous when Glenn picked the gun up, swung it until it pointed toward the street. Staring down the sights as he lined up an imaginary target. "How much?"

"Sixty dollars."

Glenn released a humorless chuckle. "I thought you were going to make me a deal."

Alonzo gave a halfhearted shrug. "Okay, fifty."

"I was thinking more like forty."

Alonzo sighed while scratching the side of his face, considering the offer, then gave a quick nod. "Forty-five. Plus, four percent more for the state."

"Goddamn government. Seems it gets greedier every year. You've made a sale. Ring me up." They walked over to the cash register. Glenn pulled out his wallet. Plucking out fifty dollars. He dropped it the counter right along with Miguel's picture.

Alonzo dropped his change, wrote out a receipt, and handed it over. "Who's the *niño*?"

Glenn tensed at the man's nonchalant attitude. He brought three pounds of chromed steel and oiled walnut down hard across the knuckles of Alonzo's right hand. The man screamed when bones cracked. Wide-eyed with pain, he stepped back, cradling his damaged hand against his chest. But not far enough back to keep the muzzle of the Python from stabbing him in the throat. From the corner of his eye, Glenn saw the curtain to the back room jerked sideways. He snatched Chesty from his holster, thumbed the hammer, and aimed without looking. The figure in the doorway froze.

"Come on out where I can get a good look at you. Hate for this thing to accidentally go off. Then we'd have to deal with the cops with their paperwork. Not to mention the mess your boss would have to clean up, the brains, blood, and all."

The figure moved closer with his hands raised, a tall beefy man who looked like he wrestled bears in his spare time. He wore a t-shirt that looked like it had been tattooed on. His pockmarked face was hard as stone, and his dark eyes cold as knapped flint. Glenn couldn't read anything in his features beyond a bland indifference, but he didn't need to. His eyes told the story. They said he would gladly twist off Glenn's head and dry fuck the hole left behind.

"Now that I have your attention, here's what we're going to do. You're going to tell your friend over there to sit back and mind his own business. Then you're going to take another look at the picture. Then you can tell me again whether or not you recognize the boy. After we're done talking, you're going to pinky swear you'll never do business with him again. Then pass the word to your cronies to leave him alone. Then maybe I won't pull either trigger."

Alonzo turned his head to speak to his friend, but Glenn could tell his heart wasn't in it. "Jorge, don't do anything stupid. I got it all under control."

Both men waited while Jorge leaned back against the wall, letting his body weight take him to the floor. Silently, the man dug into his pocket to pull out a handful of penny Tootsie Rolls, which he started to peel, one by one. Jorge then popped the turd-colored candy into his mouth, then rolled the wrapper into a tiny ball before he flicked it away. Eat and repeat.

"Yeah, I know him. Sometimes he brings in stuff to sell. Usually, it's junk, but I give him a few dollars for his trouble. I do it for a lot of the boys in the neighborhood," Alonzo said.

"Is that how you recruit your dealers?"

"I don't know what... urk—" Alonzo stopped talking when Glenn jabbed the Python's muzzle hard against his throat.

"Easy, man. Yeah, sometimes. They bring in junk. I give them a little grass to sell in their neighborhoods, with nobody being the wiser."

"Thought so." Glenn pulled back, easing the pressure. "But not this kid. Not for you, or your friends. If you do, I'll be back. But next time, I won't be so nice about it."

Alonzo stretched his neck while he rubbed his throat, his eyes making promises Glenn knew his ass couldn't keep. "Okay, we won't touch him."

"But you didn't pinky swear."

"Are you serious, man?"

"As a mother's love for her first-born child." Glenn holstered his Colt, then stuck out his fist, with his little finger extended like a society dame sipping tea. A nervous Alonzo stuck out his own and they hooked pinkies. Then Glenn made him repeat his promise.

"Now, don't you feel better? I always do when I've wrapped up a case. It seems to take the pressure off." He picked up his change and shoved it in his pocket. "It makes me feel like such an adult, you know, doing adult stuff for adult reasons."

"You *loco*, man."

Glenn pointed at the swollen hand, now turning an interesting shade of purple. "I would have somebody look at that if I were you. Never can be too careful. You know what they say about most accidents happening at home."

Taking his purchase, now tucked into a brown paper bag, Glenn left the shop to see the pair of deputies leaning against his fender. One sipped on a straw sticking out of a Dairy Queen cup. The other used a plastic spoon to scoop up a chocolate sundae, already turning soupy in the heat. Glenn nodded and dug for his keys. "Boys."

The sipper sighed and dropped the cup down by his thigh. "You wouldn't be trying to interfere with our investigation, would you, Helka?"

Glenn held up the bag. "Doing a little shopping. Only eight more months until Christmas. I do try to avoid the last-minute rush. You can't ever find what you're looking for after everything has been picked over."

Sipper snarled. "You're a wise-ass, Helka. I don't know what Sheriff Gaines sees in you."

Soupy Sundae put his cup down on the hood in case he needed to get fractious. Glenn ignored him and grinned at Sipper. "He likes my sunny disposition and winning smile. We both belong to the same social clubs, casual drinkers anonymous. Then we joined the Whiskey of the Month Club together. April's selection was a real smooth Scotch. Beats the hell out of the fruit punch you boys like to drink."

"We've been watching Ortega for a while now. Trying to get something on him and his friends. We don't need you throwing a monkey wrench into the works."

"Y'all have such wild imaginations. I'm surprised you haven't figured out how to take down the whole organization by now, since it's so obvious."

"Huh? What are you talking about?"

"The kids, you pair of dipshits. If you want to bust him, look at the kids."

"Kids?" Sipper sounded confused. Soupy Sundae picked up his cup and scooped out another bite.

Glenn sighed and turned to toss his package in the front seat. He didn't want to mess up Ortega's prints, you never know when something like that might come in handy. "Yeah, the kids, the ones who come here every day. They bring in junk, then walk out with a little cash. Only they leave with more than cash. They also leave with dope to sell in their schools and neighborhoods. Tell Charlie that Ortega's using them to move his product. Is that simple enough for you?" He jangled his keys meaningfully as he continued moving toward the driver's side. "If you *have* figured out what I'm saying, then get your butts off my car. Unless you want to move over to the other side and use your ass to polish that fender."

They stepped away to let Glenn reach his door. Once inside, he pulled out, on his way to find Miguel. He planned to explain the facts of life to him. The real facts of life, not that birds and the bees bullshit any kid can pick up on the street.

seven

ALONZO STOOD behind the counter while his sister, Lucinda, wrapped his hand. Starting at his wrist, she wrapped the gauze around until only his fingertips showed. He moaned when she tightened the bandage against the swollen flesh.

"Don't be such a big baby, *hermano*. You should go to my clinic. Then we can X-ray it and check for broken bones. I'm betting you have a couple." She ran tape around to hold the bandage in place and gave him a pat on the arm. "There, I can't do anything more. Not here."

"I'll stop by when I get the time after I get me some payback against the *hombre* that did this."

Lucinda gave him a look of disgust. "How you gonna do that? You can't even take a piss by yourself. Who are you going to get to give your little boy a shake? One of those dumb asses you have working in the back? You better watch out, if you do. You might start to like it."

"Don't worry about me. I'll work it out. There is a lot of *putas* in town who would like to have the job."

"Don't be so nasty."

He knew his cavalier attitude made her furious but figured she should be used to it by now. Alonzo cradled his hand while Lucy stuffed the medical supplies back into her bag then dug out a sample package of pain pills she slammed on the counter. Brushing her long black hair back, she slung the bag over her shoulder. "If you don't want me worrying about you, quit calling me to patch you up every time something bad happens. I swear to God, *hermano*, when will you stop being so stupid?"

"I will be fine, Lucy. Now go back to your clinic so you can take care of all those poor wetbacks, and their brats." He looked down at his throbbing hand, tried to make a fist, and winced, ignoring her when she stormed out.

"Hey, Alonzo."

Ortega looked up at his sister's back as she left. That's when he saw Manuel standing in the door, his lips cocked in a sneer. The wide brim of his straw cowboy hat shaded his face, which half hid the scar slashed down his left cheek. Pearl snaps gleamed on his western-cut shirt, colorful as a macaw. Fancy metal caps covered the long-pointed toes of his Mexican-style cowboy boots, his jeans tucked into the tops.

"What happened to you, *hombre*? Did somebody fuck you over?"

"You might say that, but the sonofabitch is going to pay for it. I have a job for you and Jorge. Now fetch me a beer from the back so I can take these goddamn pills."

"Do I look like your bitch?"

Alonzo met him scowl for scowl. "You look like a man who works for me. One who likes to get paid."

Manuel shrugged and headed for the back of the shop. Biting his lip, Ortega hissed in pain, grabbed his wrist, and squeezed, hoping that would somehow ease the throbbing, but it didn't. Instead, it shot up his arm before it worked its way down to settle atop his bladder, pressing down harder and harder. Sweat trickled down the side of his face, leaving an irritating itch. He looked up, hoping the breeze from the overhead fan would waft down to offer a bit of relief.

"Sonofabitch, that asshole is going to pay for what he did to me. Then that little prick Miguel is going to get it for ratting me out."

"Here's your beer, *jefe*. Now, what did you want us to do?" The glass bottle clinked against the counter. He looked up at Manuel, with the hulking figure of Jorge close behind.

Alonzo lifted his bandaged hand and waved it in Manuel's face. "You dumb shit. How am I supposed to open it with a busted hand?"

"Sorry." Manuel grinned, grabbed the bottle, pulled out his key chain with a church key attached, and pried off the cap. Ortega used his teeth to rip open the pill packet, then washed down three of the pills.

"Who gave your hickey, *jefe*?"

"What?" Ortega touched his throat where the cock sucking bounty hunter had shoved the barrel of the Python. He turned around to check it in a mirror, staring at the round bruise that did, indeed, look somewhat like a hickey. "The guy who did this has an office over on Main Street. I want the two of you to pay him a visit. Tell him who you work for to make him understand what it means to fuck around with Alonzo Ortega. Make sure you take some heat with you. Don't be afraid to use it."

"What about the sheriff? I hear they're buddies."

"Fuck the sheriff. If he gets in your way, you can deal with him. Just do it."

Manuel patted his hip and flashed a gold-filled grin, one that sent shivers climbing Alonzo's spine. He knew his man was a half-crazy, soulless bastard. Hell, sometimes Manuel even scared him.

Taking a breath, Glenn eased his grip on the steering wheel. He had decided what needed to be done about his Miguel problem, to keep him busy and off the streets. First, he needed to talk to his friend Danny Pratt. Danny had opened a gym on Fleet Street where he trained boxers of all ages. Glenn hoped it would be the perfect diversion for a teenage Miguel to keep his dumb ass out of trouble and away from people like Alonzo Ortega.

Glenn pulled into the nearly empty parking lot where a sign hung over the building that said *Danny's Boxing Gym* with a pair of boxing gloved above it dangling by their strings like baby shoes. A cinder block propped against the front door held it open so a breeze could help push out the stink of leather mingled with sour sweat. He had known Danny for donkey's years when the man had been an up-and-coming welterweight before the burnout hit. Sometimes all it takes is one devastating loss to end a boxer's career. Danny's happened when he stepped into the ring with Manuel Gonzales a decade ago as a warm-up to Gonzales's championship bout with Curtis Cokes. His fifteen-and-three record eventually turned into a seventeen and ten record that caused his purses to drop down so low he could have made more as a blind beggar selling pencils. That's when Danny realized he needed a career change.

Leaving the cool comfort of his car, Glenn stepped inside, pausing to blink until the weak fluorescent lights caught up to the South Texas sun. He listened to the echoing slap of leather against leather for a moment as someone worked the heavy bag, the scrape of the jump ropes against the concrete, and the rhythmic bounce of the speed bag. All mingled with the grunts of several boys throwing punches in one way or another. Add the sounds to the smell of sweat, rosin, and stale cigarettes, it could have been any one of a hundred gyms he had spent time in when he was younger.

Glenn crossed the wide-open room after he spotted Danny leaning on the apron, watching a couple of young fighters going at it. Faces buried in headgear, they wore ridiculously large gloves that flailed in the air like a bear swatting a swarm of bees while trying to steal their honey.

The third man in the ring was Doc Hearn, who had been hanging around the local boxing clubs since Glenn fought in the Golden Gloves. That seemed a century ago. Glenn sidled up beside Danny to watch the fight, his friend so focused he didn't notice he had company.

"Were we ever that awkward when we started?"

"No. I remember someone who was as light on his toes and as smooth as Sugar Ray. Before he got old, fat, and couldn't walk without tripping on his two oversized feet. I heard about what happened at the Sunset; you must be all kinds of stupid to pull a stunt like that." Danny twisted his neck enough so he could look Glenn over and shook his head in disgust. "You let a club fighter do that to you?"

"I didn't come here to talk about my shortcomings, but in all fairness, the guy had one hell of a right hand. I want to talk to you about Paloma's little brother."

"I know Julio. He has shit for defense. Anybody in half-decent shape should have taken him out in three. So, you want to talk about business?"

Glenn nodded.

"Let's take this into my office." Danny pushed off the ropes, raising his hand to signal for Doc to take over. Glenn followed his long-time friend into a cramped office. Stacked forms covered the desk. Yellowed posters of past fights decorated the walls, leaving barely enough room for a pair of chairs. Squeezing in, Glenn flopped into a hard, wooden chair while Danny dug out a bottle and a couple of glasses and poured them both a drink.

"What's the deal with your *chica's* little brother?"

"First, she's not my *chica*. Second, don't let her hear you calling her that. Third, Miguel's a teenager, a modern-day euphemism for asshole, and he's in full bloom. I'm trying to figure out a way to keep his wise little ass out of the juvenile lockup. I'm hoping you can do for him what you've done for a lot of the other troubled boys in town."

"How bad is it?"

"I went to have a conversation with Alonzo Ortega. I told him Miguel was off-limits."

"Ortega, huh?" Danny took a swallow and sighed. "That's bad, but it could be a lot worse. What do the boy and his sister think about it?"

"Haven't talked to them yet. Thought I would put it to you first."

"I would be glad to help, but you know we can't save everybody. First, they have to want to be saved."

"Yeah, but you and Doc have saved your fair share."

"Bring him around. Once I get a look at him, we'll see how it goes, but no promises. You can't force a kid to save themselves."

Glenn finished his drink and reached for his wallet, slapping a C on the desk. "I'm covering his tab. If it doesn't work out, consider it a donation. I have a job to do in Mexico first, so I won't be able to bring him by until sometime next week."

With their business wrapped up, Danny returned to ringside while Glenn headed for his own office.

The downtown area was pretty much deserted except for the Woolworths. It had been a long day, and his stomach wasn't shy about telling him it needed to be reminded what food tastes like. Glenn figured he had screwed around enough so far. Now it was time to set things in motion for his trip down to Jalpa.

Climbing out of his car, he stood there for a moment to give the sweat that had soaked the back of his shirt time to dry, then headed upstairs. Glenn had grown to hate those creaking narrow things with the loose railing. He never understood how Paloma could do it in heels. One had to be half mountain goat to climb the things. The light at the landing always seemed to be burned out, but the rent was right. He found Paloma seated behind her desk, working on the accounts. Paco sat half sprawled out on the battered office chair, thumbing through a three-year-old *Field and Stream*.

Glenn said. "Didn't realize you were interested in fishing."

"I'm not." Paco flashed the cover that showed a big mouth bass the size of an RV leaping out of the water, its mouth opened wide enough to swallow most household pets and still have room for one of the kids. "Where you going to find something like this on the Texas/Mexican border. I think you need to upgrade your reading material."

Glenn headed to his office while stripping off his jacket, then hung up his rig in its special nook. "To what?"

Tossing the magazine down on the table, Paco flashed Paloma a smile and followed. "*Playboy* is pretty cheap. It also has lots of good articles."

"Get real, kid. All that naked skin would burn your eyes out. If I did that, Margarite would have mine for buttons on her favorite sweater. No *Playboy*." He pulled the painting back and put away his toys, including his latest addition from the would-be street bandit. "I don't think Paloma would approve. Believe me, you don't want to get on her self-righteous side. The lectures alone could put you in a coma if you survived them."

"What's the plan, my man?"

They both sat. Paloma brought Glenn a bottle of Shiner beer, the sides already streaked with sweat. The icy brew soothed his parched throat, leaving a pool of coolness in his gut. "Thanks. You read my mind, Doll. I needed that after the day I had. Paco, I need you to go across the border to secure a vehicle we can use to transport the body, something inconspicuous. Paloma, give him what he needs, cash. I want to be on my way to Jalpa by morning. We'll meet at Rosa's, across the border."

"Okay, but I want to talk to you about something first." Paco cut his eyes toward Paloma, indicating he wanted privacy.

She caught the signal. Clearing her throat, she asked, "Will two hundred be enough?"

Glenn took another swig. "Probably, but better double it. Worst case scenario. Now I just want to rent, not buy the damn thing, understand?"

Paco nodded. "Sure, boss."

"I better run by the bank before it gets any later," Paloma said.

"Pick me up a sandwich or something. My belly's starting to wonder if one of my less moralistic associates has managed to cut my throat. It needs some convincing I'm still in one piece." He waited until the office door closed, then sat back to nurse his beer while he waited for Paco to explain his situation.

"It's about my dad. Something strange happened in the bar this morning. While I was stocking the coolers, a couple of guys came in. I heard them talking. That's when I noticed they sounded a little odd, I mean in the way they talked. They had accents like they were from east somewhere. I went to get another load of beer, but when I got back, they were gone."

"What's so strange about that?"

"You know my dad. Nobody walks into O'Rourke's for the first time without him buying the first round."

Glenn shrugged. "There might be lots of reasons for that. They didn't want to drink, were lost, or could have been asking for directions."

"Those men knew my dad, called him by name. If I didn't know better, I would say he was scared." Paco dropped his chin to his chest, staring at his hands that curled into fist, like he wanted to hit someone, or something, but he wasn't sure who or what. "And if my dad is scared, I think I have a reason to be scared."

Glenn finished his beer and dropped the bottle into the trash. "Seamus, scared? I don't believe it. That man would wrestle a longhorn and kick a rabid javelina in the balls. If he were scared, it wouldn't be about himself, but because of you or Margarite."

"Before we leave, can you ask around? Maybe see if you can figure out what's going on?"

Paco looked desperate. Glenn could see how the boy's worry ate at him. He knew Seamus to be a hardheaded Irishman, who loved his family and was about as loyal as a bottle-raised pit bull. He knew there weren't too many decent places in town for a couple of strangers to stay. If they have any accent other than Texas or Mexican, they should stand out easy enough.

"Sure, kid. I'll ask around tonight, while you go across the border to find us some wheels. Now, when Paloma gets back with the money, I want you to go pack enough stuff to last a couple of days."

Glenn heard someone clear their throat. Swiveling in his chair, Glenn saw an angry Paloma standing in the door.

"I'm back, *jefe*," she snarled. "I heard what you said." She walked in, slapping the bank envelope on his desk. Glenn spotted the top of Jackson's high pompadour peeking out, backed by a fan of more bills. He knew Paloma had a temper, and right about now it seemed to be sizzling in the habanero range. Glenn pushed the money across to Paco, jerking his head toward the door. The boy was smart enough to grab it without saying a word and vanish, leaving his boss to deal with the problem.

Paloma stared after him. If looks could kill, Paco didn't have long to hang around this mortal sphere. When they were alone, she turned on him like a bad batch of chili. "What about me?"

Glenn squirmed in his chair, his fingers tapping out a nervous tattoo. "About that. I've been thinking..."

Glaring, she crossed to his desk. "Don't think. Just do it. You need me with you."

"But Miguel..."

"He can stay with my cousin Beatrice, and her husband. They can watch him until we get back."

"But school..."

"He doesn't need me to get him to school. Besides, he doesn't go half the time, anyway."

"I don't have time to..."

"No, you don't. Now quit looking for excuses and say to me, 'Paloma you are more than welcome to go. I am just a helpless and stupid *gringo* who can't get along without you. I will probably be killed if I don't have you there to keep me out of trouble.'" Her angry voice sounded bad enough, but the hand gestures told him he might be treading on dangerous ground. Her finger waggled hard and fast, like a six-year-old playing cowboy. Glenn was afraid the damn thing might go off from sheer determination.

Glenn started to say something else, but the hard look she gave him with her smoky brown eyes caused the words to freeze in his throat until he swallowed and turned them into acquiescence.

"Okay, but don't overpack. We'll just be there for a couple of days. This is a business trip, which means we won't be making any unnecessary stops along the way, so make sure you pack enough shit for your lady parts."

Her face relaxed enough for a smile to flicker around her lips. "That's better. Now that you're showing a little bit of sense, I can go home to check on Miguel." She turned to walk out but called back over her shoulder, "And by the way, my lady parts are fine, if it's any of your business."

Having several errands to run before he headed into Mexico, Glenn locked up and followed her down the stairs. He stood beneath the awning of the electronics store, pulling out a Lucky to feed his nicotine demon while he waited for her to reach the bus stop. He would have offered to drop her off, but Paloma had already turned him down too many times. Said she didn't want the neighbors getting the wrong idea, seeing a *gringo* dropping her off so late. After she climbed on the bus, Glenn scanned the street. That's when he spotted the two men climbing out of an old Chevy pickup and heading his way. One he recognized easy enough. Jorge from the pawnshop had been sitting behind the wheel. It was hard not to remember someone who looked like they were built on the chassis of a Ford F-350, a well-used older model that could still pull stumps out without straining. The other guy had had his booted feet propped up on the passenger window, showing off his Mexican cowboy boots. Him, Glenn didn't know, but of the two, he looked more dangerous, the kind who would pull the wings off flies for fun. Someone who wouldn't hesitate to hang a kitten on a clothesline by its tail so he could use it for target practice. They both looked serious, which didn't bring Glenn much comfort, like they were ready to do some payback damage to a nosy PI who had embarrassed their boss.

eight

GLENN EASED BACK into the shadows of the doorway, unsure if he had been spotted. Regretting he had locked his guns away, he figured they would come in right handy now and considered going back to fetch them. But Glenn knew Charlie would frown on an old-timey gun battle playing out on the street of McHenry when civilians could get themselves caught up in the crossfire. Instead, he considered making a run for his car, but he knew he wouldn't make it before they caught him. Hell, he wouldn't make it from beneath the electronics store awning if they were carrying.

Glenn peeked out again, cursing when he only saw the Tootsie Roll eater. The guy wearing the pointy-toed jam makers had vanished. Glenn knew they were called jam makers because, by the time the wearer finished kicking the shit out of somebody, they looked like they had been turned into strawberry jam. He decided a strategic retreat would be the smart thing to do. He backed down the hallway until he reached the back door where he stepped out into the dirty and narrow alley lined with dented trash cans, most of which were overflowing. A few of the potholes were filled with what smelled like sewer runoff and looked deep enough the Loch Ness monster could have used them for a summer home and Moby Dick could have been his neighbor—they could have borrowed eggs or sugar from each other or swapped recipes. The brick walls were dirty with exhaust and oily smoke from delivery trucks. The whole area smelled of sun-cooked garbage. The alley was not meant for the weak of stomach.

Glenn looked toward the corner, wondering if he could make it to his car while the two men headed for his office to discover he wasn't there. Feeling good about outsmarting Ortega's stooges, he put a bounce in his step, despite his sore ribs. Glenn even considered whistling a little tune.

Until the boot wearer stepped around the corner to block his way, his right hand reaching for the small of his back under his worn denim jacket.

Glenn glanced over his shoulder and saw Jorge had stepped through his back door, blocking any potential escape route. Glenn stopped and raised his hands. "Let me guess, Alonzo Ortega, right?"

"You done messed with the wrong man, *gringo*." Boots flashed a gold-filled smile that stretched the scar on his cheek like he had been sleeping wrong on his pillow.

"Shit, man. If I knew he was going to bear a grudge, I might have been nicer."

"I heard you were a smart ass."

Glenn kept a close watch on the man's hand he had placed behind his back, but the anticipated weapon never appeared. That was the thing about guns. When you point one at an individual, you rightly knew the caliber. With the gun pointed at you, that hole at the end of the barrel could grow as big as a cannon. He had seen some .45s pointed his way he could have stuck his head in and not crowded his ears.

A moment later, a hand the size of a dinner plate, the kind a café would have served their lunch specials on, grabbed Glenn's shoulder, squeezing hard. He wanted to groan from the pain. His knees felt a little wobbly, but he didn't want to give those two men the pleasure.

"It's time for us to go on a little ride. The man we work for wants to see you."

"You can say his name, it's not like it's a dirty word or something. Well, maybe it means something dirty in Spanish. I better check on that before I embarrass myself in mixed company. Don't want to be yelling dirty words in church, Spanish or otherwise."

"Make him shut up, Jorge," Boots snarled. "I don't care what you have to do."

Glenn heard the chirp of a siren coming from behind. He looked back to see a car pull into the alley. The driver turned the rooftop gumball lights on as it rolled closer to the three men, weaving back and forth to miss the most egregious potholes, the ones that could be Nessie's or Moby Dick's summer homes.

Boots dropped his hand from his back and stepped away from Glenn. "Shit, it's that nigger sheriff."

"What are we going to do, Manuel?" Jorge chirped in Spanish.

"Okay, Manuel," Glenn deadpanned, but kept his hands up, hoping he could sweet-talk his way out of the situation. "You really want to do this out here in front of God and everybody?"

"Goddamn you, I should shoot your white ass right here before your nigger friend can reach us, and then I can tell Alonzo we took care of you."

"You could, but I doubt you would get very far. What say we call it a draw for now? You go your way. Maybe I won't tell Charlie the extent of our conversation."

"This ain't over, *gringo*." Manuel signaled to Jorge it was time to leave. The big man released his shoulder. He imagined he knew how Atlas felt when he talked Hercules into taking his place. Glenn rolled his shoulder when they vanished around the corner.

Charlie stopped with his driver's side window rolled down. It let slip some of the cool air, strongly tainted with coffee and cigarettes. That would have been enough to make Sylvia or Sheila spit nails since he was supposed to be on the nicotine wagon. Charlie said, "Appears you've been riling the locals."

"You got it all wrong, Charlie. I'm the life of the party, always looking for ways to make new friends. Some people just don't take to me the first time."

"I'll admit you are an acquired taste. You look like you could use a drink," Charlie suggested.

"I probably could, but only one."

"Hop in. I'll drive us both around to O'Rourke's."

Glenn eased his way into the passenger's seat and laid his head back, holding that position until they reached the bar. "I need you to do me a favor. Paco said a couple of guys came into the bar earlier. Seems they spooked Seamus. I haven't had time to check them out, but I'm up against the wall here with this job in Mexico. I can't do much until I get back. Maybe you can keep an eye on them and make sure they don't cause any trouble."

"Sure, anything specific?"

"Not really, he's just worried."

The problem with drinking with Charlie is that one drink turned into another, the alcohol flowing like the conversation. On occasion, Charlie would need to unburden himself, and who better than a fellow jarhead to dump your shit on.

"Sometimes I think it's time for me to hang it up. I've been dealing with the people around here for too long. Did I ever tell you how I ended up with this job?"

Even though he had heard the story several times, Glenn saw no harm in hearing it again. His friend only brought it up when he needed some kind of assurance he was doing the right thing. With the clack of pool balls, Hank Williams being lonesome then Patsy Cline being blue spilling out of the jukebox in the background, and a couple of cold beers to lubricate his tongue, Charlie began to talk.

"I retired from the Marines in sixty as an old Gunny, coming home to a place that had more crackers and peckerwoods per capita than Georgia and Alabama put together. I needed a job because, despite all my experience, there ain't no career in killing North Koreans or Chinese on the Texas border, although there were some who wanted to see those skills turned on the Mexicans crossing the border, but it wasn't to my taste. I've always considered myself to be one of those live and let live sorts." Charlie used his thumbnail to cut through the wet circles his beer had left on the table.

Glenn drew a line through the condensation on his beer bottle.

"It seems the old sheriff in McHenry had other ideas about which laws should be enforced and which ones could be ignored. He got caught with his hand in the cookie jar with so many crumbs under his fingernails he couldn't have gotten them clean with a wire brush. I think the breaking point came when he was caught taking money to turn a blind eye on the cross-border marijuana trade. The Rangers hauled him off. They ended up locking his ass up over in Jim Hogg. That's when some concerned citizens talked me into tossing my hat into the ring, much to the chagrin of some of McHenry's leading white citizens, some who had more than a passing acquaintance with pointed hoods, or planting flaming crosses on people's lawns."

About here in the tale is where Charlie always got a little wound up. Understandably.

"Believe me when I tell you I heard my share of *nigger this* and *nigger that* thrown my way from the good folks of McHenry, mostly in the name of Jesus. Telling me about the proper place of us Black folks in this world. But to the surprise of all those good white Christian people, they soon realized the balance of power had shifted, but they weren't ready to let go. Hell, that rotten bastard, Johnny Hightower, ran for reelection with their support while he still had his ass locked up in jail."

Glenn inserted his line, like a dutiful member of the chorus: "I remember my dad talking about those days. Laughing at all those tight-ass Church of Christ or Southern Baptist people who were shitting their pants because a colored man dared to run for office."

Charlie nodded, taking a sip from his drink, just enough to keep his throat oiled while he stretched his story out. Not that Charlie was particularly narcissistic, but he sometimes did take pleasure in hearing his own voice. "It wasn't long after that when the burning crosses and nooses hanging from trees showed up all over town, like ugly Christmas ornaments. Sylvia begged me to let it go, but I wasn't ready to. I refused to let those people run me out of my town for wanting a job that needed doing right. When that didn't work, then came the drive-bys with gunfire, trying to intimidate the people into voting the way they wanted them to, or stay at home and not vote at all. But I kept on going out, meeting people, shaking hands, telling them what my plans were." Charlie waved his empty to Seamus, who nodded that he'd bring another round.

"That's how you learn about the quality of your community, going out to meet the people, listening to their problems, finding out what they need. Then understanding the difference between need and want.

What they needed was someone who would uphold the law for everyone."

A slice of light drew Glenn's attention as a couple of locals left the bar and a handsy couple stepped in from the heat, sliding onto barstools down toward the shadowed end of the bartop.

"I worked the colored neighborhoods, as well as the Mexican ones, as hard as I could, as well as the poor whites who had been forced to put up with Hightower and his heavy-handed deputies beating the hell out of them, locking them away for minor infractions, costing them more in bail money than most of them earned in a month. I knew I didn't need all their votes, just enough to offset the privileged white ones, since all the Blacks and Mexican voters outnumbered them about five to one. Plus, many of them were veterans of World War Two and Korea."

The redhead looked me in the eye while her hand wandered from her man's knee up toward his crotch. *Jesus.* The smack of Charlie's bottle onto the bartop drew my attention back to his story. He was headed toward the finish line now.

"It all came to a head the weekend before the election. The "Charles Gaines for Sheriff" election committee had bought a billboard on Highway 83 with my face plastered all over it. Ten-foot high, twenty-feet wide, my pearly whites shining in the middle of my Black ass face below a tan Stetson." Charlie sighed wistfully while rolling his drink between his hands.

"The picture was one of my best. You could say I looked right handsome. At least Sylvia said so, until those sons of bitches desecrated it by painting 'N-I-G-E-R' across it in big white letters—the illiterate bastards couldn't even spell nigger right. Then they tore down my posters, stole my yard signs, did everything they could to sabotage my campaign. Everything they could to intimidate the voters. Know what I did then?"

Charlie sat back, waiting for Glenn to say something. "Charlie Gaines, I've heard you tell this story near a dozen times, drunk and sober. So, I have no idea what you did."

His friend laughed, but it didn't slow him down, not when he was so close to the end. "The day of the election, they even showed up at the polling station ready to shut it down or drive off those they didn't want voting. I showed up right after with a forty-four-ounce Louisville Slugger, with a dozen other veterans backing me up. You see, Glenn, you might can walk up to a Black man, spit on him, and call him *nigger* or *boy* to make yourself feel like a big man. But when that *boy* is six foot four, weighs near two hundred and fifty pounds, who spent twenty-six years in the Marine Corps? Well now, it doesn't have quite the same effect as going against a sixty-year-old teacher or an eighteen-year-old high school student. Because you insult *that boy*, he's going to fight back."

Glenn dutifully nodded his assent.

"After that, the people voted. We stood guard over the collection boxes until all the votes were tallied. Then that corrupt sonofabitch Hightower was out on his ass. On top of losing his job to a Black man, he got fifteen years in federal prison." Charlie set his glass down and grabbed his hat, ready to call it a night.

nine

ALONZO REMAINED stoic behind the counter, although his impatience had begun to show. He stared at the skinny kid with long blonde hair, thick and greasy, that hung down like dead snakes. Alonzo imagined the boy smelled like a wet dog who had rolled over in a pile of fresh cow shit. Blondie stood gnawing nervously on his thumbnail, eyes darting from side to side, like he was trying to make a pick in three-card monte. The kid bounced on his feet like a toddler who'd had one bottle too many and whose bladder was about to explode. Alonzo stared at the portable television next to the cheap clock radio while shaking his head. "That's my final offer."

"Come on, man. It's got to be worth more than that," the boy whined. One of them high-pitched, why-can't-I-have-my-own-way whines.

"Five bucks, no more."

"But I gotta have more. I just gotta. I heard you were cool, man. That you buy stuff, man. What's wrong with my stuff?" The kid's eyes were red, and the pupils were so dilated they were rimmed with a nearly invisible band of gray. The small scars on the inside of his arm told Alonzo everything he needed to know about why the boy seemed so anxious. Crashing wasn't pretty, and Blondie seemed to be coming down hard.

"It's old. Cheap. I'll bet it's stolen, too. Maybe I can offer you something besides cash."

"Like what, man?" Blondie crossed his arms, absentmindedly scratching the inside, although he couldn't do much, not with the way he had gnawed his nails down to the bloody quick.

"How about a couple of joints. It's primo stuff, *amigo*." Alonzo smiled to show his sincerity, something he had learned to fake a long time ago. He found it to be good for his business. If he could get the people to believe he was being honest, it made it so much easier to screw them over. A little thing he picked up while still a kid going to church.

When he had spent time as an altar boy, he'd had a ringside seat to watch how the priest would hustle the widows and mothers out of rent or food money they could hardly afford to spare. The priest had claimed it was God's divine will that the bishop would get a new car every couple of years, with chrome wheels, leather interior, and a cassette deck. Vestments weren't cheap. If they wanted the priest to pray for their souls, they damned well better be willing to come up with God's share.

"I don't know, man. I need something stronger than grass." Blondie scratched harder until even his bitten nails began to gouge his skin and leave tracks of red welts like he was playing connect the dots with his needle marks.

"I don't deal with anything stronger. Once you ride the pale horse, it can only take you to one place. Customers ending up there ain't good for building repeat business."

"Ten bucks, dude. Ten bucks will get me what I need." The whine became strident, like a tree full of cicadas begging for attention.

The bell over the door rang. Alonzo looked up to see Manuel come in, with Jorge on his heels. Manuel moved with the smooth flow of a cat. One foot barely touched the floor before the next mincing step. The tension on Manuel's face told him something had gone wrong. Alonzo hit the no sale key on the register. The drawer popped out with a bell like chime. He pulled out a sawbuck and slapped it on the counter. "Take it and get the hell out of here. This is a one-time offer. Don't come back here thinking you'll get the same treatment."

Blondie grabbed the bill and stuffed it in the front pocket of his dirty Levi's. "Thanks, man, you're a righteous dude. I'll tell everyone I know how you helped a brother out."

"Yeah, yeah. Now get out."

Blondie vanished through the door, never looking back. Probably afraid Alonzo would change his mind. Alonzo nodded for Jorge to flip the closed sign over and turn the lock.

"What the hell happened?" Alonzo snarled before Manuel spoke.

"He wasn't in his office, but we caught up with him in the alley behind his building. Had him all ready to bring to you when that nigger sheriff turned up to stick his nose into it. We had to beat it."

Alonzo's face turned ugly with anger, dark as a hurricane threat. He looked to be ready to do as much damage. "Goddammit. How can that sonofabitch be so lucky."

"We checked around, but the word is he shut down his office so he could go out of town for a few days."

"So, he's going out of town? Where?" Alonzo leaned on the counter. Careful of his damaged hand, he ran his fingers through his hair. "If he's locked the place up, that means his girl has some time off, or she's gone with him. If anyone knows what's going on, it will be her little brother. Find that little shit Miguel and bring him here. Don't hurt him, but you can scare him enough so he craps his pants."

"Sure, *jefe*. Like a baby." Manuel laughed. The taciturn Jorge just nodded, blank-faced, as they turned back to the door.

Once they left, Alonzo had nothing else to do but be patient. He had never been known for being a patient man.

After a half-hour, Alonzo heard the alley door rattle when it swung open. Then the backroom light clicked on. A moment later, Manuel stepped through the beaded curtain followed by Jorge, who dragged a scared Miguel with him. The boy tried to put on a brave front but failed miserably.

"What do you want with me?"

Alonzo chuckled. "*Chico*, it's a good thing you're young. Means you got control. Strong muscles to keep that asshole of yours clenched tight.

Otherwise, you might be shitting all over yourself. You were an old man, I guarantee your pants would be filled right about now, and you would be smelling like a park toilet during August."

"I ain't done nothing."

"No?" Alonzo held up his bandaged hand. "An *amigo* of yours paid me a little visit this afternoon. Warned me to stay away from you. He left me with this."

With Manuel between him and the front door and Jorge blocking the way to the back, Alonzo knew Miguel had nowhere to go, even if he did try to run. "That wasn't me, I swear. I had nothing to do with him coming here."

Smiling broadly, Alonzo stepped from behind the counter, crossing the floor until he stood within striking distance. "So, you know who he is."

Miguel nodded. "He's my sister's boss. Calls himself a private investigator, but I think he's a shitty one."

Alonzo laid his good hand on Miguel's shoulder, digging his fingers in until the boy winced, folding over to one side. "And where would I find this shitty dick when he's not in his office?"

Manuel sniggered like a schoolboy who got his first look at a pair of girl's panties. "That's funny, *jefe*, a shitty dick." Aiming the next words at Miguel, he said, "Is he doing your sister, *chico*? Is that how he gets a shitty dick? I know a lot of *putas* who like to butt fuck, claim it saves them a lot of money on pills and rubbers. Your sister like to grease up her shitter? To show her boss a good time?"

Miguel's face went red, his eyes burning from tears of shame. His chin dropped to his chest, words spilled out low and harsh. "He's going to Mexico. My sister said some rich white lady hired him to go down there to bring back her son's body. She's going with him, making me stay with our cousin."

"Where?"

"Across town."

"No, you dumb shit. Where are they going?"

"My sister said they were going to Jalpa."

Alonzo looked at Manuel. "You heard the *niño*. You two go after this shitty dick. Make sure he doesn't come back."

"Wouldn't it be easier to wait until he gets back to take care of him, *jefe*?"

"Yeah, probably. But I don't want to wait that long for you to bring me his balls in a paper sack after you make him eat his own fucking dick. I don't care if you have to follow him all the way to Chapas to get it done."

Miguel's head jerked up. "But my sister is with him. You can't hurt her. Please."

"You heard *el muchacho*," Alonzo said. "Don't do anything that could hurt his sister, understand?"

"Sure, *jefe,* sure. We understand." Manuel's grin said otherwise. He watched the boy's face go pale, like he was about to be sick, but he didn't respond.

"Good, now take the boy home."

Jorge grunted and clapped his meaty hand around Miguel's neck then steered him toward the back door. He moved fast, causing Miguel to stumble, but the big man's strength kept the terrified boy on his feet.

Alonzo grabbed Manuel's arm and held him back until the beaded curtains fell back in place, then leaned in to speak in a low voice. "I don't care what it takes, or who gets hurt. You don't let that sonofabitch come back here in one piece. Or anyone else you find with him."

Flashing his gold-filled grin, Manuel nodded and patted the butt of his pistol. "*Sí, jefe.* Just like at the Alamo. We take no prisoners, hey?"

ten

GLENN ROLLED out of bed and shut down his alarm, his head a little worse for wear after his evening with Charlie. He leaned to one side to stretch, testing his ribs. He didn't scream, nothing was punctured or causing him to spit up blood, so he figured he was on the mend, even if he was still somewhat sore.

Dosing himself with some aspirin, he dressed, grabbed his bag, and made sure he locked the door behind him, for all the good it would do. The door lock was so cheap, the only ones that might not be able to jimmy it were small desert animals and the mentally incompetent. Hell, even a stiff breeze might be able to break in, make itself at home by drinking his beer and watching dirty movies on cable—if he could afford cable.

Glenn slid behind the wheel and pulled out, heading back toward McHenry where he parked in front of his office. A quick look around showed no sign of the beat-up pickup. He figured neither man was smart enough to hide it while keeping an eye on him. Jorge hanging around Main Street would be about as conspicuous as parking the pickup in a drugstore window.

He climbed the stairs only to discover Paloma had beat him there. She had a pot of coffee brewing and a box of mixed donuts open on her desk, filling the room with the smell of sugar and the elixir of life in the form of slow-roasted magic beans. "Anyone ever tell you that you are an angel, Doll?"

"Yeah, usually dirty old men with impure thoughts who think saying nice things will help them get into my pants." She poured him a cup, sliding it across her desk.

"I'll cop to the impure thoughts part, but I'm too young to be a dirty old man. Also, I don't think your pants would look good on me."

"Keep telling yourself that." She sat behind her desk, two-fingered a donut and bit down, glazing her lips with flakes of sugar.

"I'll have you know I'm considered an upstanding member of the community. I have a job, pay taxes, am kind to small animals and children. I will help an old lady cross the street faster than a Boy Scout can slip on his bandana."

Paloma licked her fingers and grabbed another donut. Glenn figured he'd better partake while he still had the chance. He grabbed a still-warm cinnamon roll the size of a hubcap and bit down. The damn thing nearly melted in his mouth, so sweet it made his jaws ache. By then, Paloma had grabbed her third donut.

Glenn said, "You keep eating like that, you might not be able to hold onto that figure much longer."

She rolled her eyes. "I didn't realize you were that interested in my figure. Besides, I eat like this only when someone else is paying. Did you call Fatima to tell her you would be gone for a few days?"

"I did. You need to remind me I promised to pay Burt a visit when we get back. I'm not sure what my dad is paying her, but it ain't half what she deserves, considering what she has to put up with."

While they sank into a companionable sugar and caffeine haze, Glenn's thoughts turned to the previous evening when the two men trapped him in the alley until Charlie showed up. It didn't take much for him to realize Alonzo Ortega had plans to give him some kind of payback for that busted hand. Glenn just needed to figure out how he would deal with it after they completed their current gig.

He had begun to think about switching to something a little stronger than coffee to help deal with the pain when Paco came through the door wearing a grin a shit-eating possum would have been proud of. "I got us a ride, *jefe*. Hey, cool, donuts."

Paco grabbed one, devoured it, and grabbed another while Paloma poured him a cup of coffee.

"Good. Let's finish up here so we can be on our way."

Once the coffee and donuts were depleted, the small group rumbled down the stairs. Paloma toted her bag down to the sidewalk, refusing Glenn's offer. That's when Glenn spotted a long, low-slung black vehicle with a boxed back end and high fins trimmed with chrome pulled up next to his car. Paco went over to it, proud as a new papa. "There it is, *jefe*. What do y'all think?"

Glenn stared at it for a moment, as if trying to absorb what he was seeing. He said flatly, "That's a hearse."

Paco's grin faded, replaced with a look of confusion. "Yes, a fifty-seven Chevrolet Bel-Air. It cost me just twenty-five bucks to rent it for a week. Plus, it has an eight-track player. I should have thought to bring some of my tapes. Maybe we can pick up some new ones along the way."

"What part of inconspicuous do you not understand? We're stealing a body. It would be nice if we didn't do anything to draw the attention of the *federales*."

"But we have to move a body and casket, don't we? So, what better way than to use a car designed to haul caskets?"

"Yes, but—"

Paloma cleared her throat loud enough to quell their arguing. "Paco's right. If we are caught with a body, it's best if we have it in a hearse, not be caught hauling it inside some kind of delivery truck. We might stand a better chance of bluffing our way through by claiming there was a mess up in the paperwork."

Paco bobbed his head. "Sure, that's what I thought, boss."

Glenn closed his eyes with a sigh. "Okay, but we have to cross deserts and mountains to get to Jalpa. Then drive back the same way. You want to do it in a damned car that's almost twenty years old. Then, to make things worse, that thing probably doesn't even have air conditioning."

"But it does—it's mounted in the passenger side back window."

"Mounted in the side window?"

Paco went a little red. "Yeah. In Mexico, when you don't have a lot of cash, you have to figure out how to do things, like rig an air conditioning system to keep yourself and your cargo cool."

"You mean, like a body."

Paco nodded. Then waited to see how Glenn would react. After a minute, Glenn ducked his head, shrugging to show he was surrendering. "Okay, you win. This round."

"If you boys are done playing, I want to get my bag stowed away and run across the street to the Rexall for some personal stuff," Paloma said.

"I'll get your bag," Glenn said. "Just hurry up so we can get on the road before it gets much later."

Seeing his chance, Paco leaned close and spoke in a low voice. "Did you have a chance to check out those two men?"

Glenn shook his head. "I left the office last night intending to go over to the hotel, but a couple of Ortega's goons tried to highjack me. Lucky for me, Charlie came along in time to scare them off. I explained the situation, and he said he would keep an eye on them until we get back."

"The guy who runs the pawnshop?"

"Yeah. He also deals drugs."

"Thanks, *mi amigo*. I don't know what's going on between them, or much about my dad's past. He never talks about it."

"Most men don't."

Paloma returned with a small bag that couldn't have held much. But since she said she needed personal stuff, Glenn knew those things didn't need much room. "I'm ready if you two are. It's a long way to Jalpa."

"About five hundred and thirty miles," Paco said. Glenn stared at him until the boy blushed. "I checked."

Glenn shrugged. "That's like a day drive to Dallas."

"Except that the roads in Texas are a lot better," Paco said. "No telling how many detours we may have to take before we get there."

With their bags stowed, Glenn steered around to the passenger side. He let her take the center spot while he took a moment to study the little A/C unit that stuck out the side. It looked to be held in place with foil tape and spit. A rusty streak ran down the side where condensation run-off had discolored the paint, making it look like it had a bad case of the shits.

"I figure we'll take Mexican Highway 40D far as we can," Paco explained after Glenn climbed in, referring to the main east to west Mexican thoroughfare.

"Sure, you've got the wheel." Glenn's eyes were drawn to Paloma's legs, her feet straddling the transmission hump, canted so her knees were forced together. The wide bench seat left plenty of room for Glenn to slump against the door. He pressed his head against the cool glass, hoping it would ease the pain. The aspirin were not quite doing their job. After Paco started the car, he heard the low hum of the air conditioner kick in. A moment later, cool air spilled over the back of the seat.

Taking his time, Paco nudged the behemoth down the street to the border bridge and crossed over. Circling the town center of Nuevo Prado, they were able to bypass the crowds of tourists. They picked up speed when they drove by the cobbled-together hovels that passed for housing on the south side of the border. The dusty yards were filled with dirty kids playing with washboard-ribbed dogs who chased the hearse with snarling yelps and indecipherable cries. Seems no matter what country you find yourself in, they always had neighborhoods on the other side of the tracks. Trouble was that most of Mexico happened to be located on the other side of the tracks.

Minutes later, after several twists and turns, they reached the two-lane highway. Glenn, trusting in Paco's ability to get them going in the right direction, decided it would be a good time to take a little nap.

Jorge rode shotgun while Manuel took the wheel of his old Chevy pickup, the two men crossing the bridge with no problem after flashing their IDs. They soon left McHenry and the United States behind. It felt as if they had traveled twenty years into the past. The road turned from smooth concrete to poorly laid asphalt, then to rough, cracked bricks filled with potholes big enough to hold bullfights in. Taking his time, Manuel found a place to park where they could spot the shitty dick or his friends when they came across the border. Jorge had followed the clueless kid into town last night, watching while he picked up the old Chevy hearse and drove it back to McHenry.

Manuel had a pair of field glasses trained on the outhouse-sized building where the border guards checked papers, asked questions, flirted, and pocketed the occasional bribe. You could tell the ones who took bribes by the way their uniforms fit. If they looked like a ten-year-old wearing their papa's clothes, they were either honest or too stupid to know how to collect money from the day workers crossing the border.

Jorge kept himself busy peeling Tootsie Rolls, popping them between his constantly moving jaws. His eyes locked on the bridge like an eagle searching for a rabbit, he bolted upright, pointing a finger the size of a chorizo and spraying brown sugar-juice when he yelled in Spanish, "There goes their car!"

Manuel followed Jorge's pointed finger, trying to interpret his grunts. He started the pickup, hurrying to catch them. Reaching the highway, he spotted a hearse about a mile or so down the road. "Is that them?"

"*Sí.*"

Grinning, Manuel pressed the gas down, trying to close the distance but keeping far enough back so they wouldn't realize they were being tailed, or so he hoped. "If you're just going to respond with one-word answers, this is going to be a long trip."

"*Sí.*" Jorge didn't like Manuel much. The man had a mean streak that made him carry things a step or two too far. He didn't mind that he had to do bad things working for Alonzo, like breaking an arm or leg of someone who showed his boss disrespect. But that never seemed to be enough for Manuel, who would break both legs *and* an arm, then kick the man in the balls with his pointy-toed cowboy boots for the same offense. So, instead of talking, he turned on the radio, twisted the dial until he found a Tejano station. With the speakers blaring, he leaned back to look out the window at the passing scenery. He dug out another small Tootsie Roll and lazily peeled it before popping it into his mouth. Sticking his hand out the window, he let the wrapper flutter like a tiny flag before releasing it, watching in the side mirror until it vanished.

eleven

THE REAL WORLD intruded into Glenn's sleep, a sleep so deep dreams hadn't bothered to manifest in the dark, blank corridors of his mind, leaving the cobwebs and self-pity intact. It began with the hot blast pouring in through the hearse's vent window, heavy with the taste of dust tainted with the seared plants disintegrating under the power of the arid wind. Then came the tickling slide of sweat down the side of his neck, like ants marching across his gritty flesh, followed by the incursion of the sunbaked glass pressing against his cheek. He sat up, wiping the sweat and drool off the side of his face and blinking to clear his clouded vision. Glenn checked Paloma sitting next to him, spotting the growing wet spots that stained her blouse. She had undone the top few buttons and spread the lapels wide open to expose an interesting amount of flesh. Beads of perspiration dotted her skin and slid slowly toward that lace-covered valley she usually kept hidden, turning the top of her bra dark with sweat. Sometimes stifling heat can trump modesty.

"What happened?"

"Sorry, boss," Paco said. "The air conditioner quit working."

Glenn cranked his window down to increase the airflow. The wind hitting his sweaty body did help cool him down. He heard a sigh of relief come from Paloma as she gathered her hair to pile it on top of her head and held it there.

"*Gracias a Dios*," she said. "I couldn't get around you to roll the window down. That feels so much better now."

The good news for Glenn, the pain in his head had almost faded. The bad, he felt like he had been sheep-dipped and hung out to dry, but the drying part hadn't worked worth a damn. He stared through the windshield at the one-lane ribbon that seemed to stretch off into haze-shrouded mountains. Their snowy cap made them look like pimples on a teenager's ass. The hearse was flanked by a dusty landscape dotted with patches of yellow-green beneath a merciless sun that reflected off the mica-peppered rocks and caused them to twinkle like stars. To Glenn's mind, it didn't look any different than some stretches of West Texas.

He swallowed hard, then licked his chapped lips. "How long we been on the road?"

"About three hours," Paco said.

Running her hand over her neck to wipe away the sweat, Paloma said, "The air quit working about a half-hour ago. It still blows, but just hot air."

"That's going to make for a tough trip." Glenn groaned, feeling his bruised muscles cramping up. He had no way of relieving them other than trying to stretch, which was hard to do while confined to the front seat. He needed to get out so he could move around. "How soon before we reach a place where we can stop?"

Paloma grabbed a folded map off the dash and passed it to Glenn. He unfolded it until he found 40D coming out of Nuevo Prado. With his fingertip, he traced the highway across the creased paper. The roadway had been marked in red, with long dashes joined with occasional blue lines. "This doesn't look like highway 40."

Paco cleared his throat. "It's not. They shut down 40 for construction. We're on the Monterrey-Reynosa highway. It's kind of the scenic route."

"Dammit, it's also a lot longer and slower."

"Yeah. There is that," Paco agreed.

"How much more time are we talking about here?"

"Gee, I don't know. It's not like I drive this way every day, *jefe*."

"We're no longer on the main highway, the A/C is gone, what else can go wrong? Do you know what this kind of heat will do to a body before we can get it home? It's going to blow up like a fucking party balloon, is what. His mother won't be very happy to see that."

"Will you two knock it off. It's too hot for this kind of stuff. You." Paloma punched Paco in the arm. "Keep your eye on the road until you can find a place to stop. Preferably a place where we can get something to drink and freshen up. Now you." She punched Glenn. "Stop being such a butthead. If you hadn't decided to take a nap, you would know what had happened. So, don't be blaming Paco. As for the body, it's not the end of the world. We'll figure something out when we get to Jalpa."

The ride became a little quieter after that. Before long, Glenn spotted a sign that said *Petrol de 25 Kilómetros*. He figured that to be about twenty miles. A half-hour later, he spotted a lone building alongside the road with two ancient pumps out front. Several vehicles were parked around it. Some looked to be held together with spit, duct tape, and baling wire.

Paco drifted off the road until he eased up alongside the pumps. They were old-style, with hand cranks to reset the counter. The building looked to be thrown together with leftover scraps, peeling paint exposing the bare wood in places. The clapboard sides were half-covered with battered, rusty metal signs hawking everything from Coca-Cola to tires and auto parts. The corrugated tin roof would normally turn the building into an oven, cooking those inside like your memaw's gingerbread cookies, if not for the massive swamp cooler mounted on the side. The fly-specked windows were almost obscured with smaller handmade signs offering a variety of beers, snacks, or food from the kitchen.

Glenn climbed out, pausing to stretch to get blood flowing back into his limbs after sitting so long. He held the door for Paloma while she scooted out of the hearse, stretching her bare legs until they touched the ground. He sympathized with her sigh of relief and watched while she shook her head and fanned herself with her purse while walking toward the station's screen door to vanish inside. A sweat stain spread across her ass, making her yellow shorts uncomfortably transparent, enough so he could make out the cut of her panties. The image gave Glenn ideas he shouldn't be having since Paloma was a good Catholic girl and not given to those sorts of thoughts. If she were, she had managed to keep them well hidden from the likes of him.

Paco grabbed the handle on the side of the pump, cranking it around several times to reset it. The sound jerked Glenn's thoughts back to their current situation, making him blush with shame at where his thoughts had gone. Turning to look up at the sun, he let its radiant heat bake the bruises on his face.

"Might as well fill her up while we're here. You see if you can find someone who can figure out what's wrong with the air conditioner."

"I don't think we need that." Glenn wiped his fingers across a spot where the fins had been bent over. They came away covered in oil. "Looks like it got hit by something that punched a hole in the coil. Most likely a rock. We can't spare the time it would take to get it fixed." Disgusted, Glenn wiped his hand on his jeans. "Looks like we're stuck using the two-sixty method to keep us cool."

Paco slapped the roof of the hearse while the gas pump dinged behind him. "If we can get this beast to do sixty. The good thing is we'll soon be in the mountains where it will be a lot cooler."

Glenn looked at the corrugated peaks in the distance pressed against the washed-out sky, like a lower jaw dug up from an ancient grave, missing half its teeth. "Won't come soon enough for me. When you get done, let's grab something cold to drink before we hit the road again."

"Maybe they have some decent eight-track tapes for sale. Check them out, will you? Preferably some Motown or one of those funky British bands."

Paloma stepped into the interior, where it was cooler but not by much. She let the screen door slam shut behind her before pausing a moment to let her eyes adjust while they swept across the dingy room. The counter lined the wall to her right, and a few wooden tables with chairs were scattered across the room, with even fewer customers sitting around them. A couple of old men washing their food down with cold beer warily watched the stranger in their midst.

Paloma spotted the kitchen through a small pass-through in the back wall. A large drink cooler sat in the corner, with the bottles chilling in an ice bath. The rest of the walls were covered with flickering neon signs that buzzed like a swarm of angry flies. A single, creaky ceiling fan tried its best to move the heavy air. The large swamp cooler rattled in the window while it filled the station with its mildew-tainted air before it spilled out through the screen door. It managed to keep the heat down a bit, but then she could hear the way it struggled, clanking and squealing like a pig with its snout caught in a snare.

She crossed to the drink cooler and reached in the icy water to pull out a bottle of Coke, knocking the cap off with the opener on the side. She took a long drink, relishing the way the carbonated drink tickled her throat to open up a flower of coolness in her belly. She let go with a little belch and rubbed the chilled glass alongside her neck while crossing to the counter to talk to the old man working there.

"How much...uh, *cuánto*?"

"*Cinco pesos.*"

Paloma dug in her purse. "*Americano?*"

"*Sí.*" He smiled widely, exposing his brown teeth.

Paloma thought it seemed a little high, but considering they were out in the middle of nowhere, there wasn't much reason to haggle. The quarter she laid on the counter vanished. Turning around, she spotted an old man hunched over his beer bottle smiling at her. He wore a battered cowboy hat tilted back to expose a shock of long gray hair that fell over a dark and wrinkled face. He motioned for her to join him with a gracious wave of his hand.

She sat, and he extended a dry, calloused hand with gnarled knuckles. "My name is Mack. It's been a long time since I had a chance to talk to a pretty young girl in my language."

"Paloma." She stuck out her hand. He wrapped his around hers for a quick squeeze. No intimacy involved, just a desperate need for a friendly face from what he considered home. "What's a man like you doing hanging around here?"

"Live here now, but I sure do miss my old place outside of Taos. Ain't seen it in about fifteen years. Where you from, pretty lady?"

"McHenry, Texas. If you don't mind me asking, why can't you go home?"

"Well, seems me and some folks back there got into a tussle over a slight misunderstanding about who owned certain heads of cattle. I decided it would be better for my health if I went away for a while. Mexico seemed like a smart alternative. Last I heard, they hadn't allowed I was in the right. They seem to be still holding a grudge against me."

"So, you were a rustler." Paloma couldn't help grinning.

"Let's just say I had developed a discreet way of redistributing livestock."

"Do you have any other special abilities?"

He grinned. "You mean besides getting the odd traveler to buy me a beer when they come through?"

Despite his admission about his past, Paloma started to warm up to Mack. She checked around the room but saw nothing but a few locals. "Seems like business isn't all that good."

"It's been better. Now let me show you something." He grabbed a paper napkin, rolled it into a tube, then dug a piece of string out of his pocket and handed it to Paloma. Mack held the rolled napkin between his fingertips.

"Take the string. Use it to tie any kind of knot you want around the middle of the napkin, then hold it tight at both ends," he said.

Curious, she tied a double square knot and pulled it until it creased the soft paper. He then had her hold it out straight in front of her, the ends wrapped around both her fists with the napkin in the center.

"Now watch closely." He reached out to wrap his hand around the napkin and string, muttering a few words under his breath before sliding his hand toward her left. The napkin moved until his hand touched hers.

"Now look at your knot," Mack instructed when he pulled his hand away. She pulled it close enough so that she saw it still seemed perfect, even if it had moved several inches to one side.

"That's amazing, how did you do that?" Paloma asked in that sweet voice.

"I'm not done yet. Watch close now." Mack took his finger and thumb and pinched the string between the knot and Paloma's left hand. Then slid it the other way, while he muttered under his breath again. The knot soon touched her right hand. She watched in amazement when it slipped along the string with a gentle vibration.

"Okay, now check it again." His wide grin exposed his tobacco-stained teeth.

Paloma unwound it from her fist, checked the knot closely, and tugged on the napkin, but it didn't move because it was still firmly held in place. She tossed it on the table. "I'm impressed, but what did that prove?"

"It's magic! Don't you like magic tricks?" Mack took a healthy pull from his beer, draining the bottle.

"I don't believe in magic," Paloma admitted.

"More's the pity, then. It's just a trick. A very good one, but still a trick." Mack grinned at her over the top of his empty bottle, giving it a shake. Paloma took the hint and headed for the cooler to get him a beer, paying for it at the counter. She set the bottle in front of Mack. He took the salt shaker and sprinkled some on the top before he caught the rising foam—a poor man's margarita without the lime.

"Thank you. So, where are you headed from here?"

"Me and my friends are headed for Jalpa."

"Nice place. You got business there?"

Paloma cocked her head, trying to read the man across the table from her, wondering if he might have an ulterior motive, or maybe just nosy. "I'm not sure I should answer that. You seem awfully curious about what our plans are."

Mack laughed, then touched his forefinger to the side of his nose. "What else have I got to do but sit around here, drink beer, ask questions, and play the jukebox? Except the jukebox is always broke. When it ain't, all it plays is Tejano music. To my ear, it all sounds like country Cajun with a lot of yipping going on. Ain't none of them good as a Hank Williams song." He sucked on the neck of his beer, not letting the foam created by the salt escape.

Paloma grinned. Leaning in, she lowered her voice like she had a big secret to share. "Okay. I'm traveling down there with my boss to escort a young boy's body back home to Texas. He didn't want me to come. I had to force him to let me tag along. He thinks it's too dangerous a job for a woman."

"Sorry to hear that, but he might be right. Mexico's not the safest place in the world, not now with all the drugs being smuggled across the border. That being said, I know for a fact that we men can be real assholes when it comes to you ladies, thinking we know what's best for you. Even better than you do."

Paloma laughed then reached across the tabletop to pat his gnarled hand. "I'm sure you don't mean all men."

"Sure, I do, since I am a card-carrying member of the male persuasion, I can attest all men are assholes. But some men are bigger assholes than others. I like to think I'm at the low end of the scale most of the time, but not all of it. It's when a woman finds a man that's only a part-time asshole that she figures she believes she's found a good one. Of course, we have been known to mellow out with age, which means an old asshole is almost always a better man than a young asshole, unless he's an old, bitter asshole who thinks the world has done him wrong. Then you won't find a bigger asshole than that." Paloma grinned her agreement.

"Plus, all you pretty girls are asshole magnets," he continued. "The plain girls don't draw as many. But then again, the assholes they do draw can be the worst of the lot, since they think they can treat that poor girl like crap because they have nothing to lose. But they're usually wrong—they have a lot to lose, but they never seem to realize it."

Glenn and Paco stepped in the open door, glancing around. Glenn spotted Paloma and crossed the room to join them while Paco paid for the gas, spending a few minutes haggling over the difference between dollars and pesos. When he finished paying, he spotted a rack of eight-track tapes against the wall and browsed for music. Glenn grabbed a chair, giving it a spin so he could straddle it.

"Who's your friend, Doll?"

"Glenn, this is Mack, an American from Taos, New Mexico. He lives down here now."

Mack grinned and stuck out his hand. "Ah, the asshole."

Glenn gripped the offered hand but looked hard at his secretary. "I have had better introductions. But I'm sure Paloma will tell you, none more apt."

Dropping her eyes, Paloma felt her face grow hot. "He's joking, *jefe*."

"Sure I am." Mack winked. "I don't get much chance to talk to many Americans anymore. It's been a pleasure to spend time with your pretty young lady."

"I thought we should grab a bite while we're here since breakfast didn't sit all that well with me. Maybe Mack can recommend something."

The old man shrugged. "Pretty much anything Graciela can whip up in that little kitchen back there is damn good, but I'm partial to her *gorditas* or the *chalupas*. She also can put together a pretty mean *carnita*."

Glenn nodded and waited for Paco, who sat down with a frown. "Nothing but Tejano music, not one decent rock band anywhere."

"Too bad," Glenn said, sending him to place their food orders, with beers for the two men. None for Paco despite his argument since he still had driving duty. While they ate, Mack entertained them with a few more tricks. Then they swapped a few lies, at least he and Glenn did.

After they finished their meal, Glenn and Paco headed for the car, but Paloma stayed back a minute. She reached into her purse to pull out a five-dollar bill, laying it on the table. "For your next few rounds."

Mack looked down for a moment, then looked into her brown eyes. "I didn't mind hustling you for a drink earlier. It's a silly game I like to play. But I put on a little show to earn it. I did nothing for this."

"But you did. Look at it like this, it's the least I can do for someone who can't go home again. Maybe we'll see each other when we come back through. You made me do some thinking. I don't believe it's in a man's nature to be an asshole, but it's what our society has expected him to become. It's like having a bad teacher. If they teach you wrong long enough, in your mind it becomes right. Then pretty soon, you don't know any better. But things are changing. Maybe not fast enough, but they are changing."

"You think so, pretty lady?"

"I know so, or else I wouldn't be here." Paloma cocked her head, sharing a warm smile. "I'll think of this as the parable of the asshole." With that, she hurried to catch up to her friends, sliding into the seat while Glenn held the door. He jumped in after he let loose with a beer and bean belch.

Ready to chastise his rudeness, Paloma caught him reaching out to adjust the side mirror. "What are you doing?"

"Keeping an eye on the road behind us. There's a pickup parked on the shoulder a good ways back that looks a little bit too familiar."

Paloma started to twist around, but Glenn grabbed her shoulder and said, "Don't."

Paco started the hearse and eased out onto the highway, picking up speed until he had the old beast pushing the speed limit, ignoring the groans coming from the front end when they hit the dips doing forty. Paloma peeked over Glenn's shoulder to look in the mirror and saw an old truck pull onto the highway behind them, picking up speed.

"Be careful, Paco. Looks like we picked up a tail." Glenn kept watching in the mirror while the truck grew larger as it closed in.

twelve

FRIDAY NIGHT in McHenry wasn't the most entertaining of places unless you happened to be in O'Rourke's pub. Even at that, it seemed to run at 33 RPMs in a 78 RPM world. Sometimes when the place was extra crowded, it would move up to 45 RPMs, but that Friday wasn't that kind of night. The jukebox sat silently in the corner while a handful of customers loitered around the pool table, hugging the cue sticks like slender lovers, straddling and pressing them against their crotch while the colored balls chased each other across the table with a little assistance. The television screen at the end of the bar flickered gray on gray while the tinny voice of the announcers spilled out. The Astros were playing at home. Several of the regulars had hunkered down to watch the game, groaning like women in labor when things didn't go Houston's way and sounding like a bunch of geezers at Mardi Gras when they did. Even after all his years in America, Seamus had never warmed up to the game of baseball. And even though cricket might be beloved by the English, in his mind, that seemed reason enough to hate it. He believed, if you were going to play a game with a stick and ball, hurling would be the thing to watch.

Seamus stood in his usual place behind the bar, working the keg handles like an old-timey church organ, filling mugs until the foam slopped over the lip. Or popping tops off bottles and setting them on pasteboard coasters printed with the O'Rourke's logo to catch the bottle sweat, leaving the bar ring-free.

Margarite handled the tables, serving those spread around the pub, turning and twisting like a ballerina with her usual grace and dexterity. When dropping off the drinks, she always had a smile for the customers, old or new.

She returned to the bar carrying a tray of empty glasses, dropped them on the bar, and pooched out her lower lip to blow a loose strand of dark hair from her eyes. Seamus grabbed the mugs, dropped them into the tub of soapy water, then gave them a quick rinse before setting them aside to dry. Occasionally he would cast a nervous look toward the door.

"What's bothering you, *mi amado*? You've been acting like *un gato en celo* since I got here. Pacing, frowning like a priest during confession. Spilling drinks, forgetting to laugh at Henry's jokes, even the ones you haven't heard before."

Sighing, he set up a couple of shot glasses, topped them from the bottle of Bushmills Black Label he kept under the bar, and tossed one back. Dropping his head, he stretched his arms out to grip the bar. "I think I may be in some trouble. I had a couple of visitors drop by earlier today."

Margarite paled and she closed her eyes. "*Madre de Dios*, who were they?"

"Men I knew when I first came over. They came down from Boston to look for me."

Barry Hudson called for another round. Margarite raised her hand, palm out, to signal him to wait. "What did they want?"

"Said they needed to talk to me."

"When?"

"Tonight." That's when he picked up the second glass and tossed it back with a sigh of satisfaction. "I promised not to hold anything back from you about my past when I asked you to be my bride. I'll be damned if I will break that promise now. I don't believe those boys have good intentions."

"What do you intend to do?"

"Hear them out first. I may be worried about nothing."

"But?"

"I'm probably wrong about that, or else they would have no reason to be here. These are not men inclined to cross the country for a social visit." He refilled three mugs, setting them on her tray. "Now go take care of Barry and his friends before he keels over from thirst."

She grabbed the tray and turned away, but not before calling over her shoulder. "We aren't done with this, Seamus Hennessey O'Rourke."

"I know, me darling girl. I know." He watched her walk away, balancing her tray one-handed while she slipped between the tables, with a certain heaviness in his heart. Margarite dropped the beers Barry had been caterwauling over, staying long enough to share with him and his friends a few light-hearted words to soothe his impatience before moving on.

It was getting on to closing time when the door opened to let the two strangers step inside. They paused to sweep the room with narrow eyes. Seamus knew that look. Out of habit, they were checking out his customers, thinking some might be informers. Checking the ways in and out. He had done it himself often enough in the olden days. When you weren't sure who you could trust, first rule, always make sure you had a safe way out in case things went to shite, which they often did. Owen led the way to the end of the bar, where both men took a seat well away from the others still huddled around the telly, listening to the post-game wrap-up show.

Seamus might not have been happy to see the men, but like a good publican, he made them feel welcome. "Owen, Paddy. What is it you'll be having, now?"

"A couple of pints."

"Best if you be sticking to the Irish whiskey, considering why you're here."

"That's a grand idea, Shammy. Perhaps we should have a little of the Black Bush, then. Since this is a special occasion. We can drink to each other's health or the good life in the hereafter."

Seamus fetched the bottle with three glasses, giving each a generous dose. Before taking a drink, he offered a toast. "Here's to the t'irty-two. May it happen soonest, God willing."

They lifted their glasses and solemnly tossed the drinks back.

Seamus refilled the glasses, allowing them to have a more leisurely drink. "Now, what are you boys doing here, as if I didn't know."

"We can hold off to talk until after you call time. Isn't that right, Paddy?"

"Sure, this is a wicked fine place you have here, a wicked fine place. We're in no hurry."

Grunting, Seamus left the bottle for them to share and went to service his other customers. He kept glancing at the clock, silently urging the slow-moving hands to get to midnight so he could announce last call and clear the place. Then he and the lads could get their business done.

The sudden spate of conversation at the end of the bar told him the wrap-up show had ended. Still talking about the game, the regulars started to settle their tabs before they headed home, paying their respects, drifting out by ones or twos. Before long only the four of them remained. Margarite went around to clean the tables, gathering up the dirty mugs and glasses. Seamus noticed her casting worried glances at the pair of strangers, at least they were strangers to her.

"Let's get this done with." Seamus stopped in front of the two men, pausing to pour himself a fresh drink.

Staring at his glass, Owen spoke without looking up. "Ah, Shammy, Tony Magan sends his regards."

"I thought he would have forgotten all about me by now. Fifty-one. that's a long time ago."

"You know how the old man is, he never forgets. He's not very good at forgiving, either. Not after what happened with his protection money back then. If we let one man get away with betraying his comrades, you never know when it will end."

Seamus gave them a hard look. "That's not the way of things. No matter what you've heard."

"It doesn't matter, the Southies always takes care of their own, good or bad."

"You came all the way here to tell me that? Or for me?"

Owen poured himself another drink and scoffed. "Not just you. There are a few others around the country who Tony feels he still owes a debt."

"You got nothing to say about this, Paddy?"

Patrick frowned. Reaching down, he pulled a gun out of his waist-band and laid it on the bar. "I'm just a soldier who follows orders, just like you were back in the day. Nothing personal in this at all."

"Soldiers is a mighty highfalutin way of referring to yourself, consid-ering what we did." Seamus looked at the gun, a beast of a thing with a bore big enough to shove his little finger in. He felt the sweat trickling down his face. "I hope you won't be offended if I take it personal, now."

"Not at all." Patrick picked up the weapon, thumbed the hammer back, and extended his arm. Seamus sucked in air, closed his eyes, flinching when he heard the first shot.

Margarite had left the men to their talk as she worked her way around until she slipped through the rear door where she managed to duck into the back office unnoticed. She went straight for Seamus's desk, searching for the revolver she knew he kept there. She never approved of him having a gun in the bar, but she understood the necessity. For the first time, she was relieved at the sight of it. Panting like a pup in summer, she removed the box of shells, and with shaking hands, she made sure all six chambers were loaded before she dropped it into her apron pocket. Margarite paused a moment with her eyes closed, curling her fingers to clench the apron while she tried to get her breathing under control. Closing her eyes, she made a quick sign of the cross. When she felt calm enough, she returned to the front of the bar, hoping no one had noticed the few minutes she had disappeared.

The men were still facing Seamus, talking in a way she couldn't hear what they were saying. Her breath caught when she spied one of them pulling out a gun and laying it on the bar. Then she saw the look of defeat on her husband's face, and it made her want to scream. Margarite's plan had been to work her way to Seamus' side while the men were talking and somehow slip the gun to her husband. But those men had other ideas. The quiet one picked up his gun, cocked it, and pointed it at Seamus.

"No," Margarite whimpered while standing behind the men. Then she reached into her pocket and pulled out the gun. Unable to watch, she raised the gun, closed her eyes, and pulled the trigger. Ignoring the way it kicked, she didn't stop until the explosions ended with metallic clicks of the hammer striking air. Dropping her head, she sobbed until a shaking hand gripped her shoulder, took the pistol, then gently pushed her back until she collapsed in a chair.

"Jayzus and Mary, mother of God." Seamus dropped to a knee and reached out to cup her cheek. Her tears washed over his hand, him half afraid to question the miracle of how she managed to kill the two men, shoot up half the bar, but miss him entirely. "What have you done, woman?"

Sobbing, she threw herself into her husband's arms, gripping him with a fierce hug. "I didn't know what else to do, *amado*. I couldn't let them take you away from me and Paco. They shouldn't have come here, not after all these years."

"Maybe so." He looked at the two men crumpled to the floor, the overturned stools, the shattered bar mirror. The broken liquor bottles filled the room with the strong aroma of spilled liquor mixing with the acrid stench of burnt powder.

Patrick raised his head, managing to flash a grin while blood leaked across his cheek as he wheezed from the hole in his lung. "That's a wicked fine woman you have there, Shammy."

"You be right about that," he agreed, still holding the sobbing Margarite tight. She had her arms tucked against his chest and head under his chin, trembling like a kitten abandoned in a storm.

"You did fine by yourself." Patrick's head dropped back to the floor. "Ah, where is a priest when you need one? For all the sins in my life, I could use a little absolution about now. Tell a dying man the truth, boyo, so I can go in peace."

Seamus shook his head. "I did not steal from Tony. True, I ran, so you can call me a coward if you wish. The truth is I was sixteen at the time. Not near ready to be a man when the order came for me to..."

He stopped when he saw the light had gone from Patrick's eyes and his breathing had stopped. The man was now beyond explanations. Seamus promised himself he would light a special candle for the two men at Sunday's mass. It was long past time for him to pay a visit to the confessional to get absolution for his sins.

Clenching her skirt, Margarite stared at her husband. Her dark eyes wide and wet, she said, "What are we going to do?"

"We have to clean the mess up and hide the bodies. I think I know just the place."

thirteen

WHEN THE HEARSE STOPPED, Manuel eased off the gas to let his pickup drift over onto the shoulder of the highway. They rolled to a stop a mile or so short of the small gas station. Ignoring the loss of the breeze, he looked out at the flat plain dotted with scattered Joshua trees with their tufted limbs and a lone yucca plant sprouting with sword-like leaves, impossibly sharp and dangerous. He imagined a wandering troop of conquistadors from five-hundred years ago pausing to pluck them for weapons, then using them to attack a small Aztec village, chopping off heads or limbs and gutting women and babies in hopes they could bring the heathens to Jesus.

Shaking his head, he looked back at the road-side station, watching as the driver climbed out and moved around the back of the big hearse. "I got to take a leak. Get the field glasses out of the glove box so we can keep an eye on that *gringo* bastard."

When he stepped out, the truck groaned like a skinny whore under a fat john—all complaints, no pleasure. Stretching first, he went around the rear to check the tire. Standing with his back to the highway, Manuel dug his dick out then let it wave in the sauna-like air while he relaxed his bladder. Eyes closed, he sighed at the sudden relief, listening to the way his stream splattered against the rocky ground, like someone crinkling a sheet of notebook paper. He'd about finished when the spattering sound seemed to mingle with a baby maraca. Cracking an eye, Manuel looked down to spy a coiled rattler a step away, its lifted tail a shimmying blur. The flat, triangular head pointed straight at him, its forked tongue flickering like it was tasting him and was in the mood for Mexican. The sight caused his bladder to clamp down until his piss stream slowed to a meager dribble. The last drops splattered on the toe of his right boot because his dick curved like a Carl Hubbell bases loaded, three and two pitch.

"Shit." Manuel yelled as he jumped back. His loose dick flopped in the breeze until he could get it tucked away, praying he didn't get it caught when he jerked the zipper up, which he accomplished more by luck than effort. An itchy bead of nervous sweat formed below his hairline, slipping down the side of his face, followed by another. Then came several more when he dragged his foot back, making a rasping sound as the sole slid over the coarse gravel—he was terrified any sudden movement could cause it to strike. "I hate fucking snakes... Jorge?" His voice sounded weak and high pitched in his own ear. He wasn't sure his companion had heard him. "Jorge."

"*Qué?*"

"Rattler." From the corner of his eye, he saw Jorge's head stick out the window so he could look back. Manuel's bladder began to hurt again from his unfinished business. He was half afraid he would piss his pants.

Still speaking Spanish, Jorge said, "So? What do you want *me* to do about it?"

"Get out here and kill the sonofabitch, that's what I want. Now hurry."

The door gave a rusty scream when the big man pushed it opened and climbed out, causing the truck to bounce on its worn-out springs. He flashed a look of disgust at Manuel and marched over to the snake. Then he stomped down, crushing its head before it could strike and kicking it hard enough to send it sailing out among the cactuses.

Falling back against the side of the truck, Manuel wiped the sweat on his sleeve. "Goddamn it, you know I hate those slimy bastards. They make my skin crawl."

"All that pissing and moaning over a fucking rattlesnake, dude."

"Screw you. Give me those goddamn field glasses."

Jorge extended the glasses with a mocking grin that infuriated Manuel. He hated that the sonofabitch saw him in a moment of weakness. Snatching the glasses, he stomped around the truck and climbed in. Leaning out the window, he pointed the glasses toward the hearse, trying to get a closer look at their targets. Manuel ignored his partner getting back in. He saw the tall *gringo* standing next to the pump while the girl vanished inside. "We'll wait here until they get back on the road."

The big man said nothing. He just pulled out another Tootsie Roll, peeled it, popped it into his mouth. He chewed slowly, like a cow at its cud. Manuel watched him for a moment, the constant chewing, smacking, and grunting playing on his nerves until he wanted to smash something. "Where in the hell do you keep all those damned things. You've been eating one after another since we left Texas. Don't you ever run out?"

Jorge shrugged, worked his jaws, and spat a stream of Tootsie Roll juice out the window. Staring across the road at the dusty land dotted with clusters of faded green going the color of crackers. Then there were the piles of something that had the look of abandoned stacks of giant tortillas. It looked like the sun had tried its damnedest to bleach all color out of the world. Muttering under his breath, Manuel returned to watching the little gas station, ignoring the trickles of sweat that slid down his face. He still needed to empty his bladder but was afraid he might stumble across another snake.

The two men sat there, waiting patiently for about an hour before the three figures came out and climbed into the hearse to continue their journey. Manuel waited a few minutes to give them a head start before he started the truck, then pulled back onto the highway, keeping well back so he wouldn't arouse their suspicions. When he did make his move, he wanted it to be a surprise. He figured the mountains would be the perfect place for the hearse to have an accident. If he planned things just right, it would be weeks or longer before the wrecked car and the bodies would be found. That should make Alonzo as happy as a tick on a hound's ear.

Glenn watched while the mountains swallowed the sun. They sucked it down into the earth like a kid with a red grape, then orange and red streamers reached up to pull the pale sky down with it, leaving a velvet blanket full of pinholes in its place. A few high, wispy clouds flew across the sky like cotton candy escaping a carnival midway joint. In the desert, the light went quick, like it had things to do and needed to be somewhere else. The road curved like a licorice whip as it stretched out toward the foot of the mountains and began its gentle climb.

Almost without notice, the air became cooler. Glenn knew the temperature would drop even more now that the sun had gone down. Maybe uncomfortably so. He still kept a close eye on their tail, watching the men behind them who would close the distance before falling back until they were a barely recognizable dot. The driver had experience and enough skills that most people might not realize they were being followed.

"Who are they, *jefe*?" Paloma asked when she caught him checking the side mirror again.

"If I had to guess, Doll, I would say they were a couple of Alonzo Ortega's men."

"Why in hell would a small-time marijuana smuggler be following us?"

Glenn looked at Paloma with surprise. "You know who he is?"

"Don't be an idiot, of course I do. Everyone in my part of town knows who he is. His sister runs the free clinic over on Houston Street. He runs a pawnshop. But everybody knows it's mostly a front for his drug business."

"Why didn't I know that until recently?"

Paloma stuck her arm out next to his, contrasting their skin color, a stark reminder of their different places in society. That made his face turn an unappealing shade of red. "Gee, I don't know, *gringo*. Why do you think? Now, I'll ask you again. Why would they be interested in us?"

"Well, I might have had a little run-in with the man, and I might have accidentally dropped something on his hand, breaking a few bones."

"What did you accidentally drop?" Her eyes narrowed with anger.

"A fully loaded Colt Python."

"Mother of God, you stupid bastard. Why in the hell would you do that?"

"Hey, Doll, I found out he was using school kids to sell his drugs and thought, if we had a civil conversation about it, he could be persuaded to change his ways." Even as he said it, Glenn realized how stupid it sounded, but he was all in now, and couldn't backtrack if he wanted to.

"Why would you break his hand if you were just having a civil conversation?"

"I felt like I needed to get his attention first."

She closed her eyes, and he heard her mutter under her breath. "You're a dumb ass to go in there, trying to act the martyr to save kids you don't even know from that dangerous maniac—wait a minute." She turned to look him in the eye. "Does this have anything to do with Miguel?"

Glenn felt his face burn even hotter. He turned away to look out the window, hoping she wouldn't notice.

"Never mind, that's answer enough. When we get home, I'm going to kill that little bastard. I'm going to take a stick and beat him like a piñata until the stupid comes out of his ears. It's bad enough he started skipping school, but getting involved with a drug dealer, selling that poison to his friends? I'm going to lock him up in his room until he's thirty."

"Whoa there, Doll. I know you're upset, but he's a kid just doing stupid kid stuff. He needs to learn his way in life like we did. We just have to make sure he doesn't stray too far."

"Shut up, Glenn. I suppose you weren't going to tell me." Paloma slumped back and crossed her arms.

"Well—"

"I said shut up. How could you keep something like that from me? I ought to... ought to... oh, I don't know what I ought to do, but I'm pissed off at you right now. He's my little brother and you were going to keep it from me?" Twisting in her seat, she brushed her hair back from her sweaty face, her eyes slitted with anger, and she began punctuating her words with punches to his arm as her voice gained volume. "*Me*, who has raised him. Who took care of him for the past six years since our mother died while also taking care of *you* like you're a toddler who can't keep his fingers out of his nose because he thinks what he finds there is some kind of dessert!" She lay her head on the back of the seat, staring up at the dirty headliner. "I can't believe you weren't going to tell me."

"Look, Paloma, I'm sorry. And I figure man is about the sorriest creature in this world. I believe it's in his DNA. Probably left over from caveman times when he was always *sorry*ing to his wife about bringing nothing home for supper but a terror-dactyl or a bronty-sore-us to make burgers with before they invented the bun. We've been apologizing ever since."

"I don't give a hot damn about your apology. Don't talk to me right now."

They drove on for a while, Paloma staring straight through the windshield, stewing in her anger until Paco broke the silence. "Uh, hey, y'all?"

"What, Paco?" Glenn said since Paloma still wasn't talking to either of them.

"I think they're making their move now."

Glenn looked in the side mirror to see the truck closing in, the rusty grill giving it the appearance of an angry, snarling beast about to take a bite out of the hearse's ass. "Hit the gas, Paco. See if you can outrun them. Damnit, I wish I had my guns right now."

"Where are they?" Paco pushed the gas pedal to the floor. The behemoth of a vehicle reacted slowly, but the speedometer needle did begin to climb.

"In a special compartment in the bottom of my bag."

"Lot of good they're going to do us in there."

"Listen, boy. You *know* what the penalty is if we get caught carrying them on this side of the border. The *federales* don't have much of a sense of humor about those kinds of things, especially if you're from the States. They just love to throw Americans in prison for that kind of stuff. And if they did, it would take a hell of a lot more money than I have to bribe our way to freedom." Glenn studied the way the mountains fell away from the highway, flanked by deep canyons between the granite hills while the terrain rose and fell like a broken washboard. He knew if that truck hit them at the right time, it could force them off the road, driving them into an abyss where they might never be found, come hell or high water or the second coming of Jesus. Glenn didn't like the idea of having to wait that long.

Despite Paco speeding up, the truck continued to close in, until, with a final surge, it slammed into the back of the hearse. The blow jolted the passengers, causing the vehicle to fishtail until Paco got the vehicle back under control. Paloma screamed when she banged into Glenn. He wrapped his arm around her shoulder to keep her steady. Panting, Paco hunched forward, gripping the wheel with both hands. "That sonofabitch is crazy. What are we going to do?"

"Pay attention to the road—here they come again." Glenn squeezed Paloma, kissed her cheek, and slithered over the seatback to land flat on his back, feet pointed toward the door. Then he yelled at Paco, "When I give you the word, get as close to the left shoulder as you can."

"Why?"

"Just do it, but don't let up on the gas."

Taking a deep breath, Paco said. "Ready, Boss."

"Now!" Glenn felt the lumbering hearse swerve hard then straighten up. He lashed out with both feet, hitting the little air conditioner with enough force to rip it free. Sitting up, he looked out the back window. In the wash of the pickup's headlights, it looked like that damned truck was about to drive up their tailpipe and mount the hearse like a horny pit bull. He watched the metal box bounce down the road, heading straight for the vehicle behind them.

Manuel saw the small box flying out the side of the hearse. It hit the road, bounced, and tumbled toward them. It bounced once more before it hit the truck and rolled over the hood. It smashed onto the windshield before he could swerve out of the way, showering them with bits of glass. Blindly, he jerked the wheel hard to send the truck sliding on screeching tires. Manuel lost control, sending them spinning off the road. The centrifugal force sent both men bouncing around in the cramped cab like dice in a Yahtzee cup. Hitting the ditch, the front end smashed into the rocky wall hard enough to whip Manuel's head forward until it slammed into the steering wheel. His nose cracked while everything went black except for a swirl of colorful stars. It took a moment to clear his head, but when he could focus, he saw a battered window unit stuck halfway through his windshield, a jagged metal corner inches from his face.

"Holy shit." Falling back, he felt hot blood pouring from his nose, which already felt three times bigger than normal, forcing him to breathe through his mouth. Jorge lay slumped against the door with a large knot growing in the middle of his forehead. That's when Manuel saw the dent in the metal dashboard that looked like someone had taken a sledgehammer to it.

Closing his eyes and panting heavily through his mouth, Manuel covered his nose, grabbed the cartilage, and squeezed while he twisted at the same time. He moaned as the knife-like pain almost made him black out again. The bones grated together, then popped back into place. Blinking to clear the tears from his eyes, Manuel studied the crumpled front end of his truck through the striations in the windshield while smoke and steam poured from beneath the hood. If they had hit a few feet more to the left, they could have ended up at the bottom of some nameless canyon where only the buzzards or coyotes would have found them. He popped the door open with a metallic groan, slipped from behind the wheel, and stumbled over the uneven ground to reach the vehicle's front, to better assess the damage. Manuel took in the bent bumper, the crumpled hood, and the driver's side flat tire. He realized they weren't going anywhere. With his broken nose, he couldn't smell, but he could taste the metal tang of the water boiling off the hot engine from the ruptured radiator, mingling with the taste of burnt oil.

"Sonofabitch. What the hell are we going to do, stuck here in the middle of nowhere?" Frustrated, he punched the fender hard enough for it to jar his shoulder.

"What?" A groggy Jorge climbed out of the cab, reeling drunkenly as he looked around, confused, his forehead now swollen to Franken-steinian proportions. Blood ran down from a cut over his right eye, leaving his face smeared with warpaint.

"I said we're stuck out here in the middle of nowhere, you dumb ox. Can things get any worse?"

Jorge nodded slowly, then slurred in English, "They can get worse. I think I ran out of Tootsie Rolls."

"I thought you didn't speak English?"

"I don't. I think I'm gonna be sick." Jorge vanished, leaving Manuel shaking his head at Jorge's second distressed spate of English. A moment later, Manuel heard retching sounds, followed by dull wet splatters.

"Shit, that's all I need. On top of a busted truck, I've got an enforcer that's sick as a dog eating cat shit. Plus, our target is long gone."

Jorge stuck his head up, dragging the back of his hand across his mouth. "*Qué*?"

"So, now you're back to normal. We need another vehicle. We need it quick, before that shitty dick and his friends can get away." Manuel climbed out of the ditch until he stood on the shoulder, looking left and right. He saw nothing but vast emptiness while the stars shed their cold light down on the all-but-empty world. Jorge joined him and passed over one of their pistols. Reflexively, Manuel checked the load before sticking it into his waistband.

Returning to speaking in Spanish, Jorge said, "What do we do now?"

"We wait. Somebody's bound to come by before long." With the sun gone, the desert began to cool down fast. Manuel sent Jorge back to the truck to fetch their jackets, along with whatever else he might be able to salvage. Which turned out to be not much.

It took a half hour but felt longer before he spotted headlights coming along one of the rough turnoffs about five miles back, the head-lights bouncing around like a couple of drunk lightning bugs trying to fuck on the fly. The vehicle soon reached the highway, turned their way, and picked up speed on the much smoother pavement. Moving into the middle of the road, Manuel half turned so that his right shoulder pointed down the road, drew his pistol, and waited.

"What are you doing?" Jorge grunted from the shoulder.

"I'm getting us a ride. Unless you like it out here in the middle of nowhere, with nothing but four-legged coyotes and scorpions for company," Manuel said, watching the vehicle while it came closer. He saw it was another pickup. One even older and more battered than his piece of shit truck now nose-first in the ditch.

"I don't like scorpions—they're some ugly sombitches. What happens if he doesn't stop?"

"Oh, they'll stop. One way or another."

The truck vanished in a dip, then climbed the rise, coming closer. The driver had to have seen him, but he made no effort to slow.

Manuel raised his hand, fired into the air once, and dropped his arm. Walking forward, he pointed the weapon straight at the driver. The truck came to a rolling stop when the driver got the message. The only sound was the ticking of the hot engine in the cool night air.

Still walking, Manuel yelled, "Get out. *Vete.*"

The door opened, allowing a small figure to climb out, his hands on the top of his head. "Don't shoot. I have no money," came out in fast, stuttering Spanish.

"I don't want your money. I want your truck."

"*Qué?*"

Motioning with his gun for the driver to step away, Manuel turned his head to look back at Jorge. "Get our stuff."

His partner stared over his shoulder, his eyes going big as he shouted, "Look out."

Manuel jerked around to see the driver had a pistol pointed his way. A bright flash was followed by a searing pain that stabbed through his shoulder, the shot echoing off the mountain, quickly followed by several more. The world slowed when he spun around to land in an awkward sprawl in the center of the road.

fourteen

GLENN WATCHED the window unit hit the road, tumble, and bounce before it smashed into the truck's windshield. The driver slammed on his brakes, causing the truck to skew sideways, the tires screaming like a dying horse as the headlights veered off in a wild direction before it vanished over the side of the road. Glenn crawled back over the seat, dragging his bag with him. Turning it upside down, he pried open a hidden panel to expose his matched Colt 1911s. Grabbing them, he hefted them in his palms and chambered a round in each. Feeling better with his weapons in his hands, he turned to watch through the rear window in case the truck managed to climb back up on the road. One of the pistols rested on his forearm, pointed at the back window. The other lay in the nest made by his cocked leg.

"You know we're going to have to pay for that," Paco said while he drifted back into the right lane, his eyes locked on the rearview mirror.

"Relax. We're on an expense account. Just remember to get a receipt for it when you turn this monster back over to its owner."

"See anything?" Paco asked. Glenn glanced at Paco, who hunched over the wheel, his eyes locked on the road.

Paloma had her head down, palms pressed against her face. She seemed to be in shock, her anger forgotten. He grabbed her shoulder, giving it a gentle squeeze until she looked up. Eyes glazed, she asked,

"Are they dead? Please tell me they aren't dead." She made a quick sign of the cross while her lips moved in silent prayer.

"I doubt it. They weren't going fast enough for a crash like that to be fatal. But I'm sure it didn't do their truck much good."

"What if they are dead or hurt?" she asked.

"Then I would call it karma. That's how the universe is supposed to work. You do bad shit, bad shit can happen to you. Doesn't always work out like that, though. There are too many times the universe lets the bad guys off without so much as a nasty word or telling them your mama is going to hear about this. Me? I try to even it out a little and make sure the bad ones pay a price, even if it's only some kind of inconvenience, like crashing their pickup and having to walk a few miles to get help."

Paco drove on while Glenn kept watch, enjoying the dry night air flowing in through the missing window. It smelled of sage and dampness coming down the mountain slopes. Before long, with the gentle rocking of the vehicle, Paloma managed to relax enough to nod off, slipping sideways until her head hit Glenn's arm. He put his gun away and shifted until she lay against his side where he could wrap his arm around her shoulder. She gave a sleepy sigh, soon followed by a gentle snore.

Keeping his voice low, he spoke to Paco. "If you feel you need to rest, pull over and I'll take the wheel for a while."

"I'm okay. I'm too wound up after what happened. We should reach the turnoff to Highway 54 soon. After that, it's a straight shot south to Jalpa. Unless we run into some more construction."

"Or bad guys, but I don't think Ortega has that many men to spare," Glenn said. He stared out the window at the mountains outlined against the growing darkness, the kind of darkness most people never get the chance to experience living so close to the cities whose lights don't seem to have an off switch. The never-ending shadow out the window was only lessened by the stars and the promise of a moon to come, the kind of darkness he hadn't seen since the jungles of South Vietnam, where the only way one could keep track of your team members had been by the sound of their breathing. You tried to keep from falling into a pit that would swallow you whole then slice you to pieces on bamboo stakes poisoned by the liberal application of human shit. In that far-away world of heat and humidity, the air felt so thick it was almost smothering, like trying to breathe water while it fills your mouth until you felt you were going to strangle on your fear.

Glenn closed his eyes, choking down the memories he tried to keep buried deep as possible until the blackness of his mind swallowed him.

Manuel lay on his back in the center of the road, his left shoulder numb and his whole face aching, staring up at the growing patch of stars. A moment later, they were blocked out by the large head of Jorge leaning over so he could check out his companion. "Are you ok?"

He groaned and reached up to feel his shoulder. His fingers came away smeared black with blood. "Of course I'm not okay, you stupid Comanche bastard. I've been shot."

"Half."

"What?"

"I'm only half." Classic Jorge—never more than a word or two, and always in Spanish. Gave Manuel a headache.

"Half, full-blooded, what's the fucking difference. Where's the sonofabitch that shot me?" Manuel rolled over to where he could push himself with his good hand until he managed to sit up. The truck still sat there, engine idling with the door open, but the driver had vanished.

"He ran off."

"Where in the hell can he run off to out here in the middle of fucking nowhere? Why didn't you shoot the bastard?"

"I did. Well, shot at, but I think I missed."

"Didn't you check for blood?"

Jorge shrugged and tilted his head to the sky, ablaze with the swathe of stars. Manuel got the message. His partner thought it would be useless to try and track anyone in the dark. He stepped in front of the headlights, ripping his shirt open to inspect his wound. The bullet had creased his shoulder close to his collarbone, hitting only meat but deep enough to still be bleeding. It hurt like hell, but not so deep that it would put a stop to their tracking the shitty dick and his companions. He would chase them all the way to hell if he had to, after what they did to his truck. It might not have been much, but the damn thing was his.

"Looks like I'll survive. Which way did the fucker who shot me go?"

Sighing, Jorge pointed. Manuel grabbed a flashlight so he could check the road for blood. He soon found droplets and followed them back to the shoulder and down into the ditch. He heard a wheezing rasp. A moment later, he found the driver sitting against a stone outcrop. In the wash of the flashlight, he saw the man's head laid back, eyes closed, face bathed in sweat. A large red stain spread across the front of his shirt. His gun lay on the ground, inches from his hand. He didn't look good, and his waxen features said he was about ready to meet up with Saint Peter or El Diablo.

"Looks like you are in bad shape, *mi amigo*."

The dark eyes opened, creased in pain, with red foam leaking from the corner of the wounded man's mouth. Licking his lips, he gasped out in Spanish, "You don't want to do anything you might regret. I work for El Toro."

"You think I give a shit who you work for? You shot me, asshole." Manuel pressed the barrel of his gun against the man's chest and pulled the trigger, twice. The body jerked, then slumped back. The stench of hot piss rose from his crotch, followed by a loud, wet fart that smelled heavily of beans. Manuel stood, wiped the mouth of the barrel against his pants, and kicked the body hard enough to send it falling over onto its side. "Tell that to your boss when you see him in hell."

Manuel limped back to the truck where he glared at Jorge, who had one hand on the driver's door, looking into the back. "There's a tarp on the truck bed."

"So what? He's a wetback farmer hauling a load of corn to the market. He probably covered it with the tarp to protect it. Did you get all our stuff, including the rifle?"

Jorge nodded but didn't look very happy. You would have thought somebody pissed in his corn flakes, took a shit in his coffee, and took away his sugar bowl.

"You can drive. We have to catch that asshole. Only he's going to pay for more than Alonzo's broken hand. He also owes me for wrecking my truck and getting me shot."

"What about unloading the back?"

"Leave it. What the hell do I care about some farmer's crops? We don't have time to throw the stuff away. It won't make much difference, anyway. Let's just get the hell out of here." Manuel climbed into the shotgun seat, glaring until Jorge got in and slammed the door.

Grabbing the shifter, Jorge stepped on the clutch and shoved it into first, causing Manuel to cringe when the gears ground together until it sounded like a trash can full of gravel rolling downhill.

"Goddammit, be careful. We can't afford to blow the transmission."

"It's the clutch. I think it's worn out," Jorge responded in Spanish while he feathered the gas until the truck lurched forward.

"Bad clutch, my ass. Drive the damned truck. Just try not to get us killed."

Jorge pushed down on the gas pedal until the truck picked up speed, but the faster it went, the more it shimmied and rattled until Manuel feared the damn thing would fall apart. He watched his partner grimace when he grabbed the wheel with both hands and leaned forward, squeezing until his knuckles were white, like he could make the truck go faster using sheer force of will while trying to hold it together at the same time.

The yellow headlights swept over the plunging canyons and thrusting prominences while they followed the winding highway. No matter how hard he tried to focus on the road ahead, Manuel couldn't see any sign of the hearse.

"Damn. Looks like we won't be catching up to them until we reach Jalpa—unless that little shit lied to us about where the *gringo* is going." Manuel settled back for a long drive, but no matter how hard he tried, he couldn't get comfortable. The seat was so worn he would swear someone was underneath, poking his ass with a stick, making it impossible to ignore. He tried to shift to a more comfortable position where the seat left his ass alone, but that only seemed to aggravate his wound. The way the old truck shook while it bounced its way down the road did little to better his mood.

Jorge switched on the radio and fiddled with the knob until he halfway found a radio station spewing out static-filled Tejano music being played between stretches of commercials. They mostly seemed to be selling Jesus and a collection of blessed relics that would cure everything from broken bones to broken hearts, along with all the diseases known to man.

The ride smoothed out some as the truck picked up more speed. Then, between the music and the gentle shimmy of the pickup, Manuel managed to drift off into a fitful doze.

fifteen

CHARLIE SAT in his office behind his big old desk in the sheriff's department, located in the McHenry courthouse, doing pretty much nothing but some deep thinking about the state of his community. Such as the problem he was having with Alonzo Ortega and his drug business. Thanks to Glenn's tip, his deputies were busting Ortega's young dealers, since most of them didn't have the reasoning ability of a bucket of rocks. They couldn't tell him much more than their name and phone number. If Ortega had any drugs on-premises, he had wised up and moved them where Charlie's deputies couldn't find them. His deputies weren't much help since their ideas were about as useful as a West Texas wildcatter's saltwater well. Hell, most of their ideas were dry holes that didn't produce so much as a methane fart.

Charlie leaned back in his chair with his fingers laced over his belly while he stared at the wood-slatted Venetian blinds over his office windows, the kind he could drop and close for privacy from the rest of the office if the mood struck. To be honest, the mood struck pretty often, and he had them closed now.

He was still pondering when Sheila's voice came at him through the office intercom. "Hey, Charlie. We just got a call from Ray over at the Hotel Paraíso. Seems he's lost a pair of customers, those two strangers who came in from the east. Says they've been missing for a couple of days, but their bags are still there."

Even though McHenry was considered a midsized town, it still had small town ethics, where strangers were looked upon with suspicion and secrets were passed along the gossip grapevine. "Did he try calling around to the whorehouses over on Beacon Avenue that we're not supposed to know about?"

"Said he checked everywhere. Claims last time he talked with them, they were on their way to O'Rourke's to have a few drinks."

"When was that exactly?"

"Ray said the day before yesterday."

"Did you give Seamus a call?"

"Yeah, but no answer. It's still early, though."

"Shit. Guess I better mosey on over there and see what he has to say."

"You could always send over one of your poor, hard-working deputies."

"Now, Sheila, don't be like that, wanting to put that sort of burden on those poor boys, trying to force them to actually use their meager thinking resources to figure out a problem. Besides, it'll do me good to get out of here for a bit. It'll give me a chance to stretch my legs. Show the people of this town I'm still cock of the walk around here."

"Right. You're such a hard man, Sheriff Charlie Gaines. You have those citizens of dubious character shaking in their boots lest you expose their peccadilloes and chicanery."

He ignored her jibe, grabbed his Stetson, and ran his fingers along the brim before putting it on. These were the same men Glenn asked him to keep an eye on. So far, he had managed to do a hell of a job if they had been able to vanish without a word.

The short walk from the sheriff's office to the bar left him drenched with sweat and his shirt tacky with sunburst stains under his arms. The bar's inside lights were on while the neon signs flashed in the bar's windows, a sure sign of occupancy. Charlie always liked the place. He spent many an evening sitting in one of the corners, sharing drinks with Glenn or a couple of his deputies. More than a few were spent hanging around the pool table, shooting for drinks with Sylvia on his arm, but it seems those times were buried a few years in the past. The Irishman had a way of making everyone feel welcome. It would be a shame if something happened to endanger that.

Charlie stepped into the cool darkness, removed his hat, and wiped his brow while scanning the interior. Seamus stood behind the bar while Margarite made her way around the floor, wiping down the tables, both working hard to get things set up for the day's coming business. Although it was still early enough that there were no customers, Charlie knew it would soon be packed with those who preferred to drink their lunch and maybe nibble on a handful of the cheap bar snacks.

He called a soft greeting while crossing the room. "Seamus."

The Irishman looked up in surprise and cast a worried glance in his wife's direction before allowing a smile to cross his face. "Charlie, what do you be doing here? It's a mite early for a constable to be having himself a pint or three. I hope you're not bringing bad news about our wayward son and your friend the bounty hunter."

"As far as I know, those two are fine. Sorry, but this is not a social call. We seem to have lost a couple of men, those two strangers who were staying at the Hotel Paraíso. Ray said they came by here the night before last."

"That they did, sat right there at the end of the bar where they had a couple of whiskeys. Stayed until closing before going on their way."

"Did they say anything about any plans, or where they might be headed after leaving here?"

Seamus shook his head. "They stayed pretty much to themselves. Didn't bother me other customers one bit."

"What about Margarite? She know anything?"

He shook his head again. "As usual, she worked the tables while I worked the bar. She didn't have the occasion to even speak to the gentlemen."

Charlie set his hat on the bar and leaned against it. "You know, I think I will have a Coke, if you don't mind."

"Sure thing. Will you be wanting a glass?"

"No. The bottle's fine."

Charlie looked around the bar while Seamus fished a small bottle out of the cooler, popped the cap, and set it on a coaster. He spotted a few shards of glass somebody seemed to have missed, tiny pieces that caught the light like splinters of ice. Charlie also noticed an odd dark stain, almost invisible, on the floor in front of the bar. He rubbed the toe of his boot across the edge, but nothing happened. He considered it might be nothing more than a trick of the light. Picking up his drink, he pointed at the mirror. "That new?"

"Yes. It seems I had me a fit of clumsiness yesterday. Tried to pick up a bottle with me soapy hands. I turned around too quick. It slipped from my hand and cracked the mirror before the bottle itself shattered. Made one hell of a mess back here, I can tell you that."

"Ought to be more careful." He drained the bottle and dug into his pocket for some change before Seamus waved him off. "If you don't know anything, guess I'll mosey on over to the hotel. Maybe I can find something out there."

Charlie walked out with the sense that something was off, but he couldn't quite put his finger on it. Not that Seamus or Margarite acted out of sorts, but he felt something niggling at the back of his mind. He did think it a bit odd that a pair of full-grown men would be able to up and disappear like that, but they wouldn't be the first. Maybe after a few drinks, they decided to make a trip across the border, seeking out something a little more exciting than a sleepy little town like McHenry might offer. They could have met a bad end there. He needed to check with his alter ego in Nuevo Prado, see if he had any information. But like he figured, they wouldn't be the first.

The Paraíso happened to be the fanciest hotel in McHenry, which wasn't saying much. It had its heyday back in the pre-World War 2 days when people used to come from all over the state to take advantage of the horseraces and gambling across the border. But like most things, when those played out, so did the town, leaving the hotel to coast along on its reputation for a few years until people no longer cared. It wore its faded glory like an old Hollywood star, trying to appear more relevant than it actually was. But time had caught up with the Paraíso. It no longer entertained the state's elite, but now catered to the more mundane citizens of the town, some of whom were permanent residents.

He found Ray standing behind the front desk in the hotel lobby, talking with Annabelle Perkins, who seemed a bit agitated and was giving him what for. She picked up her purse and book, then stalked off, stiff-legged with anger.

"Morning, Sheriff," Ray said with obvious relief.

"Morning, Ray. Sheila told me about your wayward tenants. I stopped by to look at those boys' room. Annabelle seems to be in a mood."

"That she is. Said she couldn't sleep last, not after hearing all that gunfire the other night."

"Gunfire?"

"Yeah. You know she has that room in front. She likes to sleep with her window partially open, claims she doesn't trust the hotel's conditioned air—afraid it might suffocate her. I tried to explain to her that doesn't happen anymore, not since those units switched from ammonia more than twenty years ago, but she won't have it. Tells me she remembers what my grades were like in school." Charlie grinned while Ray shook his head.

"Anyway, she said she heard gunfire around midnight. She's afraid it's one of those Mexican drug gangs getting ready to invade and take over Texas. I told her she didn't have anything to worry about, we ain't had nobody try anything like that since Pancho Villa attacked San Ygnacio back in sixteen." Ray tapped the side of his head while giving Charlie a knowing look.

"I'll talk to her." Charlie waited for Ray to hand him the passkey and room number, then crossed the lobby to where Annabelle sat with her book before the large window overlooking the town square. It was a nice view, with the statue of Sam Houston in a parklike setting filled with trees and beds overflowing with colorful flowers bright as Christmas decorations. He took the seat next to her. She looked up, raking him with a pair of eyes sharp and bright like a hawk.

"Charlie Gaines. What are you doing here?"

"I'm the sheriff here now, Missus Perkins."

"I know that. Don't treat me like I'm a doddering old fool like Ray does. He thinks I'm losing my mind, but I'm just as sharp now as I was when I taught him back in the sixth grade, or at least pretty near. I didn't teach you, though, did I? You had to go to that colored school with the Mexican kids. Shame that, the government not allowing kids to get a proper education because society thinks you were born with the wrong color skin. Like that had anything to do with one's ability to think or learn. Ray is certainly proof of that." She paused a moment, like she had lost her train of thought, then shook her head. "I meant, why are you here. In that chair, sitting next to me."

"Ray told me you were having trouble sleeping at night. I thought you might want to tell me about it. He mentioned something about you hearing some shooting?"

"I suppose you think I'm crazy, too. A senile old woman who thinks she heard gunfire in the middle of the night. Well, I think no such thing. I know I heard gunfire, at least six shots, one after another like they couldn't pull the trigger fast enough. Then it was over. Didn't hear any more after that."

"Can you tell where it came from?"

She shook her head. "Sounded like it came from right out on the street. By the time I climbed out of bed and made it to the window, the gunfire had stopped. I looked out, but I didn't see anything. I went back to my bed to try to fall asleep but couldn't. Couldn't last night, either. Kept tossing and turning, expecting some kind of war to break out, with the Mexican Army come to take their land back."

"Maybe you heard fireworks, someone getting a jump start on celebrating San Jacinto Day."

She snorted. "You think I'm getting so old I can't tell the difference between a string of firecrackers and gunshots? Who celebrates San Jacinto Day anymore? Nobody, that's who. What person would stop at six firecrackers, anyway? If it had been a bunch of drunks or kids, it would have gone on half the night until y'all decided to shut them down."

Charlie held his hands up, palms out trying to keep her calm. "Of course not. I'm just speculating, is all. I'll check around to see if anyone else heard anything. Meanwhile, I have to get to my other duties."

Annabelle called out while he crossed the lobby to the elevator. "You do that, Charlie Gaines, but I ain't crazy. No matter what that fool over there behind the counter says or might think."

Through the closing doors, he saw she had returned to her book.

Charlie muttered under his breath, "Fine investigator you are, Charlie Gaines. You need to pay more attention to what's going on around you."

The room itself looked neat and tidy, no doubt because of the hotel's maid service. The men's bags were up on the dresser, the lids flipped back with clothes hanging out, looking like roadkill turtles. Either they didn't care to unpack or wanted to be ready in case they had to leave quickly. There weren't any personal products in the bathroom, except for those provided by the hotel.

Digging through the suitcases, he found their airline tickets out of Boston plus a few receipts. He also found a list of a dozen names matched with cities all across the country, several of which had been crossed off. It didn't come as much of a surprise when he found Seamus' name halfway down the list. Charlie pocketed the documents, and with one last look around the room, locked up and headed for the elevator.

Down in the lobby, Charlie found Ray and returned the passkey. "I want you to put those boys' things in storage until we figure out what happened. If they do show up after having a cross-border bender, don't give them their stuff. Tell them they have to stop by my office first so I can find out what kind of business they had being here. Whatever it is, it's probably not on the up and up."

"Will do, but I hope they didn't get themselves into some kind of trouble."

"If they did, I will find out eventually," Charlie said with a surety he didn't feel.

Heading back to his office, he had it in mind to make a few calls to check out the two missing men, as well as the names they had crossed off their list. Then he wanted to talk to Seamus about the list. He might know what it meant. There had to be a reason why the Irishman's name was on it. But no matter how hard he tried, Charlie just couldn't get Annabelle's story about gunfire out of his mind. He wondered if it might be somehow related to the men's disappearance.

sixteen

THE SENSATION of the hearse slowing, the sound of tires rolling on gravel, accompanied by the sudden flare of bright lights roused Glenn from his shallow nap. He eased his way upright, trying not to wake Paloma while he rubbed his dead arm. He stared at the pair of gas pumps, skinny things like movie aliens from another world, with their glass bowl heads wearing stickers like NASCAR drivers and curved fingers sticking in their ears. They were the kind you would have used before the last world war where the attendant did everything but stick his dick up the tailpipe. "Where are we?"

"La Encantada. This is where we pick up Highway 54. There's not a lot between here and Jalpa so, unless you want to *push* this big clunky monster the rest of the way or find a place on the side of the road where you can take a piss, I thought it best we stop here to fill up. That way you can take care of your business while we have the chance."

Glenn rubbed his eyes, taking in the small wooden structure beside the main building, with the crude images of a man and a woman painted on the door. If that wasn't enough to tell you what the little building was for, the smell and the flies were. Glenn said, "If my choice is between that outhouse or the side of the road, I think I would rather take a chance on the side of the road. Even if there are a bunch of dick-hungry rattlers or tarantulas who want to take a bite out of my ass while I'm taking a shit. Then I'll wipe my ass with a prickly pear."

"You can be so crude sometimes," Paloma said without opening her eyes.

"It's the street smarts you pick up dealing with low-class criminals. I'm too impressionable."

Paloma sat up, stretching, trying to blink away the stickiness that came from an uncomfortable sleep. Letting go with a big yawn, she shook her head and ran her fingers through her hair. "Can't we stop somewhere for the night, *jefe*? I feel like it's been a week since I've had a bath."

"No can do, Doll. I told you before we started that it was a non-stop trip. Not until we reach Jalpa. Then we'll see." Glenn climbed out of the hearse, pausing to listen to his joints pop and hoping he hadn't damaged anything important. He glanced at the small, one-room building with its metal displays of oil cans and cheap trinkets, with a small, corrugated metal garage almost attached to the side away from the outhouses. It looked like it had been thrown up as an afterthought. The place reeked of gas mixed with spilled oil and had what seemed to be a permanent cloud of exhaust fumes. The lights swarmed with confused moths circling around and around, searching for a moon they would never find.

The T-shirt-wearing attendant, a thin-faced little guy barely taller than Paloma, came out. He couldn't have been more than a flyweight. His dark pompadour rose over his duck ass hairstyle that glistened with oil. His Caesar Romero had been carefully trimmed above his crooked-tooth smile. With his style, he was probably a real lady killer with the local girls.

"*Gasolina?*" he asked, appraising Paloma with a leer, his eyes peeling off her dirty clothes. Exactly what a tired woman who reeked of sweat and looked like she had been dragged through the desert needed, to be hit on by a pint-sized gigolo.

Paco nodded, pointing at the standard-grade pump. "*Sí. Relleno*, uh, *tanque*, uhm, check *bajo*, uh, *bajo la* hood, uh *campana?*"

Laughing, the attendant slipped the nozzle in the tank behind the license plate and went around the front to pop the hood before he vanished under it.

Paloma turned her back and stretched with her shoulders hunched, elbows locked, her fist pointing at the ground. Looked like she needed a bell to ring. She tried to fight down another yawn, but the yawn won. "Think they have a place to wash up?"

Glenn nodded toward the outhouse. "I seriously doubt it. Unless..." He pointed to the coiled hose used to top off radiators.

"Maybe they at least have something cold to drink." Paloma made a face before she headed inside, tugging at the back of her shorts where they tried to crawl up her butt crack. Glenn reached for his pack of Luckies while watching her sashay across the rutted drive in those skin-tight yellow shorts that were starting to show sweat stains and streaks of dirt. With each step, her deck shoes stirred up a small cloud of oily dust that settled on her sweaty legs.

"*Jefe*," Paco called out while pointing to a sign in Spanish. Even Glenn understood the No Smoking part.

"Sorry. Wasn't thinking." He put the pack away, ignoring the craving that had reared its ugly head. Hell, heroin had nothing on nicotine. He had seen people walk away from the white horse easier than they could turn their backs on a pack of Camels. Glenn even considered kicking the habit one of these days, promising himself he could stop anytime he wanted to. "How much further do you figure?"

"Around a hundred miles. Which means a couple of hours, maybe more, depending on the roads. You can't trust the maps. Down here, these major highways sometimes have a way of sneaking up on you before they turn into little more than goat tracks. Driving them is bad enough during the day, but at night it can become a downright terrifying experience."

Paloma returned, carrying three large bottles called Jarritos. "This is all they had worth buying."

Taking one, Glenn studied the bottle. "What the hell is it?'

"Just drink it. It's cold, fizzy, and wet. That's all you need to know."

He drank it. Some kind of fruit-flavored drink. Paloma was right, at least it was cold and wet. A few minutes later, with the tank full, a quart of oil added, the tires checked, and Glenn feeling healthy enough to take over behind the wheel, they were back on the road for Jalpa. While his companions settled in for a nap, he managed to locate a border blaster with a gravel-throated DJ playing country music while selling miracles guaranteed to save your soul. Just send a dollar ninety-five plus shipping and handling to a certain PO box. Then either dirt from the Holy Land or blessed water from the Sea of Galilee would be sent straight to you, allow four to six weeks for delivery. It was enough to keep him company for the rest of the drive.

Highway 54 wove its way between the mountain ranges until it reached the high valley where Jalpa nestled. Glenn stared at the little town over the steering wheel, quickly realizing it was a lot different than most Mexican towns, even at night. It looked more like it belonged somewhere in the south of France, with its brightly painted colonial-style houses and shops. To Glenn's mind, it could have come straight out of a fairytale. Even the shacks surrounding the main part of the town had a surreal, otherworldliness to them, with their own colorful patterns and enclosed gardens. Then again, it may be the fatigue catching up with him, making him see things that weren't there.

Most of the cobblestone streets were a single lane wide, made more for carts than cars. They were flanked by high, narrow curbs with cut-in steps to help with the flooding rains he doubted the town ever got. There were very few street lights, but each adobe house had an external light that created its own little pool of illumination, like yellow stepping stones across the town. Occasionally the effect was shattered by pools of neon lights, like someone had smeared a thin layer of shit across a Picasso.

He gave Paloma a nudge. "Wake up, everybody. We made it."

Paloma lifted her head from his shoulder where she had left a wet spot. She looked around while she tried to wipe the sleep from her eyes and the drool off her cheeks. "Now that we're here, what are we going to do?"

"Well, since it's only three o'clock, I suggest we find a place where we can get a room, get cleaned up, try to get some rest. We can use it for a base while we go out tomorrow to reconnoiter. After that, we make our plans. Also, it will give me time to get in touch with *Señor* Esteban, Mrs. Hamilton's Mexican lawyer."

"We're going to get rooms?" Paloma asked, her excitement showing.

"A room. Like in just one. This is a job, not a vacation. You can worry about your privacy when you get home."

"I don't care, long as it has a bath with plenty of hot water." She lifted her arms while making a face. "Plus, these clothes are getting past the point of needing to be washed and encroaching into 'burn me' territory."

"I think we're all getting a little rank. I know I could use a bath," Glenn said.

With no one around to ask directions, Glenn wove his way through the small town until they found a hotel that looked to be in his price range, which meant cheap. The large painted sign read *Hotel Francia,* a four-story edifice painted a welcoming pink with white and black trim, like a Hilton fucked a flamingo.

Wrought iron balconies painted black overhung the streets. The sight reminded him of New Orleans without the all-night partying, where women would flash their tits for a couple of strings of glass beads. Which, he thought, explained how the Dutch had been able to buy Manhattan Island.

He pulled the hearse into the small lot next to the hotel, managing to wrangle it between a couple of cars, one being a Cadillac about as old as the hearse, the other a sporty-looking Corvair convertible. Both looked to be well maintained, although Ralph Nader might be pissed about the convertible.

Yawning, Paco said, "Think anyone is on duty this late?"

"The lights are on. The doors are open. If not, we'll just have to wake them," Glenn said. Grabbing their bags, they entered the lobby and found someone dozing behind the desk, but a few slaps on the bell remedied that. The place was so bright and colorful Glenn half expected Carmen Miranda to come through, doing the Samba across the lobby floor, snapping castanets like cartoon lobster claws. The place had lots of wide-open doors to let in plenty of fresh air and help keep the place cool. Glenn left the checking in to Paloma, even though he listened in.

She had a rapid-fire exchange in Spanish with the clerk. Glenn figured he understood maybe one word in five, but his ears perked up when he heard the mention of money.

"Did he just say six hundred pesos for two days?" Glenn growled.

Glenn noted the man's startled look, which meant the clerk understood more English than Glenn did Spanish, and the man quickly gave Paloma a new number.

Paloma scooped up the key while glaring at her boss. "He dropped it to five hundred. Just pay the man. I'm too tired to haggle."

She picked up her bag and headed for the elevator. Glenn slapped a twenty and a five on the desk and waited for the clerk to check his dollars to pesos conversion chart before he scrawled out a receipt. Glenn didn't ask about the availability of ice because it seems they brought their own—he shivered from what Paloma threw off her shoulders but wasn't sure why she had become so upset. Maybe she was still carrying a grudge over the Ortega thing.

Inside the elevator, Paloma stood with her back to the wall, facing the lobby, eyes narrowed, jaw clenched. She held the handle of her case with both hands and made no effort to keep the doors open. Glenn barely made it to the elevator before they closed.

Glenn glared. Paloma ignored him. "Thanks for holding it for us, Doll."

"Right now, if I have to choose between waiting for you and a hot bath, the bath is going to win every time."

"Still not sure what threw you off down there."

"I didn't come down here to watch you become an ugly American. You've become too cynical for your own good, snapping at that clerk the way you did, trying to intimidate someone who is just doing their job. Also, it showed you didn't trust me to negotiate for the price of our room."

"Hey, Doll. I didn't mean it that way. You know these people love to haggle. To them, it's almost a religion. When I heard the number, the words just jumped out."

"*Those people* on the border like to haggle because it makes the American tourist think they're getting something over on those stupid Mexicans so they can go home and crow about how they're so much smarter—about how they took advantage of those 'dumb wetbacks.' By the way, I am one of *those people*. When you insult them, you insult me. I thought you were better than that."

The elevator opened on the third floor. Holding her bag, Paloma marched past them and went straight toward the room. It had two full beds. She staked out the one nearest the balcony by tossing her bag at the foot, then moved to stand in the open balcony doors to face the cool breeze blowing in, arms crossed over her chest.

A stunned Glenn followed her in, his face burning, and he cleared his throat. "Ahem. Look, Paloma. I didn't mean for it to sound that way. I admit I'm a hard-headed sonofabitch who will probably never change, at least not much. I stick my foot in my mouth so often I have to brush my teeth with athlete's foot cream, which tastes like shit, by the way."

Paloma sighed. "Maybe I'm not used to seeing you working out in the field. Plus, it's been a long drive. You're not in the best of shape for a man your age—"

"Hey, now."

"Considering how much you've been beaten on the last couple of days, I will consider it might have rattled that brain of yours somewhat. That means you might have lost a couple of decades of social development because of it. I want you to know I probably could have gotten the room for four hundred pesos if you hadn't butted in."

"What?" Glenn felt as confused as a cat trying to piss in the corner of a round room.

Ignoring him, Paloma raised her arms over her head to give the sweat a chance to dry and sighed. "Good Lord, this feels so much better than sitting in that oven of a car. You could bake bread on that floorboard."

"What the hell just happened?" Glenn turned to look at Paco, who shrugged, dropped his bag, and closed the door.

Paloma turned, reaching out to pat his cheek. "I forgive you for being stupid. This time. But don't let it happen again. Have a seat while I take a bath and get into some clean clothes."

Paco stayed out of what was going on between the two. He stretched out on the other bed, kicked off his shoes, and laced his fingers behind his head. Glenn dropped into an overstuffed chair in the corner next to the French doors and sighed. "Okay, I guess us losers will just sit here while we wait for our turn."

Paloma looked over her shoulder, a smile toying with her lips. "What are you going to do until then?"

"If it wasn't so late, I would find me a bar where I could have me a couple of stiff ones. But this town reminds me too much of home, where they shut things down early and get up late since the school crowds have left. With never an O'Rourke's in sight." Glenn mused.

After she grabbed her bag, Paloma locked herself in the bathroom. The last thing Glenn remembered was hearing her humming tunelessly while she filled the tub. While listening, he closed his eyes, letting her insults slide into his dreams.

Manuel rode stiffly in the passenger seat of the old truck, his eyes almost swollen shut from the impact of his face against the steering wheel. His nose felt like it had grown to the size of a casaba melon. The seat still poked him in the backside, so much that he thought it might have fallen in love with him or just liked playing with his ass.

Jorge didn't look much better, but at least he had two good arms and could see out of both of his eyes. Manuel tried to snort deep enough to clear his nose so he could breathe, tasting blood mixed with salty snot at the back of his throat. It was a lost cause. Hawking, he spit out the window, but the wind threw it back against the side of the truck until it looked like it had been sprayed with Redman juice. He hated breathing through his mouth because it made him sound like an idiot. It also dried his mouth out and left his throat feeling like he had tried to gargle sand.

Manuel tried to ignore the pain, but the jolts of the truck riding on its worn-out suspension made it all but impossible. It jerked and bounced at every little dip or rough spot, like it was trying to pay him back for killing its owner. Despite all that, he did manage to doze off until they rolled into Jalpa just before sunrise.

Jorge cussed the vehicle under his breath, threatening dire consequences if it didn't hold together.

Manuel stretched. The pressure of clenching his muscles caused a new round of stabbing pain in his shoulder. "Shit. You think your cussing is going to make it run better?"

"No, but it makes me feel better. Where do we go from here?" Jorge asked, still refusing to speak English, as much as Manuel refused to speak Spanish.

"We need to figure out where the shitty dick and his friends are staying, then stake them out. Once we find them, we can look for someone who can check this gunshot. Drive around until you spot that old hearse."

"You sound funny." Jorge chuckled.

"I sound funny because I have a busted nose and can't breathe worth shit. Anybody ever tell you that you have a mean streak, making fun of people? Now, stop pointing out my problems and just drive."

It didn't take long to find the hearse parked beside a small hotel. Jorge parked across the street and glanced over at his partner. "We found them. What happens now?"

"I have no idea. We can't just go into the hotel and take them out. Find a place to pull over so I can have time to think."

Jorge pulled into a deserted parking lot and shut off the truck. Even though Manuel couldn't smell the hot metal stink mingled with burnt oil wafting up through the floorboard, he could taste it. It lay on his tongue and the back of his throat like a slug of clabbered milk, making him want to spit to get the taste out. He climbed out, needing to move around while he sucked in some fresh air. The door gave a rusty squall like a cat in heat when he opened it, stepped out, and took a moment to stretch his aching back. "Riding in that damned truck is worse than trying to bareback a rodeo bull, but you don't get a reprieve after eight seconds."

While Jorge stayed in the truck, Manuel looked around through his swollen eyes. He spotted an all-night bodega down the street, lit up by neon lights, the windows plastered with advertising posters filled with smiling people. Happy because they were drinking the right kind of beer, smoking the right cigars, or using the right kind of rubbers. "I'm going to get something to drink. You want anything?"

"*Sí, dulces.* Tootsie Rolls."

Scowling, Manuel pushed away from the truck, crossing the street while muttering under his breath. "Goddammit. Next time I go on one of these road trips, it's going to be with someone who can have a decent conversation and doesn't have a fucking candy fetish."

Moments later, Manuel returned. He tossed Jorge a plastic bag of Tootsie Rolls as big as a pillow. The big man eagerly ripped it open, digging out a handful to drop into his shirt pocket. He pulled one out, stripped the wrapper, and tossed it in his mouth. Closing his eyes, he chewed slowly while wearing a smile.

"I think you're addicted to that shit." Manuel sucked on a bottle of beer, the kind that made people smile on the posters because they knew they were gonna get some pussy because the girl thought he had good taste. A man with good taste always gets pussy, the kind you don't need to wear rubbers to fuck. He settled back against the fender, staring out into the darkness while trying to figure out their next move. "You should go inside to see if you can find out what room they're staying in and where it is."

"Why?"

"Because we need to know where they are so we can keep an eye on them, you damned fool. I want to know when they leave it, where they go, or when they come back. Watching the main door isn't enough. The two of us can't watch all the doors. What if they decide to duck out the back way, or one of the side entrances?"

They were still arguing when a sudden bang on the driver's door followed by a bright light stabbing through the interior of the cab caused the men to jump. They both stared at the Mexican cop standing there, covering them with his flashlight.

"Is this your vehicle, *señor*?" The policeman looked both men over, the light slowly playing over their swollen faces, stopping when he saw Manuel's bloody shirt.

Jorge took his time peeling the wrapper from another Tootsie Roll, ignoring the cop.

"Would you mind stepping out to show me what's under the tarp?" The cop spoke slowly in Spanish as he stepped away, pulling the door open, an invitation for Jorge to get out. He looked at Manuel, who gave him a shrug then climbed out the other side, not worried about a local cop looking at a bunch of fruits and vegetables. Hell, maybe they could bribe him by offering a couple of bushels of the stuff. The policeman had no way of knowing they had stolen the truck or killed the driver.

Moving carefully to the rear of the truck, Manuel grabbed the tarp and flipped it back, freezing while he stared blankly at the contents for a minute before groaning. "Aw, shit."

Instead of seeing a load of vegetables being trucked to market, the bed was filled with small, square, plastic-wrapped bundles stamped with a bull's head. Manuel recognized them easy enough. He had moved plenty of near-identical packages for his boss, Alonzo Ortega, over the years. They had unwittingly highjacked a load of primo Mexican grass ready to be smuggled across the border.

"Raise your hands," the cop yelled, still in Spanish, while drawing his gun.

Growling like a bear, Jorge grabbed the cop's arm with one massive paw while he used the other to club him to the ground, but not before the cop managed to get off a shot. Manuel screamed and dropped, clutching his leg while blood pooled beneath him.

Sprawled out on the street, Manuel groaned while he clutched his bleeding leg. For the second time in so many days, he had Jorge looming over him after he had been shot. His partner shook his head, like him getting shot had to be one of the dumbest things Manuel had ever done. That he should have known better, and that him getting shot was becoming one hell of an inconvenience, as well as a bad habit.

"We have to go. More police may be coming." Grabbing Manuel's leg caused the wounded man to scream. Jorge ignored him while he checked it. "Looks like the bullet went all the way through."

Sweat painted Manuel's pale face, which brought out the jagged scar on his cheek. His breath came in ragged gasps. "No shit. Help me up. I can't believe that cocksucker shot me."

"It was a lucky shot."

"Lucky for who? Certainly not for me—or him, since you knocked his ass out." Manuel grabbed his companion's large paw. Jorge lifted him to his feet, or *foot*. He couldn't put any weight on the wounded leg, but standing made him dizzy enough so his remaining leg nearly buckled. He eyed the unconscious cop stretched out behind the truck, watching the slow rise and fall of the man's chest, but he was out of it.

Jorge leaned over to scoop up the cop's gun, which he tossed deep into the shadowy parking lot. Holding Manuel, he looked across the street and spotted a man standing in the bodega's doorway, phone against his ear.

Manuel passed out before they could reach the cab. He hung off Jorge's shoulder like a broken marionette and was about as accommodating. The big man muscled his companion over to the open door and managed to shove him inside, ignoring the blood leaking from his wound. Jorge pulled out a short knife to cut the sleeves off Manuel's shirt, then used them as bandages. He hoped it would be enough to stem the bleeding until he could find someone to do a proper job. A loud wail rose and fell in the distance. Jorge slammed the passenger door and jumped behind the wheel. Working the clutch, he lurched away from the curb with a desperate grinding of gears.

With everything that had happened, Jorge thought about finding a place to dump Manuel and cut his losses so he could make a run for the border. So far, the unlucky idiot had managed to wreck their truck and get shot twice. They'd both smashed their heads so that neither of them looked like a ray of sunshine with their bruised and swollen faces. No wonder, when that cop saw them, he became suspicious. Seeing a couple of strangers in their condition at six in the morning, plus finding a truck bed full of drugs, didn't exactly cast a favorable light on their situation.

Jorge struggled hard to figure a way out of their predicament, but planning had never been his strong suit. He always left that to Alonzo or Manuel while he did the donkey work. He was still cruising around when he spotted the girl. Short skirt, clunky heels, wrist covered with cheap plastic bangles, her long, curling hair lacquered into a billowing cloud. Her purse dangled from her shoulder on a golden chain where it swung back and forth, caused by her hip-swaying walk. Only the hip-swaying seemed a might awkward, maybe because her feet were sore after a long night. Seeing her gave him an idea. Jorge slowed the truck until he pulled up alongside her, leaned out the window far enough to call out. "Hey, *chica*. How much for me and my friend?"

She turned her head without stopping, looked him and the truck over, and started to laugh. "It's late, I'm tired. Besides, you couldn't afford me. Go back to the farm where you can stick with fucking your chickens. That's more your style."

"Come on, *chica*. Don't be like that." Jorge dug into his pocket to pull out a matching pair of Jacksons and waved them out the window. Seeing them seemed to be enough to make the girl forget how tired she felt because her eyes lit up with greed. Stepping closer, she made to snatch the money, but Jorge jerked his hand back. "Not out here, but at your place. Do you have a name?"

"Susanita." Bending low, she stared through the window and gasped in surprise when she got a good look at Jorge's battered face. "*Madre de Dios*, what happened to you? Your friend, he looks drunk."

Grateful for the poor lighting, Jorge pulled out a Hamilton to go with the two Jacksons, probably more money than that *puta* could earn in a month, maybe two, even if she gave out blowjobs like politicians gave out promises. "No more questions, okay? We also need to get off the street. Do you have a place where we can hide our truck."

Susanita looked at him indecisively and bit her lip, her brow furrowed while she considered his offer. She did a quick check along the street before she stepped closer, her pink tongue slipping from her painted lips then licking the corner of her mouth. Jorge considered pulling out another ten, but he could see her greed warring with her common sense. He was sure greed would win out.

"Okay. I live just down the street. There's a garage in the back, behind a wall, where you can park. No one will be able to see your truck." She turned and started off, her purse swinging loosely at her side. Jorge eased the truck forward with a jerk as the clutch slipped before catching. He glanced at Manuel, his head lolling back against the seat, mouth open, face white with pain.

Susanita stopped after a block, pulled open a wooden gate, and motioned for Jorge to pull inside. Once the truck was clear, she closed the gate behind him. He stopped on a drive barely longer than the truck, next to a small house surrounded with flowering plants that filled the air with their heady scent. He couldn't tell a hibiscus from a petunia, but it did smell nice. Susanita moved to unlock the door and looked over her shoulder in expectation.

"Are you and your friend going to join me? I promise what you'll find inside is much better than what you'll find out here." She pushed the door back and flipped on the light switch.

Jorge took the time to pop a fresh Tootsie Roll between his jaws before he climbed out. Circling the truck, he opened the passenger door, clenching his jaws at the way the door squealed. He grabbed Manuel, looping his arm over his shoulder, and half carried him inside, into a small parlor where he dropped him onto the couch.

Stepping back, Jorge glanced at Susanita, who dropped her purse and gasped when she spied the bloody leg.

seventeen

THE MORNING SUN crested the low mountains, spreading across the land like melted butter on a stack of fresh pancakes; then came the clouds that flowed down the slopes like warm syrup. The day was getting off to a too happy start for those folks who hadn't made it into bed before the night was half over. The sunbeams found their way through the gauzy drapes that fluttered over the open balcony doors to bore into Glenn's eyes like an ice pick in a mafia movie. Seems the morning sun managed, without much effort, to hit the corner where he had fallen asleep in the overstuffed chair but left the rest of the room in a comforting, hazy shadow. The first thing he saw when he cracked an eye was Paloma curled up in the middle of her bed, half-covered with a sheet, hugging a pillow, one leg sticking out with the pale sole of her slender foot pointed at him like a raised hand giving a warning. Above it, the brown skin looked as smooth as gravy on biscuits. Snoring softly, her parted lips leaked spit that left a thin trail marking her cheek and leaving a wet spot on her pillow the size of Rhode Island. Her hair had been done up in those giant curlers the size of soup cans that, with the help of a little tin foil, could probably pick up all the television stations within a hundred miles. Her knee-length pink nightgown had ridden up high enough to expose an eye-pleasing amount of thigh, also allowing him to get a peek at her panties. Even though it seemed to be a lot less exposure than when she wore her shorts, somehow the sight seemed a lot more intimate and tantalizing. Enough to get his juices going while filling him with shame.

On the other bed, a shoeless Paco lay sprawled out atop the covers like a puppy, still in the same clothes he had on last night. He had one arm thrown over his eyes, his jaw hung open, and he wheezed like a concertina with a torn bellows.

Trying not to wake them, Glenn sat up then began to work the kinks out of his neck and back, which had become an everyday job lately. Sitting still for more than a few minutes was enough for him to pay the price. When he felt almost human again, Glenn grabbed his bag and made his way to the bathroom. Ignoring the tub, he stripped off his shirt and snatched a cloth to rub down with, doing what an honest nurse would call a sponge bath. He paid particular attention to his armpits, then his crotch, saving his ass for last. Then he pulled out his razor to give his face a good scraping, splashing on some aftershave for a teeth-clenching, air-sucking burn. He paused a moment to give his reflection a critical look, assessing the wear and tear that had piled up over the last few years. The wrinkles, scars, and gray hairs had all seemed to come out of nowhere until he felt like he was staring at a stranger. Glenn couldn't help wondering what had happened to that young Marine that came home full of piss and vinegar, ready to take on the world. He took it on, sure enough, but didn't make the count. Now, what did he have to show for it? A failed marriage, a father who had lost his grasp on reality, and a business that was hanging on by its bloody fingernails. And a teenage assistant along with a sweet young girl trying to help hold the business together while doing her best to raise her younger brother.

"You're a real success story, old man." He wiped off the last of the shaving soap and stowed his personals away. "You're an old fool desperately clinging to a young man's game. How soon before all you have to look forward to is a bottle of whiskey while you wait for your next case? Well too late, you're already stuck on that merry-go-round, and there's no sign of a brass ring anywhere in your future."

His musings were interrupted by a pounding on the door, followed by Paco's voice. "How long are you going to be in there, *jefe*? Some of the rest of us gotta take a piss, too."

Glenn opened the door, slipped his shirt on, and picked up his kit. "It's all yours."

Paloma sat in her bed with a small travel case open beside her. She had pulled the sheet up to her armpits and tucked it behind her. She stared out the balcony doors while working the curlers out of her hair, setting them in her lap. With the last soup can-sized roller gone, she shook her head, grabbed a hairbrush, and stroked it through the tangle of curls.

Glenn dropped into the chair again and reached for his Luckies. He pulled one out, along with his Zippo. With one smooth motion, he flicked the lighter along his jean leg one way to pop open the top, then reversing, causing the wheel to spin, strike the flint, and light the wick. Firing up his coffin nail, he snapped the Zippo closed with a loud click and slowly rubbed his thumb over the eagle-globe-and-anchor imprint. Laying his head back, he pursed his lips, blew a series of smoke rings toward the ceiling, and looked toward Paloma. "Are we good?"

Paloma eyed him while dragging her brush through her long dark hair. He read the question in her eyes, the one that asked whether she should let him off the hook or leave him dangling there to become fish food. It took a moment for the pity to win out, but she finally relaxed enough to show him a smile. Which lifted a mule's weight of worry off his shoulders.

"Okay, now that that's settled, we have a shit load of work to get done, primarily scouting out where they're holding the body and who might be guarding it. Then we need to figure out the fastest way out of town. The quickest way to get on the bad side of the police here is by disrupting their supply line of money. Stealing the body is going to put a lot of those pockets on a starvation diet."

"If you want to get this done, *jefe*, you two need to get out of here so I can get dressed."

Glenn sat up, hauled his bag closer, and opened it. Digging through, he pulled out a sheet of paper, scanned it, and passed it over. "Okay,

Doll. This is the contact information Mrs. Hamilton gave me about her Mexican shyster. Since I don't know how good his English is and my Spanish is shit, why don't you give him a call. See if you can set up a meet somewhere. He might know something we don't that can help us get hold of the boy. We'll meet you downstairs. Maybe this place serves a decent cup of joe, or they can steer me to one that does."

"Okay, *jefe*." She took the letter and read it with a smile. "I don't see how you ever thought you would be able to survive this trip without me, what with your special talent for pissing off the locals and all."

Paco stepped out of the bathroom, hair still dripping water, fresh clothes clinging to his damp skin. "What now, boss man? I'm starving."

"We go down to the lobby and wait until our girl here is ready." He leaned to the side to stub his butt out in the small tin ashtray, stood, and headed for the door. Pausing to look back, he said, "The shyster might not want to work with us. If that's his attitude, try to convince him it would be in his own best interest to do so."

Glenn had the urge to let loose with a wolf whistle when Paloma stepped off the elevator to scan the lobby. She had shed her secretary persona to go full hot tourist in blue shorts, even more revealing than her yellow ones had been. A striped, low-cut blouse that left her stomach bare and a pair of cork-soled sandals that added about three inches to her slim legs completed her ensemble. She also wore her hair down, with a blue scarf snugged around her neck. Her war paint had been done to perfection, and when she smiled, Glenn could feel it down to his toes.

"Let's go, Paco," he said and stood. She spotted them and crossed the lobby with her smile still intact, but maybe a couple of watts brighter, like she was auditioning for a toothpaste commercial. Her heels caused her hips to do interesting things, enough so she drew the eyes of every man in the lobby, along with some of the women.

"Hot, *chica*." Paco grinned.

Stopping, Paloma did a little turn. "What do you think, *jefe*?"

Glenn felt his face grow hot and his mouth went dry. "I think it's about time we found a place to eat because I'm getting a little light-headed. Did you get in touch with that shyster?"

"I did." She grinned at his discomfort. "He wants to meet at a little café called El Gordo's for lunch. He gave me directions."

Glenn frowned, checking his watch. His stomach had already voiced its displeasure at being put off. "Damn, there goes breakfast. I guess we can hang on until lunch, considering we all slept in."

Wrapping her arms around Glenn's, she tugged him toward the door, excited to get out and look around. "This place is so pretty, *jefe*. I've never seen anything like it. Certainly not in Coahuila, or Texas either. I wish we could stay for a few more days. Long enough to do a little sightseeing, maybe some shopping."

Stepping out into the sunlight it felt like the temperature had jumped ten degrees or more. Still tolerable, but not by much. "No way, Doll. I plan on finishing this up so we can be on the road sometime tonight. You might have a few hours to look around this afternoon to pick yourself out a few things, but this is work, not a vacation."

They found a place where they could all get a cup of coffee to give them a jolt while they waited for lunchtime to roll around. They nibbled on a plate of local *pan dulce*—not enough to kill their appetite, but enough to keep the wolves at bay. They were colorful and tasty. Glenn thought they looked like someone had shit a rainbow. Paloma called them *conchas*, and they went perfectly with the strong, dark coffee.

When the time came to find the lawyer for lunch, Glenn had Paloma ask for directions only to find out it wasn't far. They turned a couple of corners and walked a few blocks before Paco pointed. "I see it, across the street."

A weathered sign with a grinning fat man in a sombrero and *El Gordo's* in foot-high letters hung on the roof of the building. The outside looked as if someone had dipped a jungle parrot in a bucket of water and slap dashed the walls with the runoff of reds, greens, and blues spread around in no discernable pattern, atop a base terra cotta coat. There were a handful of iron tables with glass tops set up outside, each topped with a flower-filled vase. Only a couple of people sat around them.

Glenn slowed. "Did he say inside or out?"

"He didn't. He just said for us to meet him here."

"Description?"

Paloma shook her head. "Maybe we should try to find someone who looks like a lawyer."

"I have been looking but don't see a barracuda in the bunch. But I'm only used to dealing with Texas shysters. Maybe Mexican shysters look a little different, or maybe he hasn't made it here yet."

They stepped inside where the temperature dropped until it was almost acceptable, thanks to large ceiling fans with wide, palm frond-shaped blades stirring the air enough to make it comfortable without being annoying. Glenn spotted a thin man with slicked-back hair wearing a Cesar Romero mustache and dressed in an ill-fitting suit. He waved them over. "*Señor* Helka?"

Leaning over, he whispered in Paloma's ear. "Now, that looks like a Mexican shyster. Did you tell him what I looked like, Doll?"

"No. I only told him to be on the lookout for a big, ugly, American bohunk, one that looks like he does his thinking with his fists."

"Bohunk, huh? You've been spending too much time talking with Charlie, casting aspersions on my character like that. Now, let's go over there so we can make nice with the man and see what he can do for us." Glenn crossed the room with his hand extended. "*Señor* Esteban?"

"*Sí, sí.* Please sit. I am so pleased to make your acquaintance. *Señora* Hamilton informed me of your coming by wire." He gestured to the empty chairs, mopping his face with a handkerchief already limp with sweat. After they were seated, he leaned closer and dropped his voice. "Please, this situation is most exceptional. Yes, most exceptional. I don't know what to do, yes? *Señora* Hamilton had been quite sincere in her instructions for me to assist you as much as I can."

"We appreciate that, *Señor* Esteban. All we want to do is fetch the boy so we can be on our way."

"Of course. But she is a crime to take the boy. The *policía* will react, respond, with haste. You must leave soon after you are done, yes? They will be suspicious of any strangers once they discover the body is missing." He again nervously mopped his face, eyes darting around the restaurant like he expected the police to come charging out from under the tables, blowing whistles, guns in hand, to cart them all off to the local joint.

"Which is our intent," Glenn assured him. "You have a nice town here, but we want to be on the road soon as we get our hands on the boy."

"You must abide with care. *Señor* Elonzio, the funeral homeowner, and the *capitán* of the police, Hernando Lopez-Garcia, will be quite angry when they discover the boy has gone. You will be costing them much bribe money."

"Not to worry, counselor. Once we hit Highway 54 and take it to 40, we should be halfway to Texas before they figure out what happened."

"No, *Señor*." The lawyer mopped his face again. "You must stay off the highways. Once they find the boy is missing, they will block all the main roads, looking for somebody with a body with no documentation. You must take the secondary roads, yes? It will take longer, but it will be much safer."

"He's right, *jefe*," Paco said. "The people in charge around here will consider us thieves. That includes the local police. As far as they're concerned, we'll be stealing the money right out of their pockets."

"Fine," Glenn said, his frustration starting to show. "Now, how do we get our hands on the Hamilton boy?"

Esteban pulled a folded sheet from his jacket pocket and spread it out on the table. Glenn saw several marks across it. "This is a *tabla*, uh, chart, uh, map of Jalpa. I have marked where the police station is located. Here is the funeral home where they keep the body. This one is your hotel."

Glenn thought the map looked straightforward enough. He asked questions about business hours, the staff, plus all the patrol routes and their frequency. Satisfied he had pried all the information he could out of the lawyer, he folded and put the map away. "Now that our business is done, how about some grub?"

"Please, allow me to order." Esteban turned to the bar, calling out for wine along with four of the house specials.

A moment later, the serving girl brought over a couple of large carafes filled with blood-red wine and enough fruit slices floating around to make Richard Simmons smile. The lawyer took it upon himself to do the pouring, filling everyone's glass to the brim. He lifted his own in a toast.

"*Éxito.*"

"Success," Paloma echoed, then took a drink.

eighteen

AFTER PUMPING the lawyer for all the information they could get, they broke away, feeling as full as a tick on a hound's ear. Glenn gave in and forked over a fistful of money so Paloma could go out for the afternoon and browse through a few shops, giving her a chance to soak up some of the local color. The two men returned to their room, hoping for a nap to sleep off some of that lunch and wine before they had to get ready for that night. The short plan was for them to break into the funeral home after it closed and steal Darren's body. Which was also the long plan. Or just *the* plan. Maybe *liberate* would be a better word than *steal*, considering the state of the local government. If the Mexicans could do it for Zapata, then he could damn well do it for Darren. But whatever they might want to call it, the plan called for them to reunite mother and son back in Texas quick as possible.

Glenn lay stretched out on the bed while sampling some of the local brews he picked up on the way back to the hotel. He concluded that, while it might not be Shiner Bock, it wasn't half bad. At least it was better than that Rocky Mountain piss water some places tried to pass off as beer. He held up the bottle so Paco could see it. "Can we get this stuff back in Texas?"

Paco glanced over at the brown bottle with two exes on the label. "I think so. If not, you can get it right across the border. Dad doesn't carry it."

"Guess I'll stick with my usual brand then. Smuggling beer is too much work." He finished the bottle and set it on the table before he settled down. "Paco, you better get some sleep yourself. We have a long night ahead of us."

Glenn closed his eyes, trying to quiet the goings-on in his mind, thoughts of his current case, past ones, or even some he might have in the future. *A Christmas Carol* of investigative failures telling him what he should have done right. He guessed that made Paco his Tiny Tim, but what did that make Paloma or Charlie? The two voices of the present and future telling him he needed to get his shit together. Somewhere between their warnings and expectations, he managed to doze off.

Glenn stepped out of the small shower—after a long nap, on the bed this time instead of curling up in the chair—glad for the chance to wash the sticky off. He had slept the sun away. The whitewashed sky had turned an interesting shade of purple, and the stars were busy blinking the sleep out of their eyes. Paloma opened the door, weighed down with various packages and followed by a uniformed bellboy being used as a pack mule. Glenn threw a towel around his waist, tucked the end in, and yelled out. "Give a man some warning, will 'ya? Maybe a knock or something?"

The bellboy was shorter than Paloma, with smooth cheeks while sporting a full mustache. Glenn would have put him around twelve or thirteen. He grinned as he accepted a tip and tilted his monkey hat on his way out. Glenn half expected to hear an organ grinder out in the hall.

Paco welcomed her back with a laugh. It took a second for Glenn to realize his clothes were still laid out on the bed. Unless he developed the stretching ability of Mister Fantastic, he would have to step out there in his towel. The problem was he hadn't expected Paloma to come back so soon. He farted around inside the bathroom as long as he could, ruffling his wet hair with a spare towel, running his safety razor around the scars on his battered face, dousing himself with some Old Spice, then hitting his pits with deodorant in anticipation of a long night of hard work. Finally, with nothing else to be done, he yelled out.

"Coming out—cover your eyes if you don't want to be surprised." He stepped out, followed by a puff of steam-filled air. Paloma stood beside her bed covered with colorful shopping bags. She'd pushed his clothes into a pile at the foot. She wore a new, wide-brimmed straw hat with a red scarf for a band around the top.

"Damn, Doll. You buy out all of Mexico or just the local stores?"

"Nice." She looked at him with a mocking smile that caused his face to burn. Glen gripped the towel to make sure it didn't come loose and hit the floor. Not that he was all that ashamed of what he had. He just didn't see the necessity of flaunting it, not in front of someone who worked for him. Things like that tended to give a girl the giggles. That wasn't what he needed right then.

Paloma ignored him. She pulled a blouse from one of the bags to hold it up so she could model it. "What do you think, *jefe*? I even found a skirt to match."

He looked at the sun-bleached cotton blouse covered with colorful threaded designs on the half sleeves and the bosom while picking up his clothes with his spare hand. "Nice, Doll. Now, turn around so I can get dressed."

She did, but not without giggling like a schoolgirl who saw her first dick. One who wasn't impressed and wondered what all the fuss was about. Glenn grabbed his pants and a pair of clean briefs. He dressed while Paco ducked into the tiny bathroom for his turn at getting cleaned up. Once had had his pants on, Glenn dropped down into a chair to put on his socks and do up his laces. "All decent. You can turn around now."

"For you, *jefe*." She tossed him a shirt, one of those short-sleeved, V-necked pullovers that looked like it had been dipped in a rainbow. It was all the rage among the hippie set a decade ago. He did have to admit it looked pretty and fit nice. The only thing missing was a dinner plate-sized medallion or puka shell necklace to complete it, along with a year's worth of missed haircuts.

Minutes later, the three of them were out on the street after getting directions from the night clerk. It didn't take long to find a small café close to the hotel where they could have a late meal—late for them, but it seemed to be normal for most everyone else. Sitting outside where they could enjoy the view while watching the local people out on the street, they ordered dinner. Or Paloma did since both men had trouble with the local lingo. It didn't matter what they called the food, though. As usual, it was a variation on beans, meat, and tortillas, seasoned with a variety of spices before being rolled, folded, fried, or baked, with a few different garnishes. They were halfway through their meal when a voice interrupted them. "Americanos?"

Glenn looked up from his plate to spot a policeman in his brown, pocketed khaki uniform with a pair of captain's bars on his collar, his eyes hidden behind a pair of unnecessary mirrored sunglasses since the only light available spilled through the café's doors. Glenn leaned away from the table, picked up his beer, and nodded warily. "Yes, from Texas."

"Ah, Texicanos. Are you enjoying your stay in our little town?"

"We are, but we're just passing through. Thought it would be a chance to rest up and refuel. We only plan to be here for a couple of days. You have a reason for asking?" His companions continued with their meal, but a bit slower, both watching the exchange cautiously.

The captain pointed to the empty chair. Glenn nodded. The policeman flipped the chair around so he could straddle it, rocking a little, like a quarter-a-ride drugstore pony. He removed his cap and sunglasses, setting them on the table. He then reached for the water carafe, slowly filling an empty glass. He was welcome to it since none of them wanted to take a chance on coming down with a case of the Tijuana two-step. It wouldn't be a good look to have to stop every mile or so to squat on the side of the road or have their ass hanging out of the window. That would make a long, hot trip home even longer, and a lot more fragrant. Glenn got a good look at the man's eyes. He had the feeling the cop would be able to give Charlie a run for his money in the hard-ass department, except Charlie could sometimes flash a little familial tenderness. Glenn had the idea that the Mexican cop and tenderness were strangers.

"Just being cautious after what happened this morning."

"What happened this morning?"

"A pair of drug mules jumped one of my men. They beat him then stole his gun, but not before he managed to wound one of them."

"As you can see, officer, we're all healthy here."

"Hernando—Captain Hernando de Lopez-Gutierrez. After such an incident, we would naturally be curious about any strangers we see in town."

"Naturally."

"Especially if those strangers happen to be driving such an odd vehicle."

"Our hearse? Yeah, my partner here rented it, got us a good deal on it, too. I can see where one might be curious about it, though. I imagine it would be great for smuggling. But I assure you, we don't have any plans to smuggle drugs, or anything else illegal." Glenn mentally added *yet* to the end of his statement.

"Oh, I know that, *señor*. We've already inspected it."

Barking laughter, Glenn said, "All you had to do was ask. We've got nothing to hide."

"I assure you, *señor*, that most people who have plans to smuggle drugs aren't very cooperative with the local police."

"Can I assume you've also checked out our rooms?" Glenn had the forethought to hold onto Monica's letter, instead of leaving it in his bag. But he feared what might happen if they discovered his pistols in their hidden compartment. Local laws be damned, it would take a hefty bribe to get them to look the other way. He would probably lose the pistols.

"What kind of policeman would I be if I lied to you? I assure you, my men are looking through it while we speak. I'm sure it will all be for naught."

"I hope your officer is okay. I also hope you catch the bad guys."

"Probably not. Unfortunately, the market across the border is rich enough to tempt many of our people. Some good, some not so good. Those men this morning was not so good. But they are most likely long gone by now. Yet we still must make the effort to find them." He drained his glass, stood, grabbed his sunglasses and cap. "Well, good day to you, *señors*, *señorita*. I hope you enjoy your stay in our wonderful little town."

Glenn waited until the policeman walked away, then looked at his companions. "I'm glad we're getting out of here tonight. I got a feeling that guy would be all over us if we stuck around too long."

Paloma nodded. "He can smell an American dollar. Good thing we all look like we're broke."

"Speak for yourself, Doll." Glenn swallowed his beer. "With this fancy new shirt you bought me, I'm rich in the finer things in life."

"That's what everybody who hasn't any money says."

"I want to know why you're making me stay here." Paloma stood glaring at Glenn. He tried to stare down at the five-foot-three inches, one hundred and ten pounds of Mexican fury. Despite her name, he saw nothing dove-like or peaceful about her mood right then. He saw the blood pooling in her eyes while she prepared her tongue to give him a lashing with no mercy. She stuck her finger out and poked him in the chest, then raised her voice to mountain cat in heat levels. "You spent more than a day dragging me five hundred miles through a country not fit for anything other than rattlesnakes and Gila monsters while being chased by drug dealers who tried to run us off the road, hoping to kill us. Now you want me to stay here just when the exciting stuff is about to happen?"

"I don't know about that. All those things sound pretty exciting to me. I thought you could be our backup, in case we get busted. If that happens, we'll need somebody on the outside who can lawyer for us. It only makes sense, if that police captain comes after us."

"Why do I have to be the one? Why can't Paco do it? Give me one good reason."

"One, I need his muscle to help with the body. Two, he can't speak Mex worth a shit, despite what he thinks. Three, he ain't pretty, or sexy, enough to convince the cops to let us go if we do get caught. Are those enough reasons for you?"

Paloma clenched her fist and stomped her foot. "Oh, you... you... you *man*, you. You think just because you have a pair of balls, it makes you something special. I got news for you, all it takes is one quick kick to put you both on the floor, crying like babies."

"Come on, Doll." Glenn unconsciously covered his crotch with both hands. "Be a sport. Let me do my job. Okay?"

"Be a sport? I was a sport when I rode down here between the two of you, putting up with your stinky man sweat, belches, and farts. I was a sport when you ran that truck off the road, probably killing those men. I was a sport when you lied to me about my brother being involved with that drug dealer, Alonzo Ortega. I was a sport when..."

"Okay, Doll, I get it. I get it. But I didn't lie, technically."

"No, *you* don't get it, Glenn. That's the problem. Come hell or high water, you just don't understand. You never will." She dropped down heavily on the edge of the bed, her back stiff, arms crossed, glaring. "And don't you dare say you're doing this to protect me. That just makes you sound cowardly and pathetic."

"Uhm. We'll be going now. Okay?" He took a step toward the door without turning around, not sure if showing his back to Paloma would be a wise move, considering her mood. Plus, there were so many things near at hand that weren't nailed down. She didn't say anything, so he took another step, then another, until he bumped into Paco and forced him out into the hall.

"I've never seen her so mad," Paco said after Glenn closed the door.

"You and me both, brother. And I've been on the short end of that spitfire temper more times than I can count. Let's get going, we still have a couple of stops to make along the way."

The stops Glenn referred to were to pick up supplies and top off the tank. After a few blocks, he had Paco pull into one of the small shops. "What are we after?"

"We need a couple of good flashlights and several cheap coolers we can fill with ice. Like I said back in Nuevo Prado, we can't drive across Mexico with a body and no way to keep it cool. Unless you have a better idea."

"No, no. That's a good plan," Paco agreed, but Glenn heard the doubt in his voice, or maybe it was just nerves. Two flashlights, six ice chests packed with block ice, a case of Topo Chico mineral water, and a full tank later, they were back on the road. He kept an eye out for a tail but couldn't find one. Which either meant the captain hadn't had time to assign someone or, if he did, they were damned good.

They had already done a walk-by recon of the funeral home earlier that evening, pretending to walk off their meal while they took in some of the local color. Glenn had a pretty good idea of the layout of the place, at least on the outside. The building sat in the middle of the block, a garishly painted adobe building covered with murals. It had a large double-wide door, elaborately carved, flanked by a double set of iron-barred windows. A sign above it announcing the *Elonzio e Hijos Funeraria* had also been painted in neon-bright colors, like down there they considered even death to be a festive thing. Or else funeral homes were damned hard to find without the bright colors to show the way.

Paco slowed when they reached the building. The windows were dark, but light spilled down the narrow drive that went up the side then vanished around to the back, where Glenn assumed the loading dock was located.

"Pull in there, so we're not out on the street," Glenn directed.

"What if someone sees us?"

"A hearse behind a funeral home? What's suspicious about that?"

Paco eased the clumsy behemoth up the slanted drive until they reached a small courtyard, where the loading door had a shaded cover that extended out about five feet. Climbing out, Glenn checked the back of the building, paying particular attention to the door. "I don't see any sign of an alarm system."

"If they have one, it will most likely be covered in fur and have four legs," Paco said.

"If they did, we would be hearing them trying to fight their way through the door by now." Glenn grabbed the knob to give it a twist, but it wouldn't budge. Sighing, he dropped into a squat and grabbed his picks. "Go down to the corner where you can keep an eye out for the cops or anyone else."

He hated picking locks for a couple of reasons. One, it seemed like such an invasion of a person's privacy, and he always felt guilty going into a place where he hadn't been invited, but not enough to stop doing it. That kind of guilt he could live with, so long as it paid well. Two, he wasn't very good at it. Fortunately, the quality of door locks in Mexico was far below those he usually ran across in Texas, but it still took him several minutes to get the tumblers to fall.

"Come on, Paco." Glenn kept his voice low, hoping it wouldn't carry out to the street. Snapping his flashlight on, he stepped inside, holding the door open until Paco joined him.

"Now what?"

"We need to find the cooler where they store the bodies." Pointing his light at the floor, Glenn used the glow to find his way down the hall. The first door turned out to be a supply closet, the second a small office. The third turned out to be the right one, a large room with cheap shelves and a raw concrete floor with a heavy metal table in the center. Beneath it, he spotted a large, grate-covered drain. Sweeping his light across the floor exposed several dark, striated patterns that all flowed toward the drain. He didn't want to know what caused those stains, but he had a pretty good guess.

Across from the door sat a large commercial cooler. Glenn chuckled and crossed the room. "Jackpot."

Paco stood frozen in the door, his face a mask of disgust. "My God, but this place stinks something awful."

"It's the embalming fluid, along with whatever else they use down here to preserve the bodies, but mostly embalming fluid. Now, come on."

"You sure this is a good idea? What if his spirit doesn't want to be moved? I mean, he's been here for a while now—what if he likes it here? Shouldn't we have a priest here or something, just in case?" Paco kept his voice low, speaking in kind of a hushed whisper. Like he was afraid of rousing someone, or something.

Glenn pointed his light at his friend. The brightness caused Paco to squint until he raised a hand to shade his eyes. "You mean to do an exorcism, like in that movie with the demon-possessed kid that came out last year? Look at it this way Paco, if that kid had his druthers, would he choose to be buried here with a bunch of strangers? Or back home with his family?"

"Back home, I guess."

"Then if he wants to go back home, what the hell have you got to worry about? His spirit should be happier than a pig in shit that we're doing this. He'll get to see his mama, and she'll get to say her goodbyes all proper with a church service, probably some hymns, and everything."

"Okay. I get it. But that doesn't make this place any less creepy."

"Why are you whispering? There's nobody here but us and a few bodies. I don't think they're going to be raising a fuss about the noise."

"I don't know, it just seems like the right thing to do. It's respectful."

Glenn dropped the light, letting it sweep toward the cooler where he spotted a light switch next to the door. He hit it and light came on inside, spilling through the small window in the thick cooler door. He stepped inside and looked over the several bodies stored in heavy plastic bags, all neatly laid out on the shelves, three high. He recognized the bags easy enough. He had carried more than his share of them out of the city of Huế, back in Vietnam. Loaded them on helicopters to be sent back to Da Nang where they would be sorted. Many were filled with friends and brothers, or at least parts of them, the parts they were able to find after both sides finished bombing the hell out of the city.

Glenn shook off the chilling memories, feeling the tightness in his chest whenever they popped up. It didn't take much for them to come up. Sometimes it took nothing more than a smell, a sound, an image, or a sight like those body bags to send him back there. Closing his eyes for a moment, he mentally stomped it down, then added a couple of extra nails to that mental coffin lid, hoping it would keep them at bay for a while longer. Breathing hard with his face bathed in sweat, Glenn reached for the paperwork attached to the first one. The form had been filled out all in Spanish, so he passed it to Paco. "Here, you read it."

He scanned the paper. "I can't read Spanish. I can speak it a little because of my mom, but why in the hell would I ever want to read it?"

"You can't figure it out?"

"Maybe, *jefe*. Give me a couple of minutes." Paco pointed his light at the form, his face flushed with embarrassment.

"Let's make this easy for you, What's Spanish for name?"

"*Nombre*, I think."

"Then find *nombre* and look at what it says beside it. We're looking for Darren Hamilton, or something so close it could pass for it." Glenn took one side of the cooler, while Paco worked the other.

"Found him," Paco said, pointing at a body on the bottom shelf, making sure he stood far enough back so it couldn't touch him if it decided to unzip its bag and climb out so it could shamble around the room in celebration of going home.

"Have to make sure." Glenn hunkered down and reached for the zipper tab. He pulled it down far enough to get a look at the face, wrinkling his nose at the rotted-chicken smell. He was just a kid, barely old enough to chase tail, definitely white except for the bruised eyes and blue lips. His head looked like a melon the cat had slapped off the kitchen counter. It appeared to be a lopsided mess.

"Yeah, looks like we found our boy." He closed the bag and stood. "Now we need something to put him in. Let's go check out what Elonzio e Hijos Funeraria has to offer."

"You sure it's a good idea to go up there? It faces the street. What if someone sees us?"

Glenn looked up at Paco's face, covered with sweat despite being in the cooler. Call it worry sweat, flop sweat, or fear sweat. Take your pick, it all pretty much amounted to the same thing. Throw a kid into a situation he had never experienced before, it can start to eat at him and allows him to imagine all sorts of strange things. "Take it easy, Paco. I want to get out of here just as much as you do. Spending time in a house full of stiffs sure ain't my idea of a good time. But we have to finish the job we came down here for. That includes getting our boy inside a box so we can take him back home."

Taking several deep breaths, Paco nodded, wiped his face, and stepped out of the cooler. Glenn followed, slapped a hand on his friend's shoulder, and gave a squeeze. "We're in the home stretch. Don't fail me now, kiddo. We have just a little more to do."

Taking another deep breath, Paco nodded. "I'm okay. Let's do it."

"Atta boy."

Like most funeral homes, they kept the product up front. Something about potential customers, or family, being able to walk through the door where they could pick out their chosen ride into eternity before they took their final dirt nap. That's why the dealers keep the best-looking cars on the showroom floor. All kinds of caskets packed the showroom, from simple wooden boxes to some big enough to pass for a city bus, stripped down and set up on blocks.

One looked to be fancy enough for Pharaoh. "How about this

one, *jefe*?" Paco stood beside a copper-colored casket with silver inlays that looked big as a Cadillac, minus the tailfins.

"You do realize that we have to be able to lift it with a body inside. I mean just the two of us." They continued their search. Glenn kept a close eye on the windows facing the street. They had to duck and freeze a couple of times when headlights washed over the front of the building, spilling inside.

"How about this one?" Paco pointed to a casket set up in the corner. Wood with ornate brass handles, the casket lid was painted with a copy of Da Vinci's *Last Supper* from one end to the other. It had been shellacked to a high gloss. He grabbed the end and picked it up. "It's not very heavy."

"Pretty fancy. I would sure hate to face the hereafter in something like that. Saint Peter sees you pulling up to the Pearly Gates in that thing, he may have questions about the kind of life you led, although Jesus might be happy to see you brought a picture of all his friends. How much is it?"

Paco grabbed the price tag, leaned closer, and pointed his light at it. "Twenty-five thousand pesos."

Grinning, Glenn nodded. He figured it would be a fair payback considering how the director had tried to gouge the grieving mother. "That seems to be in Mrs. Hamilton's price range, or pretty close to what she's paid them so far. Bring it. I'll get the body."

Leaving Paco, Glenn headed back to the prep room. He had taken only a couple of steps inside when a flashlight snapped on, blinding him, accompanied by a disembodied voice that said, "Don't move, *señor*, or I will be forced to shoot you."

nineteen

GLENN THREW an arm up over his eyes to block the light as he sidestepped away from the door. The invisible figure spoke again, his voice heavy with disappointment. "Ah, *señor*. Please to raise your hands, *por favor*. I suspected you had more of a reason to be in Jalpa than a casual vacation. I keep an eye on you, only to find you are trying to rob me, a simple policeman who is only trying to support his wife and four children on a meager captain's salary."

Considering the environment and the way voices echoed in the prep room, it took a moment for Glenn to recognize Captain Hernando de Lopez-Gutierrez's smarmy voice. He raised his hands as he moved away from the door. "Yeah. I bet there's a phony mother-in-law and a couple of aunties in the equation, too. How many cousins would you reckon are being deprived because of this? Would you mind lowering the light a little?"

"Excuse me, *señor*." The light lowered enough for Glenn to make out a vague outline behind it, clutching a pistol as black as the Ace of Spades, with a bore big enough for him to stick his fist in. "Now, where is your young companion?"

"I sent him down to the corner to keep an eye out, in case we were being tailed. Seems you get what you pay for these days. So, what's the deal, Captain? You planning on shooting me, locking me up, or what?"

"There is no need for us to be uncivilized about the situation. Perhaps I might be persuaded to look the other way. For a consideration."

"How much of a consideration are we talking about, here?"

"I am not a greedy man, *señor*. Then there is the grieving mother to consider. I imagine she really wants to be able to say a proper goodbye to her poor son. Let us say, oh, three thousand American dollars."

Glenn glanced down at the floor, trying to look like he was considering the offer. With his hands behind his head, he rocked from side to side, managing to get further away from the door and closer to the refrigerator with every step. "I don't carry that kind of cash on me. I have five hundred in my wallet. Will that do?"

The captain sighed and clicked his tongue. "That's too bad, *señor*. I feel you will not have a good time in our prison. Most Americanos don't."

"Wait. I said I only had five hundred *on me*. My secretary has the rest at the hotel."

"Ah, *señor*." The captain chuckled. "You would try to cheat me?"

"Can't blame a guy for trying to save a few bucks, can you?" Glenn thought he saw another shadow behind the light. He'd hoped Paco had enough sense to get away so he wouldn't get caught. The shadows merged with a grunt and whipped around, causing the flashlight to fall. From the darkness the captain cursed.

"I got him, *jefe*," Paco yelled.

When the light hit the ground, Glenn surged forward, clenching his teeth, praying he wouldn't catch a slug. Glenn's left hand clamped down on the captain's wrist while his right fist hammered the man's chin. The policeman fell to the floor, melting like a sandcastle caught by high tide in Galveston.

Clenching and opening his hand, Glenn hoped he hadn't broken anything. "Sonofabitch, that hurts. Get his cuffs so we can lock him up."

"Good thing I overheard him talking from the hall," Paco said. "Think he's alone?"

"Yeah, I don't believe the good captain is the sharing kind. Any money involved he would want to keep all to himself."

"What are we going to do with him? We can't just leave him here."

"Sure, we can. Remember that big metal box in the showroom?"

"You don't mean...?"

Glenn grinned. "Why not? He'll be safe enough, even though it might take them a while to find him. It will give us plenty of time for a head start."

The two of them muscled the captain from the floor, slung his arms across their shoulders, and dragged him into the showroom. They dumped him into the big casket, and Paco shifted his legs so they could wedge him inside. Glenn closed the lid and locked it, giving it a pat. "Now, get the box you picked out for the boy so we can get the hell out of here."

"Wait. *Jefe*. Will he be able to breathe in there?"

"I don't know. That's not usually a problem for the residents, so I'm not sure how these things work." Glenn ran his hands along the edges. "Shit, I don't feel any cracks."

"I don't want to be responsible for him suffocating. That would make us murderers."

"Me either, kiddo. I guess we need to figure a way he can breathe in there." They compromised by unlocking the bottom half and propping it open, figuring that would allow him plenty of air and still keep him secured inside. "Since he's cuffed, that should keep him safe until we get out of here. Now get our box."

Paco released the wheel locks and gently rolled the garishly painted casket down the hall to the prep room where he popped the lid. Pale green satin lined the interior, with a large pillow for the dearly departed's comfort into the afterlife. There were plenty of pockets to store those mementos they just couldn't die without. Pictures, letters, trinkets, and such. "Looks like they put everything in here but a CB radio, but for the right price you can get that installed. All you need are the brackets for the antenna. Bet that could be mounted to the headstone."

"Forget checking out the damned casket. Just help me get the body into it." Glenn grabbed a corner strap and pulled the bag onto the floor. "You get at the feet. I'll take the head."

Even with the straps, it felt awkward, but getting Darren out of the cooler was fairly easy compared to getting him into the casket. That's the trouble with bodies, they were the most uncooperative things in the world—lift it one way, and it wanted to shift in another. Glenn had to finally scoop it up with both arms, cradled it like a baby, and drop it into the casket. Then they pushed and tugged until they had enough room to tuck in the excess body bag enough to close the lid. Glenn stood over it, dripping sweat and panting like he had gone fifteen with Emile Griffith. Hell, he was ready to toss in the towel so his seconds could carry him back to the dressing room.

He looked down at the picture of Jesus staring into his empty soup bowl. It seems whoever they had working the last meal wasn't earning his tip. They had plenty of bread and wine, but no salad or entrée. Meanwhile, everybody around him pretended they didn't see the check and were waiting for the big guy to pick it up.

"I tithe thee ten percent of the total bill," Glenn said without looking up.

"What?"

Straightening to ease his back, Glenn said, "Nothing, just talking to myself. Now that that's done, let's get him into the meat wagon."

Rolling the gurney outside, they managed to get the casket into the back with a minimum of problems. Once they had it secured, Glenn emptied the ice chest to pack the contents around the body, but he had to use Paco's pocket knife to chip the blocks into fist-sized chunks before they were able to get the lid of the casket to close.

Glenn pushed the gurney back into the building and made sure he closed the door. He hoped it would take Elonzio a while to notice the missing body and get around to reporting it to the police. Then even longer to find the captain. Securing the rear door to the hearse, Glenn slapped the roof and said, "Take the wheel, Paco. Then pick up our girl so we can blow this town for good. I can't wait to get home."

"Same here." Paco carefully backed the hearse out onto the street and steered toward the Hotel Francia. "I sure hope Paloma's in a better mood."

"Trust me, she won't be. Oh, she'll be glad enough that the job's half done and that we're on our way home, but she'll still be mad about me making her stay behind. Until I figure out a way to make it up to her."

"How are you going to do that?"

"I don't know. A woman's mind is like a Chinese puzzle box. When you think you've got it all figured out, it hits you with another surprise in a secret compartment. When we do stumble on the answer, it's usually blind, dumb luck. Then we can't figure out how we did it. Just like those damned puzzle boxes."

"My mom's not like that."

"Sure, she is. Your dad is just smart enough to know how dumb he is and lets her lead him around by the nose ring while she lets him pretend he's the one in charge."

Paco parked in front of the hotel and turned to look at Glenn. "You believe women are really like that?"

"Absolutely. Now you wait here while I go fetch Miss Hell or High Water, so we can get the heck out of Dodge."

twenty

MANUEL OPENED his eyes and blinked, confused about his surroundings. The last thing he remembered was standing in a parking lot and talking to a Mexican cop when the sonofabitch shot him after Jorge gave his ass a beatdown. Now he had been shot in the shoulder *and* leg. His ears were ringing while he tried to focus. He didn't know how long he had been out. But he hurt, a lot. Instead of a star-filled sky, he stared up at the ceiling. It was a nice ceiling, a pale blue covered with swirls. He tried to make sense of the pattern. It could have been a small horse or a large dog if either animal had two tails and five legs. He forgot about the damned ceiling when he smelled something cooking. The smell woke a raw hunger in his gut and seemed almost like something his abuela would make. A slight turn of his head to the right showed him a built-in wall niche with a sacred heart of Jesus. It was filled with burning candles and flanked by chairs with frilly covers and lace doilies spread over the arms. His wounds ached abominably. When he tried to shift, the dull ache turned to a shooting pain that wrenched a groan from his lips.

"You're awake."

He turned his head the other way to seek out the voice and saw Jorge sitting in a stuffed chair on the other side of the room, the rifle laid across his lap while he ran a rag over the barrel and stock. A mug of steaming coffee sat on the table beside him.

"Where are we?" His voice came out a hoarse whisper. He tried to swallow, only he had nothing to swallow. His throat felt like a rusty pipe that had been reamed out with a plumber's snake, and his tongue lay in his mouth like an old, discarded work boot. He tried to work up some spit, but nothing would come.

"A safe place."

With some effort, Manuel managed to twist around and drop his throbbing leg on the floor so he could look at the blanket-covered sofa where he had been lying. He sat in someone's parlor, without his pants. A bandage wrapped around his thigh, with a thumb-sized red spot in the center. His boots sat on the floor next to the sofa, and another bandage went over his shoulder and crossed his chest.

The place had a back door with a curtained window that led out to a sunlit garden where he could see the top of the rusted bed of their stolen truck. Another small square window beside the door let the sun pour in. He spotted a kitchen through a door to the right where the delicious smell came from.

"What time is it?"

"Still morning." Jorge set the rifle aside so he could dip into his Tootsie Roll stash. The big man stared down with lizard eyes while he took his time peeling the small piece of candy. "After what happened when we ran into the cop, we needed a place to stay. Lucky for both of us, I found Susanita."

Manuel stared at his companion blankly. "Who?"

"Susanita, a street whore I paid to take us in. This is her house. She bandaged up your leg and shoulder." Jorge laughed and popped the Tootsie Roll into his mouth, adding the wrapper to a pile on the table next to the mug.

Manuel cradled his head in his hands while he massaged his temples with his fingertips. "Goddammit, why did we have to end up stuck here in the middle of no-the-fuck-where Mexico. All Alonzo had to do was be patient until the shitty dick came back to us. Then we could have taken care of him without all this bullshit."

"You shouldn't cuss. The priest says that every time you say a bad word, your guardian angel loses a feather."

Manuel looked at the kitchen doorway. He spied a girl standing there, holding his freshly washed jeans. She had her hair tied back and her face scrubbed clean of makeup. A pretty thing, doe-eyed with a small, pointed chin below her full lips. She looked to be in her early twenties and was barefoot, wearing a tight t-shirt and cutoff jeans, her only jewelry a crucifix on a thin gold chain that found a nice resting place in the hollow of her tits.

"At least you speak English, not like my stupid as fuck partner over there, who thinks he's too goddamn good to speak it. Besides, priests don't tell me how to live my life, and my guardian angel seems to have done shit all for me. You live here alone?" He rubbed the outside of his thigh, being careful of his wound, without taking his eyes off her.

"Yes, for now. As for my English, it helps when dealing with the tourists. That way I don't have to put up with their lousy Spanish." Susanita crossed the polished tile floor to hand Manuel his jeans. "I managed to get most of the blood out but couldn't do anything about the bullet holes. I did the best I could dressing your wound. But you should see a doctor—your wounds need to be stitched up."

"I'll see a doctor when I get back to Texas. Right now, we have business to tend to." He set his pants beside him, inspected the bandage, and flexed his leg. He winced at the dull pain, and the icepick-like stab when he twisted it the wrong way. Standing, he hobbled over to a chair where he sat down with a grunt. Sweat dripped from his face, dotting his shirt. "I don't suppose you have something for the pain?"

She dropped her eyes while she picked at the chipped polish on her fingernails. "I might, but it will cost you."

"I already paid you," Jorge snarled.

Susanita flipped her hair back with a sneer then flopped down in an empty chair, cocking her leg up until her heel rested on the edge, painted toes pointed at the floor. The shorts gave him an interesting view when she leaned over to grab a cigarette. Lighting it up, she blew smoke up at the ceiling. "You paid for a place where you and your friend can stay, that's all. In the kitchen you'll find a bottle of mescal in the cabinet. That should help with your friend's pain until he gets to a doctor he thinks he can trust."

Popping another Tootsie Roll, Jorge added the wrapper to his neat little pile. Chewing slowly, he pushed up from the chair and vanished into the kitchen. He reappeared holding a glass and a milk bottle half-filled with bootleg mescal, with a baby rattlesnake coiled in the bottom. He shook the bottle, watching as the pickled snake did a twisting dance, before settling back down. "This stuff is probably poison."

In no mood to argue, Manuel glared at his hulking companion. Much as he hated snakes, Manuel wasn't about to turn down anything that might dull the pain enough so he could make it back home. "Poison or not, at least it might help. Pour me a glass."

Jorge poured him a drink and held it out. The woman raised her head to flash him that fake doe-in-the-headlight look. She had the eyes for it, large, round, and sensually wet. The kind of eyes a man would be able to dive into and swim laps in, before being sucked down while she treated his soul like an afternoon snack. A look she probably used to her advantage in her line of work, getting the young male tourists to think they might be half falling in love, never believing she was nothing more than a mercenary whore whose only need was to get her hands on their money.

Grabbing the glass, Manuel studied the cloudy liquid for a moment before draining it. Ducking his head, he grimaced at the oily aftertaste and the way it burned going down. "I guess I owe you my thanks for patching up my leg."

Taking another drag, she stared at him. "What happened to you? Your leg. Your shoulder. Your..." She pointed at herself and made a circle. "Face."

Manuel drank down more of the mescal, the alcohol working to relax him. "Let's just say it's been a rough couple of days. I feel like I've been mule kicked, bronc stomped, then dragged by the leg across the rodeo grounds until I shit myself. Hell, half my body feels like one solid bruise. At least the mescal is doing its job. For the moment, the pain seems to have shrunk down to a bearable ache. I hope your guardian angel can tolerate me being here for a while, or he might drop so many feathers he's liable to lose both his wings."

The whore laughed as her foot slid to the floor. Manuel poured himself another glass of mescal, the bottle now half gone. "Jorge, what about the shitty dick and his friends?"

"Still in their hotel. They haven't had time to find the boy yet."

Susanita reached over to stab her cigarette butt out, then scanned both men with narrowed eyes. "Shitty dick? Boy? What the hell are you two talking about? I only agreed to give you a place to stay, not get involved in anything illegal."

Manuel barked out a savage laugh. "So says the street whore who took in a man shot by a cop."

Susanita froze, her eyes knifing Manuel like daggers of ice. When she spoke, her voice went deep and low. "A cop? Nobody said anything about you getting shot by a cop. Maybe it's time for you two to leave since you seem to be feeling better."

"We're not going anywhere, whore, not until we're ready. What did you think happened that we would need a place to hide? Jorge, I want you to go out there so you can keep an eye on them. We need to be ready when they make their move. Whatever happens, don't let them see you. Now how about something to eat? Whatever you're cooking smells pretty damn good."

"Pozole. It's almost ready. You can have some if you put your pants back on."

"You sure you want me to do that? You might be able to make a little extra money in the comfort of your own home doing what you do best."

Jorge snickered. She blushed, then snarled, "Look, you fucking asshole, I do what I have to do to survive. That sure as fuck doesn't include any freebies, not with the likes of you. I had no interest in playing with your little dick when you were passed out. I sure as hell have no interest in playing with it now."

Grinning, Manuel grabbed his jeans and tugged them up, being careful when he drew them past his bandage.

"I don't think your priest would be too happy with the way you're talking right now. I think I just heard a shit load of angel feathers hit the floor."

Susanita pushed out of the chair and stormed into the kitchen without looking back. Grinning, Manuel motion for Jorge to give him a hand standing. The two of them followed her into the kitchen where she, still angry, served them all a bowl of the traditional stew. The food seemed to settle Manuel's stomach. Susanita calmed down but remained distant. "How long do you plan on staying here?"

"Anxious to get rid of us?" Manuel dropped his spoon into the bowl and pushed it back.

"Yes. Unless you want to pay me for missing work." She cleared the table, dropping the dirty dishes into the sink and turning the stove off so the pot of stew could cool. Leaning against the counter, she lit another cigarette and tried to stare down Manuel, like she could make him walk out the door through her sheer force of will.

Shaking his head, he sent Jorge into the other room to fetch the bottle of mescal. "We'll be gone soon. Probably sometime tonight. Once the man we're after decides it's time to leave."

"I think I made a big mistake, bringing you here. I hope I won't regret it any more than I already do."

Manuel laughed. "I didn't think whores had regrets. It's not good for business. Give her another twenty, Jorge."

He loved watching the fire in her eyes. The flash of heat made him tingle. She was one hell of a woman, one he would enjoy getting to know better if he had the time. But time wasn't on his side. Once the shitty dick left town, God willing, it would be the last time he ever saw Jalpa. Jorge peeled off a twenty and let it fall to the table. Susanita's anger didn't stop the money from disappearing down the front of her blouse.

Jorge made his way through town, heading toward the hotel. He slow-walked his way through, taking the time to admire the colorful architecture. Jalpa looked nothing like the border towns he had grown up with. It was cleaner, brighter, and geared towards the more affluent tourist who would come there to stay for days or weeks instead of hours. Shops and houses crowded the streets so there was no room for trees, but there were plenty of flower-filled hanging baskets as well as planters lining the sidewalks, filled with low, flowering shrubs or miniature trees.

Music spilled through the doorways of the shops, mostly Tejano, but some American country or rock. He slowed even more to scan the overflowing shop windows, sometimes having to slip around the sidewalk displays. Reaching one with hat trees filling the window to show off their product, he stopped. Thinking he needed a way to keep the shitty dick or his friends from recognizing him, Jorge went inside. Racks of clothes filled the rest of the shop, along with displays of accessories. Belt buckles, silver and turquoise jewelry, hatbands, all the stuff to pry a tourist from his money. He ignored the proprietor's attempt at conversation, grabbed a straw cowboy hat and a pair of sunglasses, and paid on his way out.

Back on the street, Jorge continued toward the downtown area until he reached the hotel where he knew the shitty dick was staying. The hearse still sat in the parking lot so he stepped into a nearly empty cantina, taking a table next to the window where he could keep an eye on hotel parking lot.

He ordered a beer when the waitress stopped by. She dropped off a squat bottle with condensation that slid off the side to form a small pool on the scarred table. The beer was so cold it almost hurt to drink it.

He had finished his second beer, so he ordered a third. The waitress carried two over and sat down across from him before sliding his across the table. "I'm Carmalita. You seem to be awfully interested in that hotel across the street."

Jorge looked her over for the first time. Not pretty, but attractive enough, maybe mid-thirties, dark hair with a touch of gray. Not exactly slender, but stout. More of a toss-around-beer-cases-or-unruly-drunks kind of stout, not the too-many-frijoles kind of stout. Definitely the type who could keep a man warm on a cold night. "I like the architecture."

She laughed. "You don't look the architecture type."

"What type do I look like?"

Carmalita tilted her head, tugging at the colorfully stitched bodice of her peasant blouse, as if trying to assay his character. She grabbed his right hand and flipped it over, leaning close to study his palm. Her finger traced over his callouses before turning it over to look at the back. "You're a working man, but not a lot of manual labor. Hands are too soft, but not soft enough to be an office or shop worker. You've been in a lot of fights." Her fingertip traced the scars across his knuckles.

Jorge pulled his hand back and took a drink. Scanning the bar, he changed the subject. "Not much business right now."

With her elbows resting on the edge of the table, Carmalita swigged from her bottle. "*Siestas*. Won't see many customers for a couple of hours."

"So, you picked me to amuse yourself?" Jorge relaxed, enjoying having a two-way conversation in Spanish.

"No. It's just that you've been sitting here for a couple of hours, staring at that hotel across the street. It roused my curiosity. I thought you might be like one of those movie detectives, watching a cheating husband or wife. Why else would you be watching it so close?"

"Maybe I'm a *Federale* keeping my eye on a gang of bad guys."

She laughed and cocked her head. "I don't think you're the *Federale* type, either. But you're watching for someone. Who is it? What have they done?"

Jorge stopped speaking and focused on the shitty dick leaving the hotel with his friends. He dropped money on the table without a word and hurried to follow them, leaving the stunned waitress still sitting there.

Staying on the opposite side of the street, he saw them stop for coffee and move on to the restaurant called El Gordo's, where they had dinner washed down by a few beers. Then they spoke with a Mexican cop. He couldn't hear what was being said, but they all seemed friendly enough. The cop left, and a few minutes later, they headed back to the hotel. Jorge decided it might be safe to wait in the lobby. He grabbed a newspaper and found a chair far enough away from the desk where he would be out of the way but could still keep an eye on the elevator.

Jorge unwrapped another Tootsie Roll, folded the wrapper into a tiny ball, and dropped it into the ashtray on the table next to him. It overflowed with the little paper balls. Night had fallen, and there were few enough people in the lobby that he didn't know how much longer he would get away with sitting there. During the day, it hadn't been much of a problem, but now the clerk had started to give him funny looks. Jorge considered offering him a bribe along with a lie to help the clerk mind his own business. That was about the time the elevator door opened, and the shitty dick, wearing a shirt only a faggot might think was cool, stepped out, accompanied by his Mexican friend. That saved him both the money and the trouble of telling a lie.

Dropping the newspaper, he followed them to the door where he waited to see what direction they would take. They vanished in the parking lot. A moment later, the hearse pulled out onto the street, heading toward the center of town. Fortunately, the town was small enough it would be all but impossible for him to lose it. They stopped at a shop where they loaded up with ice chests, stopped for gas, then drove on to the funeral home. While they drove around back, he waited out front, finding a nice dark doorway to stand in where he could fart or scratch his balls in peace. Hell, he could even pick his nose if he wanted. There wasn't nobody there to try to shame him or give him looks of recrimination.

He was still trying to decide what he wanted to do first, scratch or fart, when footsteps echoed in the dark, a hard heel tapping stone followed by the slap of leather soles as the foot came down. It grew louder until Jorge spotted a man moving down the street, full of swagger and confidence like his shit don't stink. He stepped into the light, where Jorge saw he wore a policeman's uniform with the gleam of silver bars on his shoulders. Jorge recognized him as the same cop they talked to at dinner. The cop turned up the driveway, climbing the slope just as easily as he had walked down the street.

Jorge waited a few minutes before he let his curiosity get the best of him. He followed the officer around the back of the funeral home. The only thing back there was the shitty dick's hearse with a wide-open rear door. Jorge slipped inside the building, sliding down the hall until he heard voices but couldn't make out the words, then the sounds of a tussle. A moment later, the shitty dick and his friend came out of a room, carrying the policeman into the front of the building where they placed him in one of the caskets—a big, chrome monstrosity fit for a drug lord who has delusions of royalty, or someone with equally bad taste. They left the lower lid propped open, so the cop must not have been dead.

Jorge waited until the shitty dick and his friend loaded up the body in the hearse and drove off. With the way clear, Jorge stepped up to the casket and slowly lifted the lid. Sure enough, the police captain lay there unconscious, with his hands cuffed. Jorge watched him for a couple of minutes before grabbing the satin pillow from under his head, big and softer than a sack full of kittens. He thought a man could be comfortable laying on something like that for a long time, above ground or under. He wondered where they hid the blanket for those who liked to snuggle.

The man moaned, and Jorge leaned in close enough to whisper in his ear. "Sorry, my man. But we can't have you fucking things up before we get that shitty detective. That might piss off our boss."

Placing the pillow over the Mexican cop's face, Jorge pressed down. The pillow smothered the struggling cop's scream, but Jorge pressed down harder, not easing off until the man stopped moving.

Leaving the funeral home, Jorge hurried back to Susanita's place, where he woke Manuel up by grabbing him by the shirt and hauling him up into a sitting position before giving him a couple of gentle taps on the cheeks until he opened his eyes.

"What the fuck are you doing?" Manuel grabbed Jorge's wrist to push his hands away.

"Time to go. They've got the body and will be ready to leave once they get the girl."

"Shit, shit, shit," Manuel growled while rubbing his face with the palms of his hands, like it needed a good washing. "Any coffee?"

Susanita showed up with a steaming mug, a heavy clay thing that could be used to beat down a mugger or drive railroad spikes in a pinch. Manuel slurped it down, ignoring the way it burned his tongue and the roof of his mouth. It didn't sober him up so much as wake him up, the caffeine giving him a boost to get his ass in gear.

"Jorge, help me out to the truck."

Susanita took Manuel's empty mug, her angry eyes boring into his.

"You should be careful of that leg. If you tear that wound open, you could bleed to death."

"I don't need to take medical advice from a goddamn whore."

"Fuck you, you sonofabitch. I don't care if you do die." She spun around and vanished into the kitchen.

"Why you gotta be such an asshole?"

"Just get me to the truck before we lose that shitty dick and his friends."

With Manuel hopping along on one leg, they reached the truck. Jorge helped him climb in, slamming the door behind him. Rubbing his tender leg, Manuel gave Susanita one last look where she stood in the door watching, wearing a thin robe that clung to her body like Saran wrap, noting the relief on her face. Jorge eased out the clutch while pressing down on the gas. The truck shook and rattled as it backed its way through the gate, then shot forward. The girl followed close enough to close the gate behind them and watched as they turned to follow the hearse out of town, Jorge doing his best to catch up.

twenty-one

BY THE TIME they'd finished loading Darren into the hearse and had left the funeral home, Glenn's anxieties were about to get the better of him. His nerves were wound up tighter than the spring in a cymbal-banging monkey. He felt like he was sitting on a hill of angry red ants, ready to chew his ass off one bite at a time and haul it off to their nest for a holiday feast, like *antgiving* or *antmas*. He wasn't able to relax until they were well beyond the outskirts of Jalpa. Any minute, he half expected to hear sirens or see the flashing lights of the police in hot pursuit, waiting to take them down for a case of body snatching and depriving all those corrupt officials of their future earnings. He kept his eyes locked on the side mirror and watched while the lights of the city shrank to pinpoints behind them. Glenn hoped the good Captain Hernando de Lopez-Gutierrez would stay tucked away in that coffin long enough for them to get clear.

"First chance you get, take the next turnoff," Glenn said. Half a mile further on, Paco turned at a nearly invisible intersection to take them off the main road. Hopefully it would be a safer route home.

A few minutes earlier, they'd managed to sneak past the dozing desk clerk with their bags, wedging Paloma's recent purchases alongside the casket in the back of the hearse, which hadn't been easy, considering how much she had managed to pick up. On their way out of town,

Glenn watched through the passenger window as the passing houses flashed by until they became more spread out the further from the city they went. Most were just vague shadow humps, windows dark, until there was nothing out there but an empty landscape. The hills below the mountains were mere smears of shadows in the distance beneath the streaks of starlight.

"How much longer, do you think, will it take to get home going the back ways?" Glenn asked.

"Hard to say, might be double. Maybe longer. It will depend on the condition of the roads. If there are roads. Some of them can be pretty rough," Paco said.

"How are you holding up through all this, Doll?"

"Surprisingly well, considering how you left me out of everything that happened. You can't keep treating me like I'm some piece of your grandmother's china to be put up on a high shelf where you can keep me safe. You need to admit I'm a valuable part of this company, a little something you seem to be trying to forget."

"Forgive me if I'm a little old school. I keep thinking that dames are supposed to be protected. Treated right and kept away from all this rough and tumble stuff."

"Oh yeah? Well, we don't like to be called dames, either, Mister Spade, or Marlowe, or whoever the hell you think you are. It's nineteen seventy-four. Disco has taken over for the big bands and swing music. You should think about getting out of the forties so you can join the rest of us here in the future where women can drive, smoke, or even cuss if we want to."

Glenn chuckled, then reached for his crumpled cigarette pack to pull out a nail. "Aw, nuts. The only swing music I'm interested in listening to is Bob Wills. I admit that I might have been a little too rough on your earlier tonight, but I was just trying to protect you. Dealing with those Mexican cops can be rough, especially if you come between them and an illicit peso."

Bending low enough to get out of the wind, he flicked his Zippo to fire off the tip. Sitting back, he filled his lungs, then held it until he got a slight buzz before letting it out it, watching as the smoke stream was sucked out through the window. The heat had gone the way of the sun until it felt almost comfortable with the windows down, letting the heavy scent of the junipers blow in.

"Sometimes I think this old world is getting a little too fast for my taste," Glenn said. "I feel like I'm the last cowboy stuck out on a range, helplessly watching while the bones of the last of the longhorns are being plowed under so they can make way for a new shopping center. For that, all I get is a happy face sticker that goes with the free pass to a retirement home. Only problem, I can't picture myself as the pipe and slippers type. I'll probably keep doing this until I die on the job, either by misadventure or natural causes. They don't come any more natural than lead poisoning."

"Lead poisoning?"

"Yeah, but I can't predict what caliber." Glenn flicked the butt out the window, then watched the cherry burn bright as it tumbled through the air, only to vanish when it hit the ground. Laying his head back, he closed his eyes, letting the shimmy of the hearse massage his sore muscles until sleep sucked him down into a dark, dreamless well.

Jorge lead-footed the gas out of Jalpa until he spotted a set of taillights ahead of him and then slowed down to follow at a safe distance. Since it seemed to be the only vehicle on the road, he figured it had to be the shitty detective with his friends. Beside him, Manuel curled up against the door, still feeling no pain from all the mescal he drank, his wounded leg sticking out, wedged under the dash, wet from oozing blood. Jorge could smell and taste it, so coppery it made his teeth ache.

He let Manuel sleep while he followed the car, using every technique of tailing he had picked up over the years—closing in, falling back, even driving with his lights off for short periods, allowing the other car to show him the twists in the road.

By the time the sun determined the moon had done a shitty enough job lighting the world and decided to roll up over the horizon to take over, Jorge's arms ached from fighting the steering wheel as the truck bounced over the ruts in the road. His head hurt from having to focus so much, like somebody had taken a pair of pliers to the muscles in his neck, twisting them into a ball.

With the world lit up, Jorge rolled his head until his neck popped, now able to relax. The car was about a mile ahead of them, and he recognized the hearse. Manuel groaned, sat up, hawked until he could spit out the window, and rubbed his face like he could wipe away the sleep along with the hangover.

"Where the hell are we?"

"Somewhere in the Chihuahuan Desert, I think. Still following the hearse."

Manuel looked around at the surrounding landscape of sand and withered plants before the day could hide it behind a veil of shimmering heat. Ahead of them, the hearse threw up a cloud of dust to mark its progress. That made it look as if it were being pursued by a giant dust devil trying to suck it off the road.

"What do you want to do?"

"Keep following until we find a place where we can get them. We could have caught them in my truck, but we can't in this piece of shit. Another reason to kill that sonofabitch—he fucked up my pickup."

Jorge grunted, not wanting to get into another discussion about Manuel's precious truck when they both knew it had been in almost as bad a shape as the one they stole. Faded paint with fenders so rusted out they looked like they were infested with iron-munching termites, it had burned oil and blown smoke like an eighty-year-old woman playing the Las Vegas slots. The seats had been worn nearly through in spots, stained with spilled alcohol and maybe a little shit ground in from those *putas* who couldn't contain themselves when they'd had their taint tickled or had wanted to practice the asshole method of birth control.

The day grew hotter, and the dust kicked up by the hearse covered them with a layer of grit when they passed through it. Dust clung to their sweaty flesh, abrasive as coarse-grit sandpaper. No matter how you moved, it dug in and left you raw. It didn't do any good to try to wipe it off. It only dug in deeper until it made things worse.

Ahead, Jorge saw the road had turned back to the south until it paralleled a set of low hills that glittered like crinkled Christmas tinsel under the sun. The hills sloped down until they were no taller than a toddler in a pair of Hopalong Cassidy boots. Seeing the road made a hairpin turn around them, Jorge realized the hearse would have to slow down to make the turn. That would give him a chance to take it out. He goosed the gas until the pickup rattled louder and shimmied like a burlesque dancer with a rash. He gave Manuel a shake. When he opened his eyes, Jorge explained what he had in mind.

Manuel sat up so he could see the car ahead of them, absentmindedly massaging his leg while he listened, keeping his hands away from the crusted blood. It appeared the bleeding had stopped, but that only made it itch. Manuel was afraid to scratch lest the bleeding start all over again, only worse.

"If you're going to try, you better do it quick. We might not get another chance like this anytime soon."

"Think you can take the wheel for a while?"

Wearing a fierce look, Manuel rubbed his leg harder. "When you stop, I'll slide over under the wheel. At least until we catch up to them."

The road veered closer to the descending hills. Jorge picked his spot and slammed on the brakes. The pickup shuddered when the brakes locked, causing the wheels to skid on the loose gravel. The vehicle stopped so fast it caused the rooster tail of dust to flip over them like a bad comb-over, obscuring their view. Jorge jerked the shifter into neutral before he bailed out, grabbing the rifle from behind the seat. Bending low, he ran up the shallow incline to the peak and threw himself belly-first onto the ground. Sighting the hearse, he led it for several seconds, then fired. Before the echo of the shot could die, the driver's side dipped, which caused the vehicle to slide onto the shoulder, nearly slipping into the ditch.

Crawfishing back down to the road, Jorge stayed below the ridge until he made it back to the pickup where Manuel had slid behind the wheel.

"Got them," Jorge crowed. He jumped into the passenger seat while Manuel shifted, gears grinding. The truck lurched then picked up speed, taking them to their final reckoning with the shitty dick and his friends.

twenty-two

GLENN HAD BEEN DOZING UNCOMFORTABLY in the passenger's seat, sweat bathing his face while the sirocco wind coming in through his half-opened window did little to offer relief other than giving him a little windburn. Or maybe it was the windborne grit scouring his face that made it raw. Through cracked lids, he watched the panoramic vista of desert sand flanking the road sweep by, pocked with stony outcrops and withered plants. It reflected the sun like a cracked mirror, the light all scattered in a kaleidoscopic mishmash. He had begun to regret the choice to leave the main highway. If they had stayed there, they would be driving through the mountains by now—those wonderfully cool mountains, where the wind smelled of dampness and green things while the sun hung in the blue sky like a Christmas ornament, instead of the glaring eye of Satan welcoming them to hell, or what passed for it in the Mexican desert.

The heat had sapped his energy, leaving him feeling limp and worn out, like an old dishrag that had been wrung out too many times. One that should have been tossed out a long time ago. Groaning, he mustered enough *want to* to turn so he could check the casket and lockdowns, which seemed to have held. He thought he heard the slosh of water inside, a bad sign. Paloma looked as wilted as fried cabbage, her hair clinging to her face in clumps while her makeup had melted to a clown-like mask. Her head wobbled with the bouncing lurch of the hearse. Paco sat hunched over the steering wheel, eyes burning like he was aiming for the finish line in the Indy 500 on nothing but fumes.

He was about to say something he thought would be witty and awe-inspiring to rally the troops, hoping he could make them feel better about their situation, when the car lurched and the wheel twisted. That sent the hearse skewing sideways, sliding across the coarse gravel toward the steep drop-off. Seconds later, Paco managed to get the vehicle under control enough to come to a shuddering stop. A dense cloud of dust wrapped them before it slowly settled over the hearse like a fuzzy blanket. Glenn let his cramped hand slip off the oh-shit strap to check on Paco, his own heart beating a tattoo against his ribs like a conga drum. His mouth had gone so dry he couldn't spit sand. The boy sat frozen, staring straight ahead, eyes wide with fear, both hands locked on the steering wheel tight enough to squeeze the blood from his knuckles. Glenn saw the nervous sweat dripping down Paco's brow, crystal droplets clinging to his lashes, causing the boy to blink through the stinging liquid. Beside him, Paloma had ducked her head against Glenn's shoulder and grabbed his arm, digging her nails in until she drew blood. The way she was all over him, he felt like he was grappling with an octopus. Glenn patted her shoulder, then peeled her fingers back until she loosened her grip.

"Easy with the skin, Doll. It's permanently attached. We're all okay. Take a breath, Paco. Take a deep breath."

"What?"

"I said take a breath before you pass out."

Paco let his shoulders fall, then eased his grip while he breathed out. "What happened?"

"I think we blew a tire." Glenn stared through the windshield. The dust cloud had thinned enough to expose the barren landscape. It looked as if they had landed on Mars. Paco shut off the engine and sat back. The only sound beyond their panting breaths was the constant ticks of the hot engine cooling, sounding like a cricket with a bad case of the hiccups.

Glancing out the side window, Glenn saw just how close to disaster they had come. The wheels were near enough to the drop-off that Glenn couldn't open the door to step out. Another six inches closer to the edge and the hearse could have rolled down the steep embankment, with no way to stop until it hit the stony hardpan below, most likely upside down. If not that, then probably on their side.

"You have to back up," Glenn said.

"But the tire."

"It doesn't matter. I can't get out until you do. Unless you want me to crawl out the driver-side door."

Paco started the car, then slowly backed up, pointing the rear at the center of the road. The hearse limped along on the bad tire to the sound of crunching gravel until they were clear.

"That's good," Glenn said. "Now let's see what the hell happened."

Climbing out, Glenn circled the car until he saw the front driver's side tire was a shredded mess, with chunks of rubber missing and frayed wires sticking out everywhere. Hunkering down, he carefully ran his hands over it until he found a thumb-sized hole in the sidewall.

Paco joined him, squatting so close they bumped shoulders. "It was fine when we made our last gas stop. What the hell happened to it, *jefe*?"

Glenn stood and used his cupped hand to shade his eyes, turning slowly while he studied the surrounding vista. "If I had to guess, I would say it looks like a bullet hole. I hope this thing has a spare."

"Bullet hole? Out here in the middle of nowhere?" Paco twisted around, his troubled eyes sweeping their surroundings, taking in the hills where they made the hairpin turn.

"Can you think of a better place for an ambush? Now, about that spare."

"It should be under the casket."

"We've got to unload the casket to get to the spare tire?"

"No. There's a compartment under it you can access from the back. I'll show you." They were unloading the spare when Paloma joined them with a warning.

"Someone's coming."

Glenn looked back down the road, saw a cloud of dust, pierced with the harsh glint of the sun off a windshield.

"Shit, this can't be good news." He took a step toward the side of the hearse, hoping to reach his bag where he had his pistols stowed. A round slammed into the ground between his feet, spraying his legs with gravel and asphalt chips a split second before he heard the shot. Glenn stopped short when a second round followed, hitting even closer. Getting the message, he stepped back and raised his hands above his head.

A moment later, an old truck pulled over onto the shoulder where the scowling driver climbed from behind the wheel and limped toward them. The passenger stayed behind his open door with a rifle leveled in their direction. He wore a savage grin while he popped something into his mouth.

"Do you remember me, *gringo*?"

Glenn looked him over, noting the blood on his leg, his waning features etched with pain, the bloodstain on his shoulder. "Yeah, I do. The chuckle twins. You and that Tootsie Roll-eating sonofabitch work for Ortega. You tried to take me for a ride back in McHenry. When that didn't work, you followed us until you thought you could run us off the road a couple of days back. What the hell happened to you, anyway? You look like shit."

The man's eyes went cold with fury as he lashed out with the barrel of his pistol. Glenn tried to block it but took a glancing blow on the side of his skull that dropped him to a knee. Paloma whimpered beside him. He touched the swelling knot, and his palm came away sticky with blood.

"Get up, *gringo*. We still have a few things to talk about. Don't do anything that will piss me off. You can see by your tire my friend is one hell of a shot." The man's humorless grin gave Glenn all the answer he needed. "My boss is very upset with you. He wants to make sure you pay for what you did to him."

Manuel looked around at the desert while a grin spread across his face. "Instead of doing it here on the road, we're going to take a little walk out there." The barrel of the gun waved toward the empty desert. "By the time they find your bodies, if they ever do, there shouldn't be nothing left but some rags and a few bones."

Glenn felt a slow burn of anger that began in his gut. He hated being caught flat. He hated it even more when he felt helpless. "If

Ortega has a problem with me, okay. But no need to hurt the boy or the girl."

The man with the gun shook his head. "A shame to waste the *puta*, but witnesses are always a problem, so it's better if we leave all our problems out here for nature to take care of. It will make our lives so much easier. Jorge, make sure they don't have any weapons."

"*Bueno*." Jorge shouldered the rifle before he moved in. He gave both men a quick frisk, flashing an ugly leer when he came to Paloma.

"Don't you touch her," Paco yelled and lunged forward to block his way. He met a fist that left him sprawled in the dirt, and he banged the back of his head against the road.

"Help your friend up, then tell him to be smart. Leave the girl, Jorge. If she's got a weapon hidden anywhere in that outfit, she can keep it."

"Manuel, maybe she put it in her pussy, hey?"

Glenn pulled Paco up. Gripping his arm, he steered the boy to the back of the hearse, where he forced him to sit. He leaned close enough to whisper. "Take it easy, kid, while I try to figure a way out of this. No sense in both of us taking another beating."

When he turned around, he saw Paloma's face flushed with anger. Her ponytail had begun to come apart, and several darks strands clung to her sweaty face.

"What did he say?"

"Never mind. What he said is too disgusting to repeat."

"All of you. Shut up. You, the shitty dick, grab your friend. We're going for a little walk in the desert. You too, *chica*. Jorge, you stay here where you can keep an eye out, in case someone comes along that can't mind their own business."

"You sure you want to do this with your leg? What if it starts bleeding again?"

"Yeah, I do. The bleeding has stopped, so I'm good. Besides, I want the pleasure of shooting this sonofabitch myself for what he did to my truck." Manuel motioned for them to move down the sloping shoulder and out onto the searing flatland below.

"I have a bottle of excellent whiskey in my bag. If you let me fetch it, we can take it with us so we can have a final drink. You know, toast old times." Glenn knew that if he could get to his guns, he would be able to end this little episode damned quick.

"I think not, *gringo*. But I'm sure the two of us will get the chance to appreciate it later. We'll even offer a toast to the memory of you and your companions while the buzzards eat your eyes and the *chicha*'s tits. Now get going."

The small group marched down the slope until they reached level ground. Glenn had Paco's arm over his shoulder to help him along, since the boy was as limp as a teddy bear without the stuffing. Paloma stumbled along behind them, looking beaten. Glenn saw nothing around them but gritty dirt, a few odd boulders thrust up from the desert floor like bleached bones, and sad-looking cacti mixed with some unidentifiable scraggly desert shrubs. He had to admit it seemed to be the ideal place to dump a body. Or three, as the case may be. Except, in this case, the three bodies would be his and his friends, which didn't make it ideal at all. He glanced back at Manuel, noticing the wet spot on the man's leg had started to grow. He was bleeding again. From what Glenn could see, it appeared to be a steady flow. Coming down that slope must have torn something inside.

"That's far enough," Manuel grunted. The leaking wound had soaked his pants down to his shin. Now it was leaving splatters on the ground. Glenn also spotted a growing red stain on his shoulder. He wondered how many times the bastard had been shot, and how many bullets it would take to kill him. Manuel's face had gone three shades whiter, the jagged scar making his face look like a piece of a jigsaw puzzle, and his haunted eyes burned with feral intensity. He noticed the gunman had stopped sweating, like he didn't have the water to spare. He looked like a warmed-over pile of turds. Glenn hoped they had enough time for the heat of the desert sun to work its magic and wear the sonofabitch down.

Manuel moved over to one of the boulders, where he sat down with a grunt. Extending his bad leg, he rubbed his thigh while keeping his gun pointed in their general direction.

Glenn let Paco slide to the ground. He sat there dazed, fingering the knot on the back of his head. Paloma stood beside him, hugging her arms to her chest, looking lost. They were far enough out into the desert that they were beyond the sight of anyone passing on the road, even if there had been any traffic. The only ones watching seemed to be a couple of circling buzzards, no doubt waiting for the blue-plate special to be served up.

Manuel licked his cracked lips. His hands were trembling like it was a job to hold the pistol up. "You pissed off the wrong guy, *gringo*."

"Yeah, it's a personality flaw I've been working on. I always seem to make a bad first impression, but I usually make up for it the second time. If he'll give me another chance, Alonzo would realize what a sweetheart of a guy I really am. I bet we could become great pals."

While he talked, Glenn slowly edged his way closer, sliding his feet across the sand without lifting, hoping he would get the chance to jump Manuel before he pulled the trigger. The thug had a glassy-eyed, feverish look, his pallor had faded to gray, and the tremor in his hand had become worse. Glenn couldn't say for sure, but the way the man was losing blood, he thought the bullet had to have nicked an artery. The heat and the walk out into the desert only made things worse. The man was an idiot. It didn't take much to aggravate a wound like that.

"You're a funny man, *gringo*. I think maybe I should shoot you last. Then you can make me laugh some more."

Glenn shuffled to the side until his short shadow lay on the ground in front of him. That put the sun in Manuel's eyes. He watched the gunman blink and shake his head. "Manuel, you could let us go, then tell your boss you finished the job."

"See? I knew you were a funny man." Manuel dragged his good leg closer to the boulder so he could lean forward, absentmindedly massaging the leaking wound with his free hand, smearing the blood up past his wrist. The coppery smell of blood had grown heavy. There was no telling how much the gunman had already lost.

Glenn only hoped Manuel had lost enough, so he tried to keep him talking. "Maybe we could make a deal. How about a thousand dollars to forget you ever caught up to us."

Manuel blinked once, his eyes staring at the ground. His gun hand dropped to his thigh, and Glenn saw how loose his grip had become. Manuel stretched his wounded leg. His jeans were soaked down to his ankle now. Red drops fell to the sand, a string of glistening wet rubies.

When he spoke, his words came out slurred. "A thousand dollars don't seem like much, not for three people."

He was determined to keep Manuel distracted, regardless. "Two thousand. Come on, man. Two thousand dollars—you can buy a lot of shit for two thousand dollars."

"I suppose you'll want to give me the girl, too?"

"Hell yeah, you can have her. If you're willing to let the both of us go." Glenn nodded toward Paco. "If you can't do that. Maybe you could let me go."

"Glenn." Paloma sounded horrified, not believing he would consider making such a deal.

"Shut up, bitch. We're talking about my life here. It's not like you've never fucked around before, so what's one more time?" He cut his eyes and gave his head a tiny jerk towards the boulder, hoping she would pick up on his meaning.

"*Jefe*, you can't." Paco moaned.

"I sure can. What do you say? Two thousand and the girl for my life. Do we have a deal?"

"I knew you were a funny man." Manuel laughed. He pulled his foot closer, leaving it neatly tucked beneath the boulder. He tried to stand but reeled dizzily until he fell back. "But I don't believe you."

Glenn stepped forward. The gun came up and Manuel fired. His left cheek stung. Manuel fired again, but his hand shook so hard it was a clean miss that whined like an angry bee when it passed his ear. Glenn smashed an elbow into the man's forehead then wrestled the gun free. Once Glenn had the weapon in hand, he stepped back, letting Manuel tumble to the ground with a groan.

"You dumb macho bastard, bringing us out here in your condition. It must be a hundred and twenty, and here you are bleeding to death. What did you think was going to happen? That you would shoot us before you walked out of here?" Glenn checked the gun's load before he tucked it into his waistband.

Manuel leaned back against the bolder, panting. "What are you going to do?"

"Head back to the road where we can take care of your Tootsie Roll-eating buddy."

"You can't leave me out here."

"I sure as hell can. Call it some tit for tat. I think we owe you a lot of tit."

Manuel's head fell back, his eyes closed, his breath coming in short little pants. "But you'll save me, won't you? You're a do-gooder who can't help himself. That's what makes you such a shitty dick." He chuckled weakly at his own joke, then coughed.

Glenn sighed while he wiped his brow, his frustration obvious. "Probably."

"That's the problem with you Americans, you all have a conscience. Especially you Texans."

"I said I probably could. I didn't say I would for sure. Your plan to shoot us didn't help you make any friends here." Glenn touched the bleeding cut on his cheek. Rising from the ground, he looked back at his companions.

"Well, that certainly was an unexpected turn of events," Paloma said. Then her eyes rolled up, and she collapsed next to Paco. A moment later she looked up, eyes red, but dry, her voice a hoarse rasp. "You know Glenn, sometimes you can be a real asshole."

Glenn shrugged. "I had to keep him distracted while I waited for nature to take its course. From the way he looked, I knew he wouldn't be able to last long."

Paloma took a deep breath. "You offered me to him in trade."

"Come on, Doll. You know I didn't mean it. I was just trying to stall for time."

"What about all those awful things you said about me."

Before he answered, a hand grabbed Glenn's ankle and squeezed weakly. He looked down at Manuel's pale, greasy face. The man's leg continued to leak blood until it formed a muddy puddle beneath him, drawing ants. His voice came out weak and rusty. "Help me, *gringo*."

Glenn stepped back until he pulled free. "Maybe you should think about making your peace. From the looks of you, I would say you don't have much time left."

Manuel went slack, his defiance crumbling to fear before acceptance set in. "So, you've decided to let me die out here."

"Like you said, *amigo*. I'm a funny man. I would offer you a farewell drink, but my bottle is still in my bag in the back of the hearse."

Manuel released a sigh, then closed his eyes. "God plays a cruel joke on me." Anything else Manuel might have to say, he saved so it was between him and his maker.

"What's going to happen when Alonzo realizes his men didn't kill us after all?" Paco asked, getting to his feet.

"I'll figure out a way to deal with Alonzo Ortega when we get back home."

"Thanks, I'm fine, by the way," Paco said.

"Good to hear it. I'm going to need your help to take out the other guy."

"How are we going to do that? You don't have that many bullets."

"Yeah, but the other guy doesn't know that."

"He might if he can count. He had to hear those shots."

"We better hope he didn't, or that the ones we have left will be enough. All it takes is one. If it's the right one."

"My leg, it's burning." Manuel moaned, trying to fumble with his belt, but rolled into a ball and vomited before he could pull it loose. The vomit pooled on the dust, filling the air with its bitter tang and drawing flies that seemed to appear from nowhere to join the ants in their feast. Glenn tried to move upwind of the stench, except there was no upwind.

"Can't we do something for him?" Paloma stepped closer while she made the sign of the cross.

"No, Doll. There is no way in hell I'm going to carry him. Not with his partner waiting back there with a rifle, ready to gun us down. We've already seen what kind of shot he is." Glenn pointed to the watery haze that shimmered between them and the road.

"I'll pray for his soul. Then you can help him back."

"I'm telling you, Doll..."

"Glenn. You owe me this." Paloma's voice cracked. He knew he had no choice. That fucking *leave no man behind* idea had been too ingrained into his psyche to allow him to just walk off, no matter what he said or might want.

He looked at Paco. "Can you make it?"

"Yeah. Still a little dizzy, but I'm okay."

"Let's go, Doll."

"Amen." She turned away from Manuel, brushing her damp hair away from her sweat-glistened face. "I'm ready, but I'm still upset with you."

"Yeah. I get it." Glenn pulled Manuel's belt off, wrapped it around his leg above the wound, and cinched it tight. Manuel's skin was so hot to the touch he felt like the man was cooking from the inside out. He grabbed Manuel's arm to pull him up into a sitting position, then slung him over his shoulders in a fireman carry, the blood-soaked pants smearing his clothes and wrecking the fancy new shirt Paloma had bought him.

Manuel didn't move. He wasn't yet dead, but he was close enough that it probably didn't make any difference. Breathing heavily, Glenn's feet dug into the loose sand, making every step hard. He led them at an angle toward the road, intending to come out far enough away from the vehicles to get across so they could come up on Jorge from behind. A trip of only a few hundred yards. They were invisible behind the shimmering veil of desert heat, at least until they reached the road.

They made it to the rising slope of the roadway. That's where Glenn dropped Manuel beneath a low-growing shrub with barely enough shade for his head and shoulders.

Falling on his back, the hot sand burning through his sweat-soaked shirt, Glenn took a moment to catch his breath. It was so hot he felt like he had stuck his head in a blast furnace. His two companions sat down beside him, their limbs slack as a forgotten puppet in a toy box as the dry air sucked the moisture from their bodies and left them dizzy.

"We've got to go." Glenn sat up to check Manuel. He still breathed in short shallow breaths, and his skin had gone clammy. "After we get the drop on that big bastard, we can send him here to save his partner."

Glenn turned to climb up to the road, but Paloma stopped him by grabbing his leg. She looked up with swollen, feverish eyes. He grabbed her hand to help her stand, arm around her shoulder to keep her steady. "Thank you for doing this, Glenn," she said.

"I hope like hell I don't end up regretting it." With the others close on his tail, Glenn crawled up the sloping roadside until he could make out the ghostly-looking vehicles. They appeared to rest on a shimmering lake at one moment, then seemed to be floating in midair the next. Staying low, they crossed to the other side to be behind the vehicles. He moved closer, slipping on the coarse sand mixed with gravel.

Glenn's panting breath sounded loud in his ears, drowning out most other noises. His salt-crusted clothes rubbed against his skin, and his raw throat ached for a drink. When they were even with the truck, he flopped down on his back to check on his friends. They looked to be in worse shape than him. Both were red-faced. Paloma's long dark hair had come free from its ponytail and hung in greasy clumps. Resting a moment, Glenn stared up at the searing sun through closed eyes. He felt like he was being slowly roasted by the desert while strangled by the suffocating air.

"I'm so dry, if I have to spit, I'll probably spit sand. You two going to make it?"

His friends nodded, too worn out to speak. Glenn rolled over to crawl up to the edge of the road until he could peek over. He spotted Jorge leaning against the side of the pickup, staring at the desert with his back toward them. Waving for the others to follow, he climbed up on the road, staying low while he darted toward the truck.

Jorge stood tall, like he had been carved from a piece of desert rock. Glenn watched him peel another one of those little Tootsie Rolls, rolling the wrapper between his fingers into a tight little ball before he flicked it away. Glenn thumbed back the hammer, which clicked loud on the dry air. The sound caused Jorge to jerk to attention. Glenn moved around the back of the truck and said, "Put the rifle down, real slow, or else I'll blow a big ass hole in both you and that bag of Tootsie Rolls."

Holding the barrel of the rifle with two fingers, Jorge let it sway to the side, bent his knees, and laid it on the road. He stood slowly, with his hands up in the air.

"Now back off until I tell you to stop." The big man moved until he stood even with the front of the truck. "That's far enough. Paco, get the gun and bring it back here."

Once he had the rifle, Glenn tucked the pistol into his waistband while he motioned for the others to stay back.

Jorge cocked his head like a curious pup and said in Spanish, "What did you do with Manuel?"

Glenn chuckled. "If you're asking about your buddy, he's back there a couple of hundred yards just off the side of the road, resting comfortably under a bush. Seems the desert got to be too much for him, considering how much blood he had lost, along with the heat."

Jorge gave a macabre little laugh. "That bastard has always been too smart for his own good. He figured he could get out of anything. I guess he was wrong this time."

Paloma stopped by Glenn's side and leaned against him. "He said…"

"I think I got his meaning. Now tell him before he can go find his friend, he's going to change our tire. Then you can get the water bottles from the back of the hearse and pass them around."

Minutes later, Jorge had the front end jacked up and the lugs off. Then he tugged the shredded tire free. Paco walked around from the back of the hearse until he stood by Glenn's side. They watched the big man work while each guzzled from one of the Topo Chico bottles, trying to replace what they had lost. "Want me to keep an eye on him?"

"Nah, I'm good."

"I do know how to handle a gun, *jefe*."

Glenn looked at Paco, noting the determined set of his jaw along with the simmering anger. "I know. But too many people think the threat of a gun is all they need. Because of that, they end up hurt or dead. A lot of them never figure out it's not the gun itself that's the threat, but a person's willingness to use it. I've had to shoot enough people to know that. That big sonofabitch over there knows it, too. So, better me than you. We can't afford for you to be in a spot where you might have second thoughts. Nor do I want to be the one responsible for you carrying such a load if you do have to pull the trigger."

"Okay." Paco accepted his explanation. He didn't seem to like it, but he accepted it. "I checked the casket. There's a lot of water leaking out, but it still feels cold."

"Yeah, I figured there might be. It's this damned heat. I hope there's enough ice to last until we reach a place where we can buy some more. There has to be someplace out here we can find that sells it."

Jorge tossed the lug wrench down, then stood, rubbing his back. "I'm done, man."

"He said…"

"I know what he said. Tell him to put the stuff away and get back to his truck. You okay to drive?"

"Yeah."

"Good. I'll keep an eye on this Tootsie Roll-eating asshole until we're clear."

After making sure the tools were properly stowed, along with the blown tire, Paco climbed behind the wheel while Glenn closed the rear door. Jorge leaned against the pickup's hood and slowly stripped the wrapper from another piece of candy.

"I considered shooting out your front tires, both of them. If I did, it would be a death sentence for both of you assholes. A day ago, I wouldn't have had any compunction about leaving either of you stranded in this hellhole. I suggest you get walking, go find your friend. After that, I don't care what the hell you do, just don't let me see you again, or I might not feel so charitable next time."

Passing the rifle to Paloma, Glenn drew the revolver. He waited until Jorge was a hundred yards past the pickup before he slid down into the front seat, turning so he could keep his eyes on the big man until the hearse began to move.

Dropping back down, Glenn closed his eyes, trying to enjoy the feel of the breeze coming in through the window. Despite it being blast furnace hot, it sucked up the sweat. That made him feel a little cooler. God, now for something ice-cold to drink.

Jorge stared down at Manuel, whose chest barely moved. Sighing, he picked up the limp body, slung it over his shoulder, and carried it back up to the road, sliding in the loose sand until he reached the road surface. From there, he carried Manuel to the battered pickup, letting his limp body slide into the passenger's seat. Stepping back, Jorge wiped the sweat from his brow with the back of his arm while he leaned against the door. He looked at Manuel, his dark face grown ashy, the swollen leg looked like it could burst through his blood-soaked jeans. His cracked lips oozed blood.

Stepping back from the truck, Jorge tried to figure out what he should do. He glanced at all the small packages of Mexican grass peeking from beneath the tarp, stacked neatly in the back of the truck. With his partner out of commission, Jorge wasn't looking forward to going back to McHenry, where he would have to explain to Alonzo what had gone wrong. About how the shitty *gringo* dick had managed to stay alive to make his way back home. If the sonofabitch didn't beat him there. Digging out a Tootsie Roll, he peeled it and popped it into his mouth, soft and half-melted. He chewed slowly while he looked at Manuel, at the drugs, then back at Manuel. All the time, the tiny cogs of his brain were spinning along while they tried to gain a little traction on a growing idea until he made his final decision.

He opened the door, grabbed Manuel's limp body, and dragged it to the side of the road. With his arms around Manuel's chest, he swung it around and let go. Manuel hit the slope with a moan, bounced once, and rolled down until he crashed into a patch of prickly pears where he lay, unmoving. "Goodbye, *el cabron*. This is where we part company. I've always wanted to see California, and with my newfound opportunity, this seems to be the right time."

twenty-three

THE ROAD HAD BEGUN to slope upward toward a range of hills in the distance, so gradually as the be almost unnoticeable. When it sunk into Glenn's heat-muddled brain, he groaned with relief that they were finally leaving the sinkhole of searing heat behind. It had felt like they had been stuck there for days, but they'd only spent a few hours traversing the wide desert. He checked the side mirror constantly but hadn't seen any sign the Tootsie Roll eater might be following them. Glenn hoped they had seen the last of him, but he wouldn't have put a bet on it. Bad people are like bad pennies—they can turn up at any time. To Glenn's mind, the best way to get rid of a bad penny is to lay it on the railroad track so the Santa Fe Super Chief can run over it, squishing all the juice from it until it looked like a dried prune that even the crows wouldn't bother with. Karma. Not that Glenn was a strong believer in karma, but he did relish the concept of justice being poetically applied.

"Hey. That sign we just passed says there's a little motor hotel up ahead, *jefe*. Maybe we could stop there to clean up after what happened to us back there. What do you say?" Paco's words pulled Glenn's mind away from the vast wasteland where it had been roaming. In his mind's eye, he still pictured the pale, sweaty face of that dumbass Manuel while he lay beneath that bush, bleeding out back in the desert. Glenn might act the tough guy when he needed to, but he wasn't accustomed to standing there, watching someone die and not reacting, no matter what shape that death might take. He had seen it too many times in Vietnam to be that heartless. Much as it shamed him to admit, Paloma had been right to insist they help the man who had tried to kill them. As long as Manuel's big taciturn partner did his part, the man should make it.

"Oh, God," Paloma groaned. "That would be marvelous after being forced to walk through the desert for what felt like forever. I bet I smell something awful right now." She lifted the hem of her blouse to gently wipe the greasy sweat from her face, the skin red and tender from their short exposure to the harsh desert sun. Glancing down, she grimaced when she saw the streaks of dirty grease. "After what those two crazy men forced us to go through, I need a chance to clean up and change into some fresh clothes."

"I hate to say it, but I think that's a monumentally bad idea, us taking time to stop out here in the middle of what could pass for hell's ugly cousin," Glenn said. "That being said, we need to get gas and check the condition of our boy in the back. And get more ice if we need it. Wouldn't do for his mother to get him back with more damage than he got from whatever crazy stunt he pulled."

Paloma scowled while she tucked her lank hair behind her ears before collapsing in her seat, arms tightly crossed over her chest. "I don't care what you say, *jefe*. If we stop, I'm going to take some time to get cleaned up. You can either leave me behind or take advantage of the opportunity yourself, even if you don't think you need to. But I'm taking a goddamn bath, and you could use one to get rid of all that man's blood."

They say a wise man knows when to hold his tongue, but nobody had ever accused Glenn of being wise. But he did know the signs of a deadly trap, a taut wire strung across a jungle trail, a pit filled with punji stakes, a sapling tied back to make a Malaysian whip, and the danger of getting between a woman and her Mister Bubbles. Besides, she was right about him needing to clean up—his clothes were stiff with Manuel's dried blood. When he raised his arm, the crusted blood flaked off, or the smell caused it to abandon his shirt.

Glenn said nothing, but after a few more miles, a cluster of small buildings grew larger as they drew closer, set in a place that couldn't feel more isolated. Across the flat expanse, there was nothing except a whole lot of nothing. Emptiness for as far as the eye could see until the road hit the hills. Six tiny cabins formed an arc, with the office in the center displaying a gray weathered sign so sand-scoured it was anyone's guess what it said. A small gas station-slash-café sat next door, not in any better shape than the motor hotel. It had two gas pumps, a screen door, and a front window filled with half-burned-out neon lights. On the side facing them, a swamp cooler hung on the side. Either that, or somebody thought the building needed a washing machine attached to the side, purely as a conversation piece.

Getting closer, Paco slowed until he could safely drift onto the shoulder before he pulled off the road into the dusty parking lot, letting the hearse roll to a stop in front of the fuel pumps.

"Thank God, we made it." Paloma reached over to give Glenn a push until he climbed out. She followed him after she reached through the missing window where the little A/C unit once hung to grab her bag. Flashing her boss a look of defiance, she turned to head for the small office, vanishing through the patched screen door. She reappeared a moment later with a towel tucked under her arm, then turned to head straight toward one of the cabins without looking in their direction. None of them appeared to be particularly well maintained. Peeling paint exposed raw wood in places, and the windows were dirty, with several cracked panes. Someone had tried to patch them with gray tape, turning them into an ugly jigsaw. Only God and the local whores knew what they looked like inside.

Lifting the hose from the pump, Paco shoved it into the gas tank before he cranked the handle. "It looks like a dump."

"I agree," Glenn said. "But I ain't about to come between that girl and her bath. Care too much about my health."

Glenn leaned back against the searing fender while he cast a longing look toward the cantina, where he imagined ice-cold beer would be available. "Well, you know what they say about beggars being choosers. If this is all they have to offer, I guess we don't have much choice."

"You wouldn't leave Paloma here, would you?"

Glenn scratched his ear while he watched the money dial on the pump spin, a rigged roulette game where only the oil companies can win and with most of that money going to the Middle East to line the pockets of some Arab sheik. "Tempting as that might be to teach her a lesson, I can't say I would. Even if her hard-headedness is throwing our schedule off a bit. Good secretaries don't grow on trees. It took me over a year to find her. Hate to have to start training another one on what I can afford to pay."

"I guess that means we're going to be here a while, huh?"

"An extremely short while. Finish gassing up while I give our passenger a check." Glenn opened the back door and crawled inside. Even with the windows down, the back of the hearse felt like an industrial oven. He saw fine-grit sand covered everything. Sweat poured off him while he wrestled the *Last Supper*-painted lid up. Inside, the body bag floated in a bath of cool water. Most of the ice had melted, leaving only a few fist-sized chunks that weren't long for this world. Glenn swished his hand through the water, then he rubbed the chilled liquid over his face. It felt so good he wanted to crawl right inside and spoon with Darren all the way back to Texas.

Instead, he closed the lid and backed out. "We've got to find more ice."

Paco nodded toward the motel office where the bulky ice machine sat out in front. "If we're lucky, the machine over there might have enough ice for us to steal for the rest of the trip."

"I wouldn't hold my breath for that."

After Paco finished pumping the gas, he went inside to pay for it while Glenn waited out in the heat. He climbed behind the wheel when he returned, waiting to see what his boss had in mind. Pushing off the fender with a disgusted grunt, Glenn pointed to Paloma's cabin while crossing the rough parking lot. Paco pulled over to park outside the door while Glenn stopped to check the ice machine. But when he lifted the battered stainless-steel lid, he saw nothing but scummy water along the bottom, the sides covered with flaking mold, which left the cantina as their only option. He hoped they would be able to buy enough there to get them to their next stop, which he hoped would be Nuevo Prado.

Glenn shook his head in Paco's direction and moseyed toward the cabin. Reaching it, he pushed the door open on squealing hinges and stepped into a dark room that smelled of dust mixed with mold. The mold smell undoubtedly came from the small window unit that huffed and puffed like a wolf confronting a brick house filled with pigs happy as shit, pointing and laughing at him through the window. Below it, an ugly, wet stain marked the wall, pooling to leave a wide, discolored spot on the threadbare carpet. The dust smell was self-explanatory. You only had to run your finger over any piece of furniture to cut a rut through the accumulation you could drop corn seeds in, then pray for a decent crop. Paloma sat on the side of the bed with her blouse flared open enough for the cool air to wash over her, her face twisted in a moue of distaste. She said, "I can't believe you paid two hundred pesos for four hours in this place."

Glenn snorted. "Me? You're the one who insisted we stop. I can't believe they charged ten bucks for this rat hole."

"Trust me, *jefe*. I would have let you pay twice that much if it meant I could have a bath or shower. Now, I'm going first. Y'all can wait for your turn in here or in the cantina."

Paloma stood, grabbed her bag, and headed for the back of the room. Taking advantage of her moving, Glenn fell backward on the bed, tucking his arms behind his head. The dust rose in a thick cloud, causing him to sneeze. "Just don't take too long, Doll. Because from the looks of this place, I'm betting the cockroaches could muster an army to kick us out if they think we're beginning to overstay our welcome."

"Very funny, *jefe*." She stopped outside the closed door. She stared at it for a few seconds before turning to Glenn. "Would you mind going in there first, just to check it out?"

After a quick inspection, he assured Paloma she would be safe. There were no creepy crawlies hidden away, waiting to pounce on any unsuspecting guest. She went in, followed by the snick of the lock. The sound brought a grin to Glenn's face. The pipes rattled when the water began to flow. A moment later there came a scream followed by a metallic crash. The door flew open, and a near-naked Paloma rushed out, clutching a too-small towel to cover her front while she put her back against the wall.

"Damn you, Glenn, you said the bathroom was clear." Paloma panted while dripping water.

"It was."

"Then what's that in the shower? It tried to crawl up my leg."

Glenn sat up, trying not to look at all that bare, wet flesh, but it was hard, damned hard. Paloma was flashing more wet skin than you could see in some Austin porn movies. "I'll check it out."

He looked in to see the shower curtain and rod were a tangled mess on the floor. Her robe hung on a hook next to the towel rack. Glenn grabbed it and tossed it out, turning away while Paloma tried to hold the towel in place with one hand and use the other to slip the robe on.

Spotting something in the tub, he hunkered down for a closer look, extending a finger to give it a poke. He picked it up, and a thick clump of hair trailed down from his fingertips, matted together with some kind of greasy gel. He carried it out, holding it up so Paloma could see it. "You shouldn't be mad at me. It looks to be more of a housekeeping problem than a critter problem."

Paloma's face twisted in disgust. "Is that hair? People hair? Ewww."

Glenn flashed a grin. "Unless the last man to rent this room had something going with one of the local goats, then yeah. But at least it's not the curly kind."

"That's sick."

Glenn dropped the hairball into the trash can before he wiped his fingers on his pants. "Me or the hair?"

"Both. Now fix the shower curtain so I can finish."

Paloma had regained her composure, and she wasn't shy about making demands. The trip had done wonders for her confidence. Glenn wasn't sure how much he appreciated the change. "I thought you were all hetted up for a bath?"

"There is no way I'm sitting in that thing. Hell, I barely want to stand in it."

Glenn rehung the rod then slipped the curtain back in place while Paloma waited, her back still pressed against the wall. She kept her attention focused on the tiny room where, it seemed, the dinge went to die. When he finished, she marched into the bathroom and slammed the door. There were no more screams, just the sound of clanging pipes accompanied by the sound of rushing water.

When she came out of the bathroom, her dark hair was still damp, the loose curls swinging around her freshly scrubbed face. But removing the dirt and sweat allowed the fatigue lines to stand out like someone did one of those "this is what you'll look like in five years" portraits of her. But she did smell a hell of a lot better, like rose water spilled over a Dairy Queen cone.

With the bathroom clear, Glenn was looking forward to cleaning up and changing into something less sweaty and dirty, hating that the day's events had ruined the shirt Paloma bought him. Even with the hot water handle cranked wide open, the water felt barely tepid, but he didn't need a hot shower. Just something to wash off the sweat, dried blood, and grit until it made him feel almost human, even if it left the bottom of the tub looking like the beach at Galveston. Staring in the mirror, he inspected the fresh knot Manuel had raised by his pistol-whipping and the cut the bullet had left on his cheek. Seems getting blindsided had become too much of a habit lately. Maybe he had begun to lose his touch. If he ever had a touch. How many more times could he put up with another blow like that before it left him punch drunk?

Satisfied that his skull had stayed intact, he scratched his beard, deciding to wait until they made it home before shaving. That would give him more time to heal a little better. Besides, there was nothing more uncomfortable than sweat on a fresh razor burn. It created a low-grade aggravation that could drive a man over the edge, which meant the itching would be a lot easier to deal with than the burn.

By the time Paco finished up his shower, Glenn and Paloma were ready to hit the cantina. But before heading across to find a cool drink, Glenn wadded up his blood-soaked clothes and stuffed them into the trash, thinking they were well past saving.

The cantina didn't offer much, just a few tables with mismatched chairs set up in front of the swamp cooler where they could get a strong breeze of the mildew-tainted air. Nor did it have much of a selection in drinks, but what they had were immersed in an old oblong washtub filled with ice. A wall-mounted opener sat above a can to catch the falling caps, and a few shelves were filled with necessities, for both humans and cars. Oddly enough, it had a large variety of candy, like that part of Mexico had a plague of sweet-toothed customers crawling in from the desert in need of a sugar rush.

Fishing out their drinks, Glenn paid the man behind the counter, then carried the bottles over to a table where they could relax for a while before they had to hit the road again. Glenn chugged his beer, the liquid so cold it made his throat ache and he felt the chill down into his belly. "Oh god, but that tastes so damned good. I would gladly kiss the ass of the man who discovered wheat was good for something besides making bread."

"That would be the ancient Egyptians. They used it for the people who built their temples."

"I don't care who it was, or the color of his ass, I would still kiss it. It could be as white as an igloo or as black as the inside of a monkey's ear, but it deserves to be acknowledged."

Glenn finished his beer. He had been considering getting up to fetch another round when Paloma gasped, eyes wide, face pale, staring at the door. He turned in his chair enough to spot a huge shadow of a man standing in the doorway, so big he could have been part of the Sierra Madre. Backlight by the sun, the big man waited there, apparently until his eyes could adjust to the dim interior.

Glenn cursed as he reached under his arm for his pistol, only to realize he's left both weapons back in the room. He hissed to keep his voice down. "It's that fucking Tootsie Roll eater, Jorge. Didn't figure he would follow us here."

"What are we going to do, *jefe*?" Paco asked.

"That depends on him," Glenn said.

Stepping inside, Jorge's eyes locked on the three of them. He let loose with a snarl of anger, jerked a pistol from his waistband. Everyone dove for cover when he swung it up and fired. Everyone except for Glenn, who snatched up his beer bottle and flung it. Jorge flinched at the flying bottle, causing the slug to miss. It slammed into the wall behind them, but it came close enough for Glenn to wish he had updated his will. He could have left his home to be used as a sanctuary for abandoned puppies and kittens. Something that would look good in his obituary. It might be enough to make his dad proud, if his dad could remember who he was.

The bottle smashed into Jorge's jaw hard enough to stagger him. Before he could recover, Glenn grabbed Paco's beer and surged across the room. Sweat trickled down Glenn's face, and his stomach went sour.

He had doubts he would be able to take Jorge, even with all his training, since he was no longer in prime shape and hadn't been for several years. But he knew how to fight dirty when he had to. Glenn figured, if it came down to throwing fists with the big Mex, he had arrived at a had-to situation.

Reaching the stunned Jorge, Glen grabbed the pistol, twisted it out of the man's loose grip and tossed it behind him while swinging the bottle, trying to make the fight more even—if a fight between King Kong and Tarzan's chimp, Cheetah, could be considered even. Jorge hunched his shoulders, and the bottle bounce off his head. That blow staggered him, opening a cut that poured blood into his eyes and down the side of his face.

Roaring in anger, Jorge threw a ham-like fist that slammed into Glenn's chest, stealing his breath and giving his heart second thoughts about whether it wanted to stay in place or move somewhere safer, like maybe hiding out behind the liver.

Clenching his jaw against the pain, Glenn raised his fist as he dropped into a boxer's crouch, shuffling sideways to try to take advantage of the blood pouring into Jorge's eye. Glenn feinted a jab, then threw a hook to Jorge's ribs followed by an uppercut. When it landed, it felt like he was punching a tractor. The big sonofabitch barely moved, only blew steam through his nose like a cartoon bull. At least that was Glenn's impression when a hand the size of his grandma Helka's favorite cast iron skillet grabbed his shoulder while a boulder-shaped fist cocked back. Glenn thought about critiquing Jorge's style, maybe offering a couple of tips on the proper way to punch before he launched his missile of bone. Instead, he opted to close his eyes so he could take his beating like a man, only hoping he wouldn't embarrass himself by shitting his pants.

But they were interrupted when a gun roared and a slug buried itself into the wooden floor at their feet. Glenn swiveled his head to see a determined Paloma standing behind the table, pointing the smoking gun. "That's enough. You!" She jerked the gun in Jorge's direction. "Take care of your business and get the hell out of here."

"Or what, *chica*?"

"Or my next shot won't be a warning." To prove her point, she fired again. The slug nicked Jorge's ear lobe. Behind him, a neon Dos Equis sign died with a spark and a sizzle.

Jorge pinched his earlobe with a grin before he licked the blood off his fingers. He turned and plodded over to the candy rack, where he picked up a box of Tootsie Roll candy bars. He set them on the counter and dug into his pocket until he pulled out a wad of crumpled bills he slapped down.

"For the candy. The rest for gasoline." He spoke loud enough for them to hear, took his change, and tucked the box of candy under his arm.

Turning to face them, the big man grabbed a piece of candy, unwrapping it like a cigar. Taking a bite, he chewed slowly. "I'm on my way to California. I've had enough of Texas and all of your bullshit to last me the rest of my life."

"What the hell did he just say?" Glenn asked, massaging his chest, not sure if he had been insulted, threatened, or invited to step outside to continue the good, old-fashioned ass-kicking.

"He said he's on his way to California. That he's had enough of Texas, and us."

Glenn tried to figure out if the man was trying to con him or telling the truth. Jorge's face was a bloody mask, making it hard to read. His dead eyes gave nothing away. He had seen that look before in Vietnam, many times, the look those crazy tunnel rats had when they shucked their shirts, grabbed a bandolier of grenades and a pistol, and dove down into a deep black pit with no idea what lay inside. At least not until you heard the screams of horror before the body count started piling up. Yeah, this guy scared him shitless, but he wasn't stupid.

"Tell him I hope he has a good trip. Maybe he can drop us a post-card when he gets the chance."

Jorge laughed, took another bite of his candy, then left. Paloma let her arm fall. She sucked in a deep, sobbing breath. Glenn took the pistol from her shaking hands and dropped into his chair, his heart beating like a Keith Moon drum solo. The other patrons slowly relaxed and returned to their tables while the soft murmuring of voices filled the background. The shaken trio sat silent for a couple of minutes until Paloma gasped. "Oh my God. I don't believe I did that."

"What the hell just happened? Where did you learn to shoot like that?" Paco asked, his voice strained, before fishing a couple of fresh beers out of the washtub cooler.

"A lucky shot. I didn't mean to hit his ear," Paloma said, her breath shuddering.

Glenn sat there with his eyes still locked on the door, half expecting Jorge to come back through with blazing guns to finish the job Manuel couldn't. "Think he told us the truth?"

Paloma reached out, laying her hand on Glenn's arm. "Maybe he's afraid to tell Alonzo what happened. If he sent those two men down here to kill us and we show up back in McHenry, he'll probably be pretty mad. I wonder what happened to his friend?"

Holding his beer one-handed, Glenn picked at the label with his thumbnail, shredding it. "He could have left him to the buzzards, for all I care. Let's finish our drinks, buy as much ice as we can, and get the hell out of here. I want to get home."

Glenn managed to get forty pounds of ice from the man who ran the gas station-slash-cantina, with Paloma's help along with twenty bucks American. They spent an hour bailing the ice melt out of Darren's coffin before they could pack him down with the fresh ice, hoping it would be enough to keep the boy comfortable the rest of the way back to Texas.

twenty-four

THEY HAD the hardest part of the trip behind them. Now they just had to get through the rest of it in one piece. With a couple of cold beers in their bellies after being freshly scrubbed—and with both of Ortega's men long gone—reaching the hills brought a certain sense of satisfaction. The noticeably lower temperatures were a blessed relief, falling into the range of being almost tolerable. It was still hot, but not suffocating. You could breathe without your throat feeling like it was being turned into a piece of jerky, and when you sweat, it didn't feel like the grease had been cooked out, leaving you so shriveled your body could be used to sand paint off a car fender.

Glenn shifted over, searching for a more comfortable position because his ass was sore from the long ride in the passenger side of the hearse. The car must have had its original seats, because there wasn't much cushion left, not after the long ride over Mexico's rough roads —most of which didn't qualify as roads, more like accidental trails. He thought his ass could trace the configuration of the springs, and Glenn imagined how the bruises on his backside would look like he had been riding on a waffle iron. Because of his size, he tended to bounce around a little more than the others, which brought no joy to his aching bottom. All in all, he wanted the trip to be done with and be tucked into his own bed. Maybe with Beth making a house call from Lilly's so she could cuddle up to his side. Then she could use her magic hands to help make amends for the past few days of discomfort.

They had reached the end of a long day of driving. The shadow of the hearse stretched ahead of them, like it was in a hurry to get home and looking forward to being parked in a nice shady garage where it could chug down a couple of quarts of cool oil while it took a load off its tires. Glenn watched the swollen sun in the side mirror, its color fading from yellow-orange to bloody red as it slid below the horizon, like a giant cookie dipping into a dirty, milk-filled glass.

They drove into the outskirts of Nuevo Prado, although it was hard to tell where the country ended and the town began, what with no welcome to sign to greet them. Nor were there any other signs, like Kiwanis Club or Knights of Columbus, to show how civic-minded the residents were. Just the occasional ramshackle building of plywood topped with corrugated iron. The dusty yards filled with rusty toys, yelling kids, and barking dogs mingled together in a tornado of activity. But the further they drove, the closer the houses became. Along with upgrades on the building material, some even had patches of grass with struggling flower beds and lights on the porches, swarming with moths flying in tiny, confused circles.

"Okay, Paloma," Glenn said, relieved since they were so close to home he could almost taste the Tex-Mex. "Now that we're here, how are we going to cross with a body if we don't have the proper paperwork?"

"I need to make some phone calls. Paco, take us to where we can get something to eat. The people we'll be dealing with would prefer some-place not too close to the border."

"You sure this is a good idea? How do you know we can trust those people?" Glenn said.

"If you want to get something across the border without being caught, these are the kind of people you need to deal with. You have to trust the experts. I know you're used to going off like a bottle rocket with a short fuse, but I'm telling you this isn't the time."

"Maybe. But I don't feel good about it. From my experience, them being experts is not a reason to put a lot of faith in them. I've seen mothers who would turn in their own sons if the money was good enough. What's to say these people won't turn us in for some kind of reward if that police captain in Jalpa gets the word out?"

"Self-preservation, for one thing," Paloma explained. "To them, it's a business. If it gets around they can't be trusted, poof, the money is gone, along with their clients. The people will move onto someone else."

"You mean, if you can't trust your local people smuggler, who can you trust?"

"Something like that." The conversation died then, everybody too worn out and anxious to get home to be chatty at this late hour. Glenn turned to stare out the window to watch the three-wheeled pedal carts moving along the side of the streets, selling everything from tamales to frozen ices on a stick. They were usually driven by weathered old men with hunched backs and toothless smiles and wearing curl-brimmed cowboy hats made of straw to shade their eyes from the broiling sun.

Seeing them plodding along made Glenn think of his dad. He wondered how the old man was doing. How much longer would it be before he had to do something about him? One of these days, Burt would lose it and hurt somebody, but Glenn hated the idea of locking the old man away. Maybe his doctor would come up with something to help stop Burt's uncontrollable fits of anger. He hadn't come up with anything yet, nor had all the specialists he suggested Glenn seek out, but it was the only hope he had.

"What are you thinking about, *jefe*?" Paloma laid her hand on his arm.

"Family problems. Something we both seem to have more than our share of lately."

She nodded with a sad little laugh. "Yes, your dad and my brother. At least one of them has a good reason for behaving the way he does. It's not Burt's fault he's the way he is."

"I know. It's what makes everything so hard, remembering the man he used to be. Before the accident."

"We're here," Paco announced.

They were so close to home Glenn thought he could smell the dirty water of the Rio Grande. If he listened hard enough, he could almost hear the jukebox playing at O'Rourke's pub. Paco stopped in front of a small but crowded tin-walled café and killed the engine. Low volume Tejano music mingled with the soft conversations of the people spilled through the open window.

Glenn stuck his head out to give the place the once over. "Where in the hell did you come up with this place?"

Paco said, "It belongs to my *tia* Ernestina. She's *familia*. The food's good, too."

"It has to be, considering its lack of ambiance. Should we wait here, or go in with you?"

Paloma pushed against his shoulder to get him moving. "I'm starving. Also, I need to use their phone and their toilet."

"Okay. Okay. Don't be a nag." Glenn climbed out, then paused to stretch, eyeing a picnic table being vacated on the side of the building. "Tell you what, Paco. I'll grab us a place to sit. You get us some grub and drinks while Paloma makes her calls."

Paloma stuck out her tongue and sauntered into the café, twitching her hips to taunt him. She managed to get a soft chuckle out of Glenn before Paco interrupted.

"What do you want?"

"Anything, just make sure the food's hot and the beer's cold. The rest is up to you. After all, like you said, it's family." Glenn grabbed the table to stake a claim before anyone else could. Relaxing, he pulled out his wrinkled pack of cigarettes, taking out his last one. He crumpled the pack, then taking aim, he tossed it toward the open-topped trash can, only to watch it bounce off the rim to join the rest of the trash piled around it. He fired off the nail, closing his eyes while holding his breath. It took a minute for the nicotine to hit his bloodstream and give him that low buzz before he slowly blew it out. He leaned his head back, letting the tension flow out of his body now that the end of their little adventure seemed to be within sight.

"Do those things make you feel good?"

He looked at Paloma, who slid onto the seat across from him. "Yeah, it does. Want to try it?"

She shook her head. "No. It's a habit I can't afford. At fifty cents a pack, they're too expensive. I bet you go through at least a dollar a day buying them."

"Used to, or more. But I cut way back. A pack will last me two or three days now. I found I wasn't getting the kick I used to. So, if I wait until the craving gets so bad my lungs are knocking against my heart asking where the fix is, the kick comes back. Maybe not as strong as I want it to be, but it's there." He finished and ground out the butt on the corner of the table. "But this is my last one until we cross the border. Did you reach your party?"

She nodded. "I did. They'll meet us here in a half-hour."

"Good. Here comes Paco with our food. We should have just enough time to finish it before your man gets here. As long as these damn moths will leave us alone. Hell, some of them are big enough to make their own Japanese horror movie, if they can find themselves a fire-breathing lizard to co-star."

Paloma dug into her food with a smirk Glenn couldn't understand, so he marked it up to bad sportsmanship on her part and dug into his own surprisingly tasty meal.

Glenn patted his belly, belched, then finished the last of his beer. Good food, cold beer, the sound of the music drifting through the café's open door, with home just across the river—life was good. He missed having an after-dinner smoke, though. He almost wished he had saved that last cigarette. He could have broken down and bought one of the cheap Mexican brands, but this close to home, he figured he could wait.

"Well?"

"They'll be here. Have another beer."

"Fine. Paco?"

"Hey, why do I have to be the one to get everything?"

"You picked the place. It's your family. I figure you would be glad to play the big shot and pay for everything. This time, tell them to pass on the fruit." Glenn pointed to the lime quarters he had removed from the bottle's neck and had tossed on his plate.

After Paco left, a small figure wearing a straw cowboy hat with an oversized shirt slid onto the seat at the end of the table. "*Señor.*"

"Beat it, kid."

"I'm not a kid. I'm sixteen."

Paloma laughed. There seemed to be something odd about the kid's voice. Glenn took a closer look. That's when he saw the long hair braided up and wound into a bun under the hat. He then studied the face, noting the delicate features. "You're a girl."

twenty-five

THE KID FLASHED A GRIN. "You're pretty smart, for a *gringo*."

Paloma laughed even harder, taking it back to a giggle under Glenn's hard look. "This is your contact? A goddamn kid, a girl?"

"Aw, come on, *jefe*. It's funny. The look on your face." She looked at him again and fell forward, laughing so hard she had to cover her face. Every few seconds she would peek between her fingers, then she'd start all over again.

"Hey. It's not that funny."

Paco dropped three fresh beers on the table. "What did I miss? Who's the *chica*?"

Paloma managed to get herself under control and wiped her eyes dry. "Meet Victoria Ramos. She's going to help us get across the border."

"Like I said," Glenn grumbled. "A goddamn *kid*. I thought you knew people."

"Trust me. This girl is building her business, so she can't afford to screw us over."

"Okay. I'm willing to give it a shot on your say-so." He glared at Paloma. "But if things go haywire, it's all going to be on you. How much, kid?"

"Twenty-five dollars a head, US greenbacks. In advance."

"So. Seventy-five bucks."

"No. A hundred."

"There's only three of us."

Clearing her throat, Victoria looked at the hearse.

"For crying out loud. He's dead. You're going to charge me for that?"

She shrugged. "If it wasn't for him, you wouldn't need me."

"You're a mercenary little bitch, aren't you? I don't suppose you would be willing to give me a receipt?"

"A receipt?" Victoria looked puzzled.

"Yeah. We're on an expense account." It took some explaining, but Glenn finally got Victoria to scrawl something out on a piece of paper, the description simply saying, "for services rendered." To pay her, he had been forced to dip into his rainy-day fund, which he usually earmarked for emergency whiskey purchases and his nicotine monkey.

Victoria scooped up the money and tucked it away. "Wait for me here. I'll be back with my ride."

Glenn watched her until she vanished around the corner. She had his hundred dollars, and he had a sinking feeling in his gut. He turned to glare at Paloma and said, "You sure we can trust this gal?"

"Yes. If she doesn't come back, you can take the money out of my bonus."

Glenn scowled. "What bonus?"

"The bonus you're going to pay me for going on this trip with you. I figure ten percent is fair. Unless you think it needs to be more."

"I got news for you, Doll. If we don't deliver the kid to his mother, we don't get paid. If your friend decides to stiff us, I don't have the cash to pay someone else to get us across the border." He picked up his beer and took a healthy chug, belching a little when he set it down. That's when a mini bike turned the corner, coming toward them like a pissed-off wasp. Victoria pulled up, her braids loose and hat hanging down her back, held in place by its chin strap snugged against her throat.

"Are you ready to go, *señor*? Or do you want to spend the rest of the night drinking *cerveza*?"

"Just getting a little reinforcement before putting my life in the hands of the world's littlest Hells Angel."

Laughing, she gunned the tiny engine. "I have more people I'm taking across tonight. It's perfect timing for you."

Glenn eyed the last swallow in the bottle before he decided it wasn't worth saving and drank it down. "Well, I guess we'd better saddle up that Cayuse and get ourselves back on the trail. How long?"

"Maybe an hour to get to the crossing."

"Then I say let's get the hell out of town." He gave Paloma a hard look. "And if things go wrong, I'm going to blame you."

"You usually do."

They piled back into the hearse, with Paco still driving. He followed the darting mini bike as it wove its way through the traffic, daring Paco to keep up. He defied the specter of death by twisting through the traffic with the reckless abandon of a Mexico City cabbie who had a death wish, leaving several cursing drivers in his wake. Despite his eratic driving, he managed to keep the girl in his sight. Glenn lost count of the close calls, afraid to say anything that might distract Paco enough that he might end up sideswiping some classic Chevy or run over one of those old men with a pedal cart. Paloma had scrunched down in the seat with her arms crossed, head tucked; she refused to look. Glenn treated the side strap above the door like an airplane seat belt, wrapping it around his hand, hoping it could save his ass in a worst-case scenario that could send them rolling or crashing through some poor person's house. Not poor as in lack of money, but poor like they were shit out of luck.

Veronica led them back out of town for several miles before she turned off onto a side road heading north. The terrain changed, as did the quality of the roads when they turned off into a new direction. They only continued to get worse, until the last one seemed to be little more than a goat track in the middle of a shallow arroyo.

"I hope like hell we don't break down out here. If we do, we're royally screwed. I don't think AAA comes out this far, even if we had a way to get in touch," Glenn said. He could breathe now but still held tight to the side strap while the slowly moving hearse rolled and bucked with each rut and dip. His spine took a beating while his ass grew sorer. The motion of the car whipped Paloma from side to side with so much energy, Glenn had to grab her and hold on tight in the hopes he could keep her from getting whiplash.

Victoria rolled to a stop where the arroyo widened, turned her toy motorcycle off, and dismounted. She walked back to the hearse while motioning for Paco to shut off the engine and kill the lights. When the headlights went off, darkness fell across them like a moth-gnawed blanket, the only light coming from the stars that managed to occasionally peek through the cloud cover.

"This girl is smart, setting up a crossing on the night of the new moon beneath an overcast sky. It kind of makes it hard for border patrol to spot them," Glenn said.

"What are we waiting for?" Paco asked when Victoria leaned into the driver's window.

"For the other people I told you about. They should be here soon. Might as well get out so you can stretch your legs."

Glenn said, "I wanted to do my leg stretching on the other side of the border."

"Suit yourself, but it might take a while to get everybody together."

"You been doing this long, kiddo?"

"I'm not a kid."

Glenn heard the anger bubbling below the surface. He hoped like hell Miguel never became that jaded, but he seemed to be on his way down that path unless Glenn could do something to get him pointed in a different direction.

"So, you started this business on your own? A fourteen-year-old taking people across the border for money."

"I said I was sixteen."

"You did," Glenn nodded. "And you lied. You're no more sixteen than I'm twenty-five. Don't worry, your secret is safe with me."

"Fuck you, *gringo*." Victoria pushed off, then went to find herself a comfortable place to wait, squatting against a dirt wall far enough away from the hearse that she didn't have to deal with them.

Paloma sighed, "You really can't help yourself when it comes to charming the ladies, can you, *jefe*?"

"I have my touch." He slumped in the seat, staring through the windshield at the river to see the wind rippling the surface, carrying on it the sour stench of the mud mingled with something dead and rotting. Alongside the arroyo, the crickets chirped a seductive sonata—seductive if you were another cricket; otherwise, it was irritating as hell. Waiting there like he was on a stakeout, he wished he still had a couple of Luckies left to help with the boredom. The hunger always seemed to be worse during his downtime. Then Glenn thought he should have grabbed a six-pack of beer from *tia* Ernestina's place.

"Enough of this." Paloma pushed her greasy hair behind her ears. "You can sit in here doing nothing, but I want some fresh air. I've been cooped up in here long enough with the two of you. So, move it, *jefe*."

Glenn opened the door with a rusty squeal, the dome light casting a dim yellow pool on the sandy ground next to him, like someone had pissed there and it hadn't soaked in. He waited for Paloma to slide over so she could follow him out. Once out in the night air, Glenn decided he didn't want to get back in. After slamming the door, he leaned against the fender and looked up at the sky, only there was nothing to look at but the bellies of a few gray clouds. It was times like that when his thoughts would turn to his dad—his failing mind. Or his time in Vietnam, walking through the elephant grass, imagining them filled with bloodthirsty gooks trying to nail his American hide. Then there were those thoughts he would have about his ex-wife, Alice. Haunting memories he didn't want to face, but they kept showing up anyway.

"Glenn?" A soft hand rested on his wrist, jerking him back from his introspection of pity. He looked at Paloma, barely a shadowy outline against the hearse. "I think the other people are coming."

Glenn turned his attention from the river to the arroyo. He was soon able to make out several faint smudges against the horizon. Glenn couldn't tell much, only there seemed to be about a dozen of them, all huddled together, moving as a group, like a herd of buffalo approaching a watering hole, trying to be wary of the meat-eaters lurking in the bushes. Victoria stood to meet them, talking low for several minutes in Spanish. Someone in the group didn't seem very happy. Voices rose to a loud whisper; fingers were pointed toward the hearse.

Paloma sidled closer to translate. "They don't like the idea that we're going with them. They're afraid the hearse will draw the border patrol's attention. Victoria's calling them cowards. Now they say we must go last after they have all crossed."

Glenn chuckled, unsure how reliable Paloma's translation might be. They seemed to be saying about ten words to her one. Glenn thought she might be leaving out the dirty words. "Sounds like we ain't very welcome."

He reached through the missing window to dig through his case until he found his guns, popped the magazines before he racked a round into the chamber. He slipped them into the rig and shrugged his shoulders. Victoria left the group and walked over to them, tight-lipped.

"They are angry and afraid."

"Kind of figured that, what with all the yelling," Glenn said.

Victoria joined him on the fender, leaning back and crossing her arms while she explained their reasoning. "They are afraid of why a bunch of *gringos* are crossing the border like this, wondering if it might be a trap. That you might be border agents."

"Funny, but I'm the only *gringo* here if you don't count the dead guy. I don't think he's in any condition to cause problems. Look, girl, all we want to do is get the boy home to his mother without causing some sort of incident. This is the only way we can do it without the proper papers."

"I said I would get you there. I have, almost."

"Yeah," Glenn said. "Now tell me, who set all this up. You sure as hell didn't decide to become a coyote at nine, eating your Sugar Pops while watching Saturday morning cartoons until you started leading illegal immigrants across the border on your tricycle. Don't try to kid a kidder, kiddo."

There wasn't enough light to make out her face, but Glenn sensed her blushing like an overripe tomato. "*Mi papá*, he used to be a coyote, until he got sick and died. I had gone with him a few times, so I knew the way. By the time the people found out what happened, I was already taking people across, and they left me alone."

"She looked up at the cloud-filled sky, then checked the glowing dial of her watch. "Are you ready to go?"

"Yeah." Glenn pushed off the fender, wishing he had another Lucky.

"The people go first. You come last, okay?"

"Okay." Glenn waited for Victoria to grab her mini bike, pushing it along the arroyo instead of riding. He slapped the hood to get Paco's attention while he and Paloma walked beside the young coyote.

Coming down the slope, they stepped into a cool bowl of dampness that dropped the temperature several degrees. The illegals took the plunge while Glenn stood on the bank and stared out at the muddy waters of the Rio Grande. The stray starlight peeking through the cloud cover glittered off the ripples formed by the wind and the shallows. The thrum of bullfrogs filled the night. He heard the occasional wet slap when a fish jumped to snatch a midair snack. The mosquitos were swarming, and hungry. Glenn fought the urge to smack the pesky little vampires, afraid the sound might draw unwanted attention. Breathing deep, he detected the musty smell of sour mud, tainted with the stink of rotting fish. A chest-high wall of reeds stretched across the opposite shore, mixed with a few willows hugging the high bank, roots dangling like fingers in the water. They were just above a hairpin turn, which caused the river to slow until it flattened. Glenn guessed it to be about thirty yards wide.

Without looking, he asked Victoria. "You sure our vehicle will make it across here."

"If you're careful. To be honest I've never had a customer who wanted to drive across. I'll go first, followed by the others. You come last. This time of the year, the water here is only a couple of feet deep. The river floor is pretty firm, so there's no worry there. I never had any trouble riding across."

Glenn snorted. "I can carry your little bike over there with one hand. Our ride has a little more lead in its ass. But I guess there's only one way to find out."

Victoria climbed on her little bike and went first, moving slowly through the axle-deep water, the muffler motorboating and sending up a wisp of steam. The people stepped out into the water, holding onto one another to form a human chain and clutching their few bundled belongings as they crossed. The dark silhouettes faded like a ghost the further they got from the bank until they vanished. He still heard the sputter of the mini bike, then the strain on the engine when it climbed out of the river.

"Okay, Paco." Glenn clapped his hands and turned away from the river. "Let's go."

Paco eased the hearse up to the edge of the river, where he stopped long enough for Paloma to get in. Glenn opted to climb up on the fender, resting his heels on the bumper while he used the hood ornament for a handle. With the lights off, Paco eased the vehicle down the bank until it nosed into the water, the bumper pushing the river back like the prow of a ship. They were nearly halfway across when a voice rang out from the Texas side of the river.

"Freeze, Border Patrol. *Policía*." Then the gunfire started.

twenty-six

MONICA HAMILTON SAT on the side of her bed, letting her fingers run through her tangled hair, thinking she probably looked like hell after the night she had. She felt like she had been tied up in a tow sack and beaten with a stick before being thrown off a bridge. She'd tossed and turned half the night, haunted by dreams mostly forgotten in the light of morning except for a few flashes of Darren's face. She stared at the picture of her with Darren she kept on her nightstand. Monica stood behind him, her chin on his shoulder, arms wrapped around his chest, hugging. Both smiling like they had no cares in the world and an eternity to spend together. He wore his devilish grin, like he was laughing at some secret he didn't want to share with the rest of the world or it might lose its magic. She always thought he took after George in the looks department, a good-looking boy whose biggest flaw was he didn't have his daddy's intensity or strength. But before the incident down in Mexico, she had hopes. Oh, so many hopes he would grow into his legacy so he could take over his daddy's business, to take it out of the hands of those vultures who called themselves friends George had appointed as trustees to oversee the company. Next to the picture sat her glass, still half-filled with last night's whiskey, the rim stained with lipstick, and, next to it, her overflowing ashtray—her attempt to self-medicate with alcohol and nicotine in hopes of sleeping through the long nights of emotional pain. It worked, sometimes too well. But never long enough.

A dull throbbing had set in behind her eyes, caused by too much drink and not enough sleep. How in the hell was she supposed to sleep when she had to get up to drive over five hundred miles to pick up Darren's body? Well, she wouldn't drive, that would be up to the hired driver, but she would be there, right beside him, for every long, agonizing mile where she would have nothing to do but remember. From the hallowed halls of her home in Highland Park down to the small grubby town of McHenry, Texas, with its one-star hotel where she would sit and wait for word from the mortuary telling her Darren had finally made it home.

Monica did her best to get past thinking about the unfairness of life. About how it had dealt her such a rotten hand, to lose both husband and son. She wanted to just crawl back into bed where she could hide from the world. To pretend Darren still slept in his room down the hall. She had done that a lot the past few weeks before reality would step in to deliver its bitch slap and another round of tears.

A knock echoed off the door before it opened to expose the dark, round face of Mattie as she peered around the edge. "Ms. Hamilton? There's a man here with a car to pick you up."

"Thank you, Mattie. Tell him I'll be down in a few minutes. Take him into the kitchen and give him a cup of coffee, maybe something to eat if he's in the mood. Leave the door open. This place needs airing out."

Mattie made a face and crossed the room where she drew back the curtains before opening the windows. "It needs a lot more fresh air in here than you can get through that door. You hurry along. Even with him in the Lord's hands, our boy still needs his mama to be strong to get him home. I'll be back in a few minutes with a cup of coffee. Don't imagine you're in the mood to eat something, even though you should." Mattie picked up the glass of whiskey, then stared at Monica, never saying a word.

"Okay, okay. I'm up. Good thing I packed last night."

Mattie looked down at the bag set beside the door and picked it up. "I'll take this on down for you."

The housekeeper vanished, taking the whiskey glass with her. Monica wished she had told Mattie to leave the drink but doubted she would have, even if ordered to. Monica knew Darren's loss had been hard on Mattie, nearly as hard as it had been on her, considering she had half-raised him for the past fifteen years. Fifteen years of watching him grow as he developed from a toddler into a near man. Now he was gone.

Monica wondered if she could ever take to a colored child the way Mattie had taken to Darren. Could that be a failing on her part, a lack of Christian compassion? Not that most of the people at her church were overflowing with Christian charity towards the other races. Did that make colored people morally superior because they could look past a child's skin color to see what lay within? Maybe Martin Luther King had been right, color and character had nothing to do with each other. Maybe the problem came from the white people's failure to accept that. "Lord, Monica. It's too fucking early to be philosophizing. You need to stop the pity, the crying, and get your ass in gear."

Monica headed for the shower, leaving a trail of discarded pajamas behind her. Standing outside the stall, she reached in to test the spray, waiting for it to get just right, when Mattie returned with her coffee.

"You're getting so scrawny your ass is starting to sag because you ain't been eating right for the past month, not to mention what it's done to those poor little things you call titties. They's starting to look like a pair of empty Bull Durham bags someone drew dots on. You need to take better care of yourself."

Monica snorted, ignoring Mattie's audacity. "Look who's talking. The dress you're wearing looks to be three sizes too big. I'm not the only one who hasn't been taking care of myself."

"Maybe so, but I can afford it, and you can't. Now hurry up, Missy. Before that nice Danny eats us out of house and home."

After Mattie left, Monica carried her coffee into the shower, drinking it while the hot needle spray worked the tension out. She finished quickly, toweled off, then got herself dressed, figuring she would be able to live with the leg stubble one more day. Lastly, she did a perfunctory application of her makeup and brushed out her short hair, noticing her roots were sorely in need of touching up. Having done all she could do, Monica hit the stairs while adjusting her hat.

"Mattie, tell the driver I'm ready," Monica called, stopping in the hallway long enough to grab her keys, drop them in her purse, and check the envelope with Mister Helka's money was still inside.

A tall young man with a linebacker's build and wearing an immaculate suit stepped out of the kitchen, licking his fingers. His blonde hair fell over his collar while forming a fringe over his eyes. He looked like he would be more at home on the beach in Galveston, wearing trunks and carrying a surfboard, than driving a hearse.

Mattie followed him out then gave Monica a fierce hug and spoke to Danny without looking back. "You better mind the speed limit. Don't you be getting any speeding tickets now. You make sure you take good care of Mrs. Hamilton, too."

"I will, ma'am."

Breaking away, Monica stepped out onto the porch, pausing to stare at the long sleek vehicle, in chrome-trimmed black, parked along the curb. The boxy rear with windows were covered with ivory curtains, chrome scrolling mounted on the vinyl-covered sides.

Danny picked up her bag, then gestured toward the hearse. "This way, Mrs. Hamilton."

Monica had promised herself she wouldn't cry, not until she saw her son again. She didn't want to be one of those hysterical women who cried at the drop of a hat. Well, evidently the whole millinery hit the floor because it turned out to be a promise she couldn't keep.

"Shit," Glenn yelled when he heard the gunfire. He dove into the water. It closed over his head, filling his mouth with its brackish taste of mud and fish shit. Breaking the surface, he coughed his lungs clear before he salamander-crawled to the passenger door. Raising his head, Glenn peeked inside. He spotted Paloma sprawled in the front seat with her arms over her head while Paco hunched down over the steering wheel, still peering over the dashboard, his eyes as big and round as silver dollars.

"Is everybody okay?"

"We're good. Who the hell is shooting?" Paco grunted.

"Not sure, but whatever you do, don't stop or we'll need a tow truck to get this thing out of here. I'll go take a look to see what the hell is going on." Glenn checked to make sure his pistols were still secure, drew one and tilted it toward the river to let the water flow out of the barrel.

Crouching low, he hurried across the river, getting an unsettling sense of *deja vu* of night patrols in the jungle, while giving his sphincter a serious workout. His asshole squeezed so hard he could hear his hemorrhoids whimper for mercy. He hated river crossings—they left you too exposed. It didn't take much for an enemy sniper to pick you off, sending you lazy-rivering downstream, usually doing a face-down dead man's float. The tension caused Glenn's belly to cramp, and his chest felt like someone had stuck it into a vise then cranked the handle as far as it would go. It didn't stop until he reached the Texas side of the river where he could crawl up onto the bank.

Able to suck in air again, Glenn wiped the water from his eyes while staying hidden in the brush. He heard voices but couldn't make out what they were saying. Taking his time, he slowly made his way toward the source. The words faded to an indecipherable buzz, and he could tell there was more than one person. Glenn reached an old, rutted dirt road, the kind with a raised hump in the middle that would knock a hole in an oil pan if you weren't careful. Figuring he was safe enough, he hunkered down to listen.

It took a minute, but Glenn spotted two men carrying rifles standing over a mini bike flopped over on its side while pointing a flashlight at something just past them. Glenn shifted around until he saw Victoria sitting on the ground in a pool of light, with her arms wrapped around her knees, cowboy hat hanging down her back. She might be just a kid, but those dark eyes of hers were as hard as any Saigon whore's, and just as mercenary. She moved her knees, forcing her shirt to hang open far enough to expose her small perky breasts, the kind all teenage girls have until they get old enough for gravity to do its cruel trick.

One of the figures straightened before he stepped back. "She's clean, Merle."

Victoria snarled with anger. "If I was carrying a weapon, I wouldn't hide it in my tits, you *gringo* sonofabitch."

Merle laughed. "I reckon you wouldn't, but better safe than sorry. Besides, who you gonna tell? Maybe those friends of yours who jackrabbited into the bushes and left you behind? They're probably halfway to Austin by now or the nearest fruit orchard."

Glenn grew coldly furious, realizing the way the men were talking, they couldn't be with Border Patrol. Probably just a couple of redneck assholes looking to have a little fun with someone they thought was an illegal. Or what they would consider fun. He had seen sons of bitches like that in Nam, having their way with the village girls. Some of the girls were willing, some not. It didn't make much difference to the men, since in their minds, they were just gooks, just as those boys thought of Victoria as no more than a wetback whore.

He stayed out of sight and carefully moved around until he reached a better position where he could eavesdrop on their conversation. "People like you should stay on your own side of the border. If you don't, you can't blame us if something happens to you. Ain't that right, Bobby Joe?"

Both men were toting bolt action rifles slung over their shoulders and passing a pint bottle back and forth, tilting it up so the occasional starlight glinted off the glass. Now he knew, not only were they a couple of redneck assholes, but were probably drunk as well. He drew his other pistol, filling both hands with hard iron, squeezing the butts until his knuckles ached.

"That's right," Bobby Joe agreed with a giggle. "You're done stuck out here all on your lonesome. I don't think there's gonna be someone coming to your rescue. That's a fact."

Glenn checked the distance between him and the men, figuring it at about ten feet. Not far, normally. But this situation was far from normal. Not that it would bother him all that much if he had to shoot the pair of them. But he did hate the idea of having to explain his reason for doing so. Plus all that judicial shit when and if the law got involved. He knew most of those involved in enforcing the law didn't have a sense of humor. They wouldn't be all that broke up over a couple of white boys raping an illegal immigrant, but if something happened to those white boys, they would most likely take a dim view of the proceedings. Glenn had to wait for a chance where he could get to them before they could react, shoot someone, then claim self-defense.

"Who's going to get her first?" Merle tossed the empty bottle out into the brush and belched.

"Nobody's going first." Victoria surged from the ground with her hands curled into tiny fists. Before she could do much, Merle grabbed her by the collar. She whipped her head around, biting the meaty part of his thumb.

"Goddamn it, you little Mexican whore." He slapped her with his free hand hard enough to knock her to the ground before he kicked her in the belly with his pointed boots. Done, he walked around in a circle, like a dog looking to take a nap, while sucking on the bite. Glenn wondered why all those assholes wore cowboy boots when most of them couldn't tell the ass end of a horse from the front.

"Just for that, I'm going first. I hope that tight little cunt of yours has juiced itself up, or this is going to be awfully painful. I just wish we had the rest of the boys here with us to take their turn."

Merle passed his rifle to Bobby Joe, and he went to work on his belt. In less than a minute he dropped to his knees, with his jeans and skivvies down around his ankles. With a rapacious smile, Merle leaned over the girl, his hand lashing out to grab her by the throat. Her face turning dark, Victoria struggled to buck him off, her fingers digging into his arm. Merle laughed, squeezing harder until she fell back. Bobby Joe stood there holding the guns, watching like a hypnotized chicken.

Having seen enough, Glenn fired a round that tossed sand between Merle's feet, yelling, "That's enough. Let her go."

Bobby Joe swung around, dropping into a crouch while awkwardly swiveling his rifle up, his movements hindered by Merle's gun. But he was too stupid to drop it. Glenn fired again. The slug slammed into Bobby's knee. He collapsed, screaming in shock as the barrel of his rifle dug into the dirt.

Merle reared up on his knees, releasing Victoria, who skittered away on her back. Once clear, she rolled onto her side, wheezing to suck air through her bruised throat, and had a coughing fit.

"Hands up, asshole," Glenn said, his voice cold enough to make a man's balls shrink up and try to crawl into his belly.

Merle's hands shot up, but good ol' Bobby Joe seemed too busy crying while hugging his shattered knee. "Who the hell are you?"

"He shot me, Merle. He shot me," Bobby Joe sobbed.

"I'll do it again if you don't shut up. You could say I'm that little gal's guardian angel. Now get up." He choked his hot anger down until it became a ball of cold fury, the difference being he wouldn't do anything rash or stupid, even if he wanted to pistol-whip both punks.

Merle stood and reached down to pull his pants up.

"I didn't tell you to get dressed. You sure seemed to be in a hurry to flash that pecker of yours a minute ago—no need to get all shy about it now." Glenn holstered one of his Colts before he moved over to where Bobby Joe lay. The boy clutched his knee and rolled from side to side.

"Hurt, son?"

Bobby Joe whimpered but managed to nod.

"Let me help you with that." Glenn leaned over, clipping him above the ear with the barrel of his gun. The boy collapsed and went silent. Keeping an eye on Merle, he picked up both rifles, spun on the balls of his feet, and flung them out into the thick growth that lined the river bank.

"What the hell?! Those guns cost a lot of money." Merle's voiced cracked with anger.

"Shut up, you dumb shit." Glenn closed in until he stood a foot away. "That was a rifle. This is a pistol. *This* is a gun." Glenn jammed the cold metal of his .45 against the kid's balls, drawing a mew of pain.

"One is for fighting, one is for fun. Now, if you want to be having fun with that pecker of yours in the future, I suggest you listen to what I tell you, or I can go ahead and blow it off right here."

"NO!" the boy screamed. He swallowed hard before asking, "What are you going to do to us?"

That's when Glenn saw just how young he was. The loss of blood to his face caused his acne to stand out, dark scars like moon craters. They were both young, not much more than twenty, if that. Just a couple of young bulls trying to show each other who had the biggest balls. Now that Merle had them hanging out in the night air, they didn't look so big. He looked like a toddler who had his ass dipped into a bucket of cold water.

"I'm not going to do anything. It wasn't me you attacked." He backed away, looked at Victoria, and gave her a deliberate wink. "I know for a fact that this girl is half Apache. Now, contrary to all those stories you heard about them collecting scalps, they preferred to cut the dicks off their enemies and wear them strung together on a necklace. Ever see some of those old pictures taken of the tribal chiefs? They all wore those kinds of necklaces, but the people who wrote all the history books thought it wasn't a fitting thing for civilized white people to learn about such practices, so they changed it to scalps. I hear the women were pretty savage in the way they would amputate a man's pecker using a dull stone knife, sawing away until it came off in her hand. They say it could sometimes take up to half an hour if it's done right. If the woman was especially aggrieved."

Glenn stopped talking for a moment. Merle started to shiver while tears painted his cheeks. "You want to show this boy what it was like? I'm sure we can find us a nice rock somewhere we can chip into some kind of blade."

Going along with it, Victoria pulled together her tattered shirt and walked up to Merle. She wrapped her hand around his dangling cock, giving it a tug until she had it stretched out far enough to lift him to his tiptoes. Then she let go with a snort of disgust. "No. It's like fishing. We always throw the little ones back." Then she slapped the crying man hard enough to rock him back on his heels.

"Feel better?" Glenn asked.

Shaking her hand, she snarled. "Almost." She drew her foot back, then kicked Merle in the balls. Hard, like a Longhorn placekicker going for a winning field goal with the clock running out. Screaming, he grabbed his naked crotch, pigeon-toed, and dropped to the ground with a choked gurgle before spewing his supper all over the front of his shirt.

"I do now." Victoria tugged her shirttails from her jeans. She tied them into a knot that exposed her belly but hid her small tits, kind of. She lifted her mini bike from the ground and straddled the seat. "I have to find my people. I need to get them to where I promised."

"Fine by me, kiddo. Your business is your business. It's got nothing to do with me."

Nodding, she flashed him a grin. Victoria jumped up to come down hard on the kick start. Twisting the throttle until the little machine sounded like a blender set on puree, she raised her voice. *"Adios, mi amigo."*

"Is that all you've got to say to me after I saved your ass?"

"Next time you want to smuggle a body across the border, I'll give you a discount." She released the brake. The little mini bike leaped forward until it vanished into the bushes. He listened as the sound of the engine faded into silence.

A moment later, a pair of headlights swept across the scene as the old hearse came bouncing along the rutted road. Glenn holstered his pistol and hunkered down beside Merle, wrinkling his nose at the sour smell of vomit and alcohol that covered the boy's clothes. "You better get your friend to the doctor. It's a shame he got shot in a hunting accident, but you know how it is out here on the river at night. Y'all've been drinking, and that causes accidents to happen. If you're thinking of telling someone about this, I don't think it would be all that hard to find either of you boys again. If I needed to. Do we have us an understanding?"

Merle managed to nod his head, mustering a raspy, "Yes."

The hearse pulled up and Paco stuck his head out the window to take in the scene—two strangers sprawled on the ground, one with his pants down around his ankles, the other with a bloody leg. "What the hell happened here?"

"Just a couple of young bucks getting a little too rambunctious for their own good. Everything's just fine now since we've come to an understanding." Glenn moved to the passenger side and climbed in next to Paloma. "Let's go home."

"Are they going to be alright? Should we help them?" The tone of Paloma's voice dredged up a feeling of guilt. Maybe not a feeling, but certainly a twinge. Not that it gave him the inclination to do anything. Maybe he had stepped over the line, but that line seemed to be moving a little further with every case. God, maybe he had been at this too long.

"Yeah, they'll be fine." He barely closed the door before Paco punched it. The spinning tires sent a rooster tail of dirt and gravel spraying into the air. Glenn looked in the side mirror to see Merle still lying on the ground, curled in a ball.

twenty-seven

GLENN WAS DOG TIRED, but at least the itching sweat was now gone, sucked away by the night breeze pouring in through the vent window. But the sticky residue from the river that made him smell like dirty fish still permeated his clothes. Now, his bladder was bitching about the tango the old hearse was making it dance. Relief washed over Glenn when they rolled past the *Welcome to McHenry* sign at the edge of town. They had managed to survive Mexico, the border crossing, plus everything the fates and Ortega had thrown against them. Now the only thing he had left to deal with was getting the boy to the funeral home. Oh, and figure out how he was going to handle the drug dealer. Somehow, he needed to come up with a plan that would keep him away from the kids, especially Miguel.

Glenn was sure he would be able to come up with something, but it would have to wait until tomorrow. Right now, he was too damn tired to think straight. He looked down at the sleeping Paloma, her head against his shoulder, mouth opened, causing a soft snore to rattle her throat. She had a thin string of spittle anchored between her lips that bowed slightly with every exhale, leaving a wet spot on his shoulder where the drool ran out of the corner of her mouth. Paco sat hunched over the steering wheel. His unblinking eyes were focused on the road like it might up and take off if he wasn't watching it.

"Paco. Are you okay?"

Paco's head jerked, then he blinked several times, rubbing his face and eyes to chase away the sandman's grit. "Yeah. Looks like we made it."

"Yeah, we did. Let's drop our girl off first. Give her a chance to clean up. Slip into something comfortable."

"Yeah. Like a nice soft bed with cool sheets," Paco said. He then yawned so hard his jaw quivered. He shook his head in an attempt to keep sleep at bay for a little longer. "Me and her both."

They rode in silence after that. Like most small towns, the local folks had already turned off the lights, kicked out the cat, and rolled up the welcome mat—a hint that, at that hour, you weren't welcome and should come back tomorrow, unless it was a matter of life or death. All that gave McHenry the eerie ambiance of a ghost town. The only things missing were some strange howls, fog rolling in, or an old prospector dragging his ass behind him, loaded down with mining gear. The downtown stoplights were set to pulse a monotonous yellow when they drove through, a gentle warning to all to watch their speed using the honor system.

They went straight to Paloma's place first. Paco pulled to the curb, and Glenn nudged her awake before he climbed out to make room. Paloma scooted across the seat, extending a healthy leg to reach the curb. He helped her pull her bags out of the back, carrying them up to the porch for her, some the worse for wear after the last couple of days.

Glenn tried to imagine how she must feel after that final lap of their long, grueling drive—especially after what happened to them out in the desert, plus the events down by the river. She had been beaten up physically, and emotionally drained. Glenn sympathized because that's how he sure as hell felt.

Standing on the steps, Paloma paused a moment, as if she were searching for the right words. Glenn hoped she had forgotten her anger about the way he treated her in Mexico and how he'd kept her in the dark about Miguel and his relationship with that drug dealer, Ortega. Now that they were safe at home, he wished she had it in her heart to be just a tad more forgiving.

Instead, Paloma lifted her arm and took a deep whiff before she dropped it with a sneer of disgust. "I don't know what y'all have planned, but the first thing I'm going to do is jump into a hot bath so I can soak the stink off me. Next time I have the great idea of helping you out on a case like this, remind me of our trip to Mexico."

"Well, since we can't deliver the body until tomorrow morning, I think I'll stop by O'Rourke's for a nightcap so we can let Paco's folks know he made it home safe."

"You need to get out of those wet clothes before you catch a cold or something from the river."

"Not so wet anymore. They're almost dry. They still smell like the river, though, which might put a few people off."

"*Jefe*." Paloma paused a second, staring at the front door. He saw her shoulders tighten.

"He's not here." Glenn kept his voice low, reading her thoughts.

"I know. Does it make me a bad sister being glad he's not?"

"No," he scoffed. "You're all worn out. You need to rest up, so you can be at your best when you two talk this out."

She picked up her bags and turned around. "I'm not mad at you anymore, just tired. Maybe after I rest up, I'll be mad again."

"That's your choice, but I'm glad you're not. I hate to be on your bad side since you're the one who makes the coffee."

He saw her strained smile. "You need to understand I'm not a little girl. I've had to take care of myself and my brother since I was sixteen. When you do that, you have to be able to deal with some of the uglier things in life. Not just here in McHenry, Texas."

"I know, Doll." Glenn nodded. He reached for his pack of Luckies, forgetting he had already smoked his last one. That was always when the claws dug in to make the cravings feel much worse. It's easy when you had a handy backup to take the edge off of a situation, but if you didn't, the nicotine monster would rear its ugly head and demand to be satisfied. Closing his eyes, Glenn cursed under his breath. "Tough, asshole. You have to wait, so you might as well knock it off."

"What?"

"Nothing, Doll. Just trying to deal with one of my many personal problems."

"You know I should still be mad at you for what you did." She stared down, the momentary void filled with the lovelorn crickets playing their symphony of desperation in the shadows.

Glenn stared at her, standing there under the stars now that the clouds had cleared out enough to give the gods a clear view of how their handiwork turned out. Her clothes were dirty, wrinkled, and stained with sweat, her hair a greasy windblown mess, her makeup worn away by the harshness of their trip. But to his eyes, she was still a damned fine-looking girl. Almost too good to be putting up with a half-assed private dick like him. A girl like her deserved better. Because of that, she made him want to try harder. Maybe not much, but a least a little. He owed her and Miguel that much. Maybe the kid had been right, that he was a lousy excuse for a boss.

Cocking her head, she studied him for a moment. "Did you ever think about wearing a hat? By that, I mean something besides a cowboy or baseball hat."

"You know I don't wear cowboy hats, or baseball. Where did that come from, Doll?"

She shrugged. "All the movie detectives wear them, at least they do in the old ones. It makes them all look so dashing. You can tell how they're feeling by the way they wear them."

Shaking his head, he looked down at the sidewalk. "I think I'm a few pounds, years, and scars past dashing."

She smiled. "I don't know. I think you might be able to pull it off."

"Fat chance. Seeing that tomorrow's Saturday, Doll, sleep in, rest up. Call me if you need me. For anything. Maybe after we settle up with Mrs. Hamilton, I'll give you a call. Then we can think about painting the town."

She scoffed. "Get serious, Glenn. This is McHenry. There's not much of a town here to paint."

"Okay. I'll take you and Miguel out for a nice dinner. Maybe the three of us can talk things over. Come up with a plan to keep his dumb brown ass out of trouble. I have a friend that owns a boxing gym. Maybe Miguel could think about taking up the sport. It would be good for him. It helped me when I was a kid. Maybe we could even find the time to discuss your ideas for improving my wardrobe."

Paloma looked up, her eyes glistening. She gave him a slow nod while she considered his offer. "I think I would like that. But it has to be a really nice place. Not Hidalgos or the Woolworths lunch counter. A place where they use real tablecloths that aren't checkered and they don't serve drinks in waxed cups with straws."

"Okay by me—you pick the place. I'll promise to use the silverware in the proper order. Hell, I won't even pick my nose at the table." He waited until she had vanished through the door. He stared at it for a few seconds before he returned to the hearse.

Paco pulled away in silence, steering the behemoth back into the center of town until they reached his father's bar. He parked out front just before closing. The small parking lot alongside the bar sat nearly empty, dark, and ignored.

"You sure it will be okay to leave the car here?" Paco asked.

"Yeah. Who would want to steal a broken-down, twenty-year-old hearse? Maybe a desperate garage band needing a ride to get to their next gig, but who else? Relax, Paco, we're home free. We go by the funeral home first thing in the morning. Once Bob takes the body off our hands, we are done with everything. Except for collecting the other half of our fee. Now, let's go get a drink."

Climbing out of the car, Glenn led the way into the Irish watering hole. Seeing Seamus standing behind the bar brought a sense of welcome relief. Finally, something familiar. Further down, a couple of old-timers clung desperately to their barstools in front of the television, watching Johnny Carson leering at a big-busted blonde while in the middle of some skit. He saw no sign of Margarite and figured she must be somewhere in the back.

"Welcome home, me buckos. I hope everything went well. Paco, go let your mama know you're back home, safe."

Glenn couldn't help but notice that something seemed a little off with Seamus, something he tried to hide behind his smile. He had the kind of look a man had when he was worried the government was about to lower the hammer, or someone close has suddenly taken a bad turn and died, leaving you out of their will after sticking you with the funeral bill.

"We all made it back in one piece, none of us the worse for wear. So, that has to count for something," Glenn said.

Seamus chuckled. "That knot on the side of your noggin to go with the cut on your face tells me a different story."

Glenn reached up to touch his cheek and flinched, not realizing how tender it was. "This? Just a little reminder that sometimes I'm not as smart as I think I am. The guy who did it is out of the picture now."

"I would ask, but I'm afraid I wouldn't like the answer."

"Probably not." Glenn slapped a five on the bar. "How about pouring me up one of those special whiskeys you keep back there. I also need some change for the cigarette machine."

Seamus gave him his change before he reached under the bar to retrieve a bottle of Bushmills Black Label. He poured four fingers into Glenn's glass, then leaned close so he could speak in a low voice. "I need you to stick around until after closing. I, uhm, we sort of have a special little problem we need your help with."

Glenn nodded and took a large swallow while Seamus shifted down the bar to refill several beer mugs. While Seamus took care of his regulars, Glenn headed for the vending machine. To his mind, seventy-five cents was too much to pay for a single pack of coffin nails, but considering the late hour, he had little choice. Ripping the top off the pack, Glenn pulled one out and lit up, which managed to quiet the growls of the ravenous nicotine beast until he turned it into a mewling kitten. He made a quick detour to the little boy's room before he returned to the bar, his bladder emphatically thankful. Taking his seat, Glenn took his time nursing the drink while the bar slowly cleared out. Paco soon joined him, sipping from a bottle of Coke, imitating his boss by hunching over the bar.

"Now, that we've brought the boy home, what's next, *jefe*?"

"After we deliver it, I think I'll take a few days off before I check to see if Hugo has any new work for us. Maybe that bank robber from Lubbock is still out there, waiting for me to bust his ass and slap the cuffs on." He stared down into the glass, studying the dark dregs like they were tea leaves ready to tell his fortune. To be honest, things weren't looking good. But between the nicotine and the alcohol, he had started to feel almost human again.

Looking up at the mirror, he caught Paco nervously toying with his bottle. Glenn had known the boy long enough to be able to tell when he had something eating at him. Plus, Paco had always been a lousy poker player. He couldn't keep his emotions off his face. Like the old joke about the dog who wagged his tail every time he had a good hand. That's Paco, and he seemed to be in a tail-wagging frenzy. "You look like you have something on your mind."

The boy blushed, which meant he wanted to ask something personal but wasn't sure how Glenn would react. "You were in the Army, weren't you, *jefe*?"

Staring down at his drink, Glenn dipped a finger in. He ran the wet tip around the rim of the glass. "Marine Corps, but yeah, I served my country."

"You fought in the war, in Vietnam, I mean?"

"Yes. Where are you going with this, Paco?"

"It's just that I've never met someone who fought in a war before. Well, I have, but not someone I would call a friend. Most of them are old men now. That made me wonder why you never talk about it."

"Because nowadays nobody gives a shit about Vietnam, or for any of us who served and fought there. Especially those who fought. To most of this generation, fighting in combat for your country is no longer a badge of honor. All it entitles you to is a severe case of disrespect. To our everlasting embarrassment, it's something this country doesn't want to remember. We—I mean the ones who fought over there—didn't come home to victory parades, but with our tails tucked between our legs in shame at the way that sonofabitch Nixon let it end. Why are you so interested in that all of a sudden?"

"It's history." Paco tilted his head to indicate the other end of the bar. "Plus, those older guys down there who hang around talking about what they did in the war, sometimes it seems that's all they want to talk about. I thought... you know..."

Glenn sighed and reached for the bottle to add a couple more fingers to his glass before he spoke. "History is what happens to other people, other countries. Usually, it's about something that happened a long time ago. But that stuff that happened to me while I was over there? That's not history; it's my life. The reason those guys who hang around your dad's bar, mostly men who fought in dubya dubya two—" He said that last with a tone of compassion. "They talk about it with one another because it's something they know they have in common. It's an experience they can share with those who were in the same boat. They know they'll be understood. You know what else me and the guys who fought in Vietnam have in common?"

Glenn waited until Paco shook his head. He leaned forward, hissing in a low voice, thick with sudden anger. "It's a part of our lives we want to forget. Just like the rest of this fucking country wants to pretend it never happened. Until it suits them."

"I didn't mean to make you mad."

"You didn't, kid. Life does a good enough job of that all on its own."

That ended the conversation, not long before the last customer made his way out the door. Seamus locked it behind him and turned off the outside lights. That's when the nervous tension in the bar took a big jump.

Turning around on his barstool, Glenn looked back at the worried owner. "Now that the place is empty, what did you want to talk to me about?"

Before getting started, Seamus circled the bar, bringing with him a fresh bottle to pour them a drink, except for Paco, who got another Coke. "I have to tell you a little story. Much as it shames me to say it, I got myself in a bit of trouble back in fifty-one. June, it was. I had come to America and settled down in Boston. There wasn't much work for a poor Irish lad fresh off the boat, so I fell in with one of the Irish gangs, Southies they called them, working for a man called Tony Magan. I was a bag boy, picking up money from the numbers and protection rackets. Then I would deliver it back to his bar.

"Seems one of the other lads who had been with him for a while became a little greedy. He started doing a little skimming, not enough to be noticed. When he didn't get caught, he started to take a little more, then a little more. When he did get caught, he started to point the finger, accusing others. I never stole from Magan, but the accusation was enough." Seamus paused long enough to take a drink. He gave Paco a look that showed his discomfort over exposing his past.

"Suspicions grew. If the finger pointed at you, you were all but done. It found a couple of men I knew, and it cost them their lives.

"Then the finger fell to me. There I was, just sixteen with only a few months in America. It scared the hell out of me. I gathered what little money I had and did a runner, terrified of what would happen to me if I stayed. I eventually made my way down here, where I settled down with a wonderful woman who managed to make a decent man out of me."

Margarite wrapped her arms around him and murmured. "*Mi amado.*"

Seamus kissed her on the cheek, holding her close. "Those men, the two missing strangers."

"They're missing?" Glenn interrupted. "When did that happen?"

"Please," Seamus said, holding his hand up to signal Glenn to wait. "Those men were from Tony's gang. They came here to kill me, thinking it was me guilty of betraying my oath to them."

"Dad."

"Just wait, Paco. Let me finish." Taking a deep breath, Seamus continued. "That's why I asked you to stay. I need your help. *We* need your help."

"So, you want me to get those men off your back?"

Seamus shook his head. "No, that's not the problem. Follow me."

Glenn followed him into the back of the bar, where Seamus stopped in front of the walk-in beer cooler and opened the door. Seamus then stepped back far enough to give Glenn a clear view of what lay inside. He spotted a canvas-covered lump but still didn't understand until Seamus grabbed the cover to peel it back, exposing a pair of stiffs. Glenn quickly recognized the pale, blank faces of the two men from the hotel.

"What we need is your help to get rid of the bodies."

Beside him, Paco asked in a strangled voice. "You killed them?"

Exhibiting far more calmness than the situation called for, Margarite stepped between father and son. "No, *mijo*, I did."

Glenn closed the cooler door, cutting off the gruesome sight before he turned a scathing look on the O'Rourkes. "Does somebody here want to tell me how the hell this happened?"

"Not here. Let's go up front." Seamus led them all back to the bar. Once he had poured more drinks, he explained how the events unfolded. Glenn drank, listened, and drank some more. He asked a few questions, listened to the answers, and did a lot of cursing. Glenn ignored how that seemed to affect Margarite's Catholic sensibilities. The Irishman soon ran out of steam, and they sat there, waiting to see how Glenn would react.

Glenn finished his drink, giving a longing look at the bottle before he turned his glass upside down. "Okay. I'll do what I can. We still need to clean up all the loose ends. Where's the gun, Seamus?"

Seamus reached under the bar, pulled out a bundle wrapped in a bar towel, and set it in front of Glenn. He flipped the towel back to expose the weapon, a gray hunk of iron with a polished wood handgrip and a lanyard ring welded on the butt.

"Where did it come from?"

Releasing a heavy sigh, Seamus leaned on the bar, his face wrinkled with worry. "You might say it's a souvenir from the old days. Something I kept from when I would make my pick-ups."

Glenn hung his head while he rubbed his temples. "That means there's still a chance the serial number can be traced. Not likely, but a chance. Bring me some rags, alcohol, and all the ammo you have for it. If you have a pair of those rubber kitchen gloves, I'll have them, too. I'll clean the hell out of it, hoping I can remove every trace of the O'Rourkes. Maybe I can fix it so we can take care of a couple of other problems at the same time. Paco, bring the hearse around to the back door. I wonder if we can get their bags from their room and get rid of them, too."

Seamus shook his head. "Ray called Charlie to tell him the men were missing. He's already been around asking about them. I said they were here but left. He thinks they might have crossed the border, looking for a little excitement."

Glenn scowled. "Whorehouses or a donkey show for the tourist, seems that's all anybody ever thinks happens in Mexico. We had a hard enough time getting one body across the border, I'm not about to try it with two, especially if they're both full of bullet holes. If we got caught, the Federales would be mighty unhappy about that. I bet they wouldn't provide their best accommodations while they sorted things out."

By the time he finished cleaning the pistol, Paco came through the back, telling Glenn he had the hearse in place.

Between the three of them, they managed to wrestle the stiffs into the back of the vehicle, wedge them against the casket, and cover them with Seamus' tarp. Margarite did her best to stay out of the way but did enough worrying for all of them.

"Where are you taking them?" Seamus asked, his thin red hair lank with sweat.

"There's an arroyo west of town that's been used for a trash dump for years. I figure throwing a couple of bodies in there won't make much of a difference, except to make the rats happy."

"Aren't you afraid somebody will find them?" Seamus said.

Climbing in the passenger's side, Glenn leaned out the window. "That's what I'm counting on. Let's go, Paco, but I need to stop at my office for a minute first."

Glenn left his partner waiting in the car and ran up the stairs. He returned in less than a minute. Paco knew where the arroyo lay and headed straight there. Under a moonless sky, they unloaded the bodies, laying them out on the ground. Pulling the pistol Glenn picked up at his office, he emptied it into both bodies. They then rolled them to the edge until they fell over the side, watching their limbs windmill while they rolled down the steep slope until they vanished in the shadows. With that done, Glenn tossed both guns down after them, kissing his forty bucks goodbye. He wondered for a moment if he could add the Python to his expense list before he put it down as a bad idea.

"Why did you do that?" Paco asked, wiping the sweat from his eyes.

"Evidence. When Charlie finds the bodies—and he will—I don't want him to have any doubts about who might have done it. One of those metal stones should be enough to knock off an extra bird for me."

Glenn looked at Paco, who stared nervously into the dark pit. "You know, you did a good job down there in Mexico. Handling all the driving and getting us back across the border safe."

"Thanks."

"I really mean it. You always do a good job, kid, ever since you started working for me. I admit I had my doubts about taking on someone fresh out of high school, but so far, you've managed to pull your weight. Which makes me think we ought to take the next step, if you're up to it."

"Next step?"

"Yeah, the next step. It's your call, though. If you think you're interested and up to it."

"Up to what?"

Glenn stared at Paco. "To adding the name O'Rourke to the business. Of course, you would just be a junior partner, for now. I might not be able to change the sign right away. But you can have your own cards."

"Gosh, Glenn. Do you really mean it?"

Paco's excitement seemed to be infectious, making Glenn grin. "I know this might not seem like the best place to discuss something like that, but yeah, kid, I do. Now get in the car. We've got us a body to deliver first thing in the morning."

twenty-eight

GLENN AND PACO were both bone-weary when they pulled around behind the funeral home. They had slept over in the office, which meant that neither of them took the time to clean up or change. Still dirty after dumping the bodies, they smelled like a bad day at the trash dump. The rear doors to the Eternal Slumber Funeral Home were propped open, showing a shadowy square cavern. Glenn climbed out to ring the tradesman's bell, then leaned back against the doorframe to wait, enjoying the momentary coolness coming from the interior. The two places you could count on having an arctic setting on their thermostats, funeral homes and movie theaters—for pretty much the same reason, to keep bodies cool. Glen appreciated the respite before the oppressive humidity turned the rest of the day to shit, which in McHenry didn't take all that long despite it being only April.

The fluorescent lights came on behind him, more like flickered into life with a low, irritating buzz that made a person's teeth hurt after more than a few minutes. An apron-wearing Bob Hanover came down the short hall. Glenn always thought Bob seemed to be a funny name for a mortician. It sounded way too happy. Good-old-boy happy. Drinking-and-hunting-with-the-boys happy. Lying-about-cheating-on-his-wife-but-keeping-his-pecker-in-his-pants happy. Like old Bob didn't have the brains God gave a pissant, bless his heart, but he was nice to his mama. If it wasn't for that handing all those dead bodies thing.

"Been expecting you, Glenn. I take it you have our customer with you?"

He nodded his head in the direction of the hearse. "All ready for you to do your magic."

"How's the body?"

"Last peek I got, he looked like Humpty Dumpty from the neck up. All the king's horses and men couldn't do shit to improve the way he looks. On top of that, he spent yesterday traveling down the back roads of the Chihuahua desert in a hearse with no air conditioning. So, your guess is as good as mine, but we did what we could by packing it down with ice. Hope it was enough to keep the meat from spoiling."

"Should've, if those boys down in Mexico did a proper embalming job. That's a big maybe. But it should have been enough to keep him fairly fresh." They spent a few more minutes exchanging pleasantries, the usual about family and mutual friends, before Bob grabbed a gurney parked inside the door to push out. "Can you help me unload him?"

"Sure. Paco, get the back door."

The three of them wrestled the ostentatious Mexican casket from the back of the hearse and out onto the gurney. Bob stepped back and mopped his face, the day already turning hotter while the sun climbed higher, preparing to be another scorcher. "Damn, what did you boys do, pick the ugliest box they had there?"

"No, just the priciest. Sorry it doesn't have a drain spigot on the end. Mrs. Hamilton more than paid for it when they were trying to bleed her dry with all those bribes added to their special fees. The ugliness turned out to be just a bonus. Don't you like Michelangelo?"

Paco stayed back by the hearse while Glenn followed Bob inside. Bob wheeled the gurney into his prep area, locking down the wheels under a bank of lights that made it look like an operating room.

"DaVinci." Bob said. "I believe it was Leonardo Da Vinci who painted the *Last Supper*, but he sure as hell didn't do the one on this box. I need to get it inside so I can crack this thing open, inspect the body, see what kind of damage he's sustained, and what it'll take to fix it. You might not want to stick around."

"Thanks, we'll pass. We still have to get the vehicle back to the guy we rented it from. Then try to explain how it ended up with all that damage. After that, I'll be in my office for a while. You can pass the word to Missus Hamilton that's where she can find me."

"Will do." Bob didn't look up, already busy working on releasing the clamps that held the lid in place.

Leaving the mortuary, Glenn saw Paco had slid back into the driver's seat, his fingers beating a drum solo on the wheel. He had an eight-track tape playing that he'd managed to dig up from god knows where. An Arlo Guthrie one. He wondered why the hell somebody would be driving around in a Mexican hearse listening to Arlo Guthrie. He jumped into the shotgun seat to hear Paco singing along about some guy on a motorcycle and a pickle. "Where did you find that?"

"Would you believe I found it in the glove box, buried under a stack of gas tickets? We drove across Mexico, twice, without any damn decent music and it was in there the whole time."

"I'm glad you didn't find it. Don't know how many times I could have sat through that. I mean, it's good music, but the repetition. You had the radio. At night you could pick up some good music."

"Yeah, but during the day, all you had were a dozen stations that played nothing but Tejano or religious music. Who the hell wants to listen to that shit?"

"There's a whole country out there that likes it, maybe a country and a half. Now, if you're done whining, let's take this beast back home."

"Okay, but I don't think Carlos is going to be very happy about what we did to his car."

"We didn't do anything to it. It was those two assholes that worked for Ortega, but you would be surprised at how much forgiveness you can buy when you offer cash money."

Paco took them across the border bridge and through Nuevo Prado until they reached a small garage surrounded by a collection of half-stripped-down cars. To be honest, it wasn't much of a garage, mostly cobbled-together pieces of corrugated metal attached to a wooden frame surrounded by mesquite trees that were hard put to provide much shade for any type of mechanicking. Paco climbed out and called for Carlos.

He ambled over in grease-stained overalls, all smiles, wiping his hands on a shop rag. Until he saw his hearse.

The words spewed out fast and hot, and in incomprehensible Spanish.

Red-faced, Paco said, "You know my Spanish isn't that good."

"What the hell, Paco—what did you do to my car, man? My baby?"

"We ran into a little trouble along the way with a couple of drug dealers."

"A little trouble?" Carlos walked around the hearse. "The air conditioner is gone, the window's busted out, the back bumper is bent, and the rear door looks like someone tried to run you off the road. What the hell did you do to the driver's side headlight and fender? Looks like you tried to play chicken with a bull, man. It's going to cost a lot to get it fixed back up."

"Sorry about your car, Carlos," Glenn said.

"Who the hell are you?"

"He's my boss," Paco explained.

"So, you're the *gringo* that's going to pay for all the damages?"

"I guess you might say that. How does a hundred bucks sound?"

"It sounds like fucking shit, man. It's going to take at least three hundred, American dollars, to fix it. I'll have to repaint the whole thing." He ran his hand over the dented fender and looked about ready to break into tears. "This car belonged to my papa. It's all he left me."

Glenn struggled not to laugh, turning it into a cough. "A hundred and fifty, then."

"If I do all the work myself, I could probably do it for two-fifty."

"One seventy-five."

"Two twenty-five, and you're breaking my heart."

"Two hundred. That's only if you give us a ride back to the bridge."

"Two hundred and I call you a cab, may my papa forgive me."

"Pay the man, Paco. We could have saved a lot of time if we had settled for that upfront," Glenn said with a shake of his head. "You Chicanos sure waste a lot of time dickering over nothing."

Carlos grinned while Paco counted out the money before he passed it over. "Yeah, but where's the fun in that? You Americanos never understand that about us. It's a way to pass the time, but you tight asses are always in such a hurry. You think if you throw money at the problem, it will all work out. Hell, you people aren't even civilized enough to take *siestas* in the heat of the day, then you get upset when we don't take you seriously? Besides, you're a Chicano if you live in LA. Down here in Nuevo Prado, we're just Mexicans."

"I'll try to remember that. Now, about that cab?"

After the cab dropped them off, Glenn climbed into his own car and headed over to check on his dad. He pulled up alongside the curb in front of Burt Helka's modest ranch-style house set on the tree-lined street where the neighbors seemed to have some kind of contest to see who could keep the most immaculate lawn. It appeared to be a disease common to most white suburbanites. His dad had caught it big time. Even with his diminished mental ability, along with the physical problems caused by the accident, he never let his yard get out of hand. Glenn had tried more than once to hire someone to take care of it, but Burt wouldn't have it. He kept running them off, telling his son the day he couldn't mow his own goddamn yard, his only son could dig a hole out front to plant him. It didn't matter whether he was dead or alive.

Glenn spotted his dad in the front yard, wearing his sweat-stained, straw cowboy hat. Limping behind his old push mower, Burt was cutting the grass that had grown less than a half-inch since the last time he cut it, most likely two days ago. The flower beds were blooming, the roses had been trimmed, and the tree trunks had been painted white up to the first forks.

Moving forward, Glenn eased into the drive of twin bricked paths, pulling up a few feet from the locked garage's barn-style doors. Inside sat his dad's '65 Caddy, locked away to keep Burt from going off to look for his wife. Glenn thought he should have had the thing totaled and hauled away after the drunk driver nailed the front passenger door right where his mother, Kitty Helka, had been sitting after leaving the late Wednesday church service. She didn't need the ambulance called out to the accident. It was too late for her. But his dad did. It took ten hours of surgery to stuff his brain back into his cracked skull, the parts they didn't have to cut away. He survived, but he would never be the same Burt Helka who had played ball with his son in the front yard. Or had sung bass in the church choir.

Instead, for some reason, Glenn had decided to have the damned thing repaired until it looked like new. Then he locked it up, except for those times when he came over to start it to keep the battery charged or take it for a short drive, doing what he could to keep it from rotting away.

He climbed out to walk across the lawn and wait for his dad on his return pass. The old man saw Glenn and stopped, frowning while he struggled to remember. "I told you, I already take the paper, but I didn't get my copy last Saturday."

"Dad, it's me, Glenn."

Burt's face brightened with a smile. "Glenn. You look different. When did you get back from the war, boy? Does your mother know you're coming? Why aren't you in uniform? You ain't let all those commie war protesters get to you, have you?"

"No, Dad. I just felt like wearing civvies. Remember, Mom's gone."

"No, I'm sure I saw her earlier. She made me breakfast. I'm a really lucky man—that woman knows her way around a kitchen. But of course, you know that. You grew up eating her cooking. Let's go see if she's got a pitcher of iced tea ready. It's sure a hot one out here." He pulled a handkerchief out of his back pocket, using it to mop his face while heading for the porch. "Kitty, come on out. Our boy's come home."

The screen door opened. Instead of his mother, the round, brown face of Fatima greeted them. "The missus has a headache. She went to lay down for a while." She lied to Burt with practiced ease, playing the game to keep him from becoming upset.

"That's too bad. Maybe you should give Doc Prichard a call. Have him stop by," Burt said, not remembering the family physician had retired five years ago, only to die two years later.

"I already did. He said she should lay down until it goes away. I'm sure she'll feel better by supper time."

"She should know that Glenn is home. How long is your leave, son?

Where's Alice? Don't tell me you didn't bring your pretty, young bride along?"

"Not long, Dad. We're not together anymore. She moved back to Fort Worth to be close to her family." His belly soured when he thought about the fights, accusations, and her threats to leave. She had never been happy about his career choice. Also, there was her habit of going to all those out-of-town dives and doing the tube snake boogie with whoever bought her the most drinks. She eventually followed through with her threats three years ago, right after his momma's funeral. At first, he believed she had gone home to Fort Worth for a visit. Until the process server showed up at his door with the papers. Glenn tried to save his marriage, acting like a teenager with a bad case of rampant dick, not wanting to break up but not having much say in the situation. Alice refused his calls, and even her family wouldn't talk to him. There was no telling what kind of horror stories she told to made them believe he was some sort of abusive asshole. Glenn shook his head to discard the memories. "You said something about some iced tea?"

"Did I? That sounds like a good idea. It's a hot one out there today." Burt removed his hat and hung it on the coat rack by the door, exposing the ragged scar that crossed his head from front to back.

"I'll fetch your drinks, *Señor* Helka."

"Fine, we'll take it in the dining room. Come in where you can rest yourself, son. Did I say it was a hot one out there today?"

"Yes, you did, Dad." Glenn looked at the walls covered with family photos. A lot were of his mom and dad when they were younger. There were more than a few of him when he was growing up. Most were from his school days, back when he played sports. The one his mom had been most proud of was a boot camp picture of him in his dress blues. It was hard to remember he had once been so young and innocent.

He followed his dad to the large dining table, so big that only during holidays or special occasions were there enough people around to fill it, but those days were long gone. The china cabinet held a collection of delicate place settings from several generations. They would be his problem one day but should have gone to a sister he never had. Fatima carried a tray in with two large glasses, each with a slice of lemon dropped in. She set them on the table, then stepped back out of the way.

Burt picked his up to take big drink. His face suddenly turned ugly with anger. With a lurching swipe of his arm, he sent it all tumbling across the table, staining the white tablecloth. "What the fuck is this shit? Iced tea? Where the fuck is my whiskey? You been stealing it again, you wetback bitch? I know goddamn good and well what whiskey tastes like. This shit ain't it." Burt stood, drawing his hand back to slap Fatima.

"Dad!" Glenn yelled as he lunged to grab his father's wrist. Burt froze with a look of surprise while he stared back at his son.

"Glenn? When did you get here? Does your mother know you've made it home? Is Alice with you?"

twenty-nine

AFTER GLENN MANAGED to get Burt calmed down, Fatima fetched his medication. They both got him dosed before they helped him into bed. Once things were quieted down, Glenn left for the office. Once there, he settled in behind his desk while leaving the lights off, and pulled out his whiskey to pour himself a generous portion into a glass. He laid his head back with his eyes closed, the loosely held glass resting on his desk, as he enjoyed a moment of silence with the chance to be alone for a while. He was trying to work up the energy to take another swallow when he heard the front door open. Without bothering to look up, he yelled out. "It's Saturday. We're closed. Check with me on Monday. I might be open by then, or I might be shacked up with Raquel Welch across the border, reevaluating my life's choices."

The door shut and he assumed whoever had been there had reconsidered their intentions until he heard the soft sound of a throat clearing at his office door. Cracking one eye, he spotted Monica Hamilton standing there in her funeral togs, a dark veil covering half her face. Her eyes were red from crying until her makeup had been smeared into a panda mask.

"Raquel Welch, really?"

Glenn smiled as he made a motion for her to come in. "More like wishful thinking."

"I didn't intend to disturb you, Mister Helka, but I thought you might like to get the balance of your pay before we leave for Dallas."

Glenn sat up, opened his bottom drawer to dig out another glass. "Have a seat. You look like you could use a drink. This might not be top shelf, but it burns real good going down. Enough to help you forget your problems for a while if you drink enough."

"Thank you." Monica sat. She carefully folded back her veil before she removed her hat. She set it on the desk and picked up the glass he had poured. "I seem to have made a habit of drinking your whiskey."

He shrugged and joined her. They drank in silence, Monica trying to burn away the reawakened pain of her loss, him figuring no dame should ever drink alone, especially a high-class one from Dallas. Just doing his part to help maintain the separation between the classes.

"I saw him, Mister Helka. Darren, I mean. Mister Hanover didn't want me to, but I insisted. I had to see him one last time. I'm sure he did the best he could, but I imagine it's like trying to put a jigsaw puzzle together. He said he would have done better with more time, but I want to get my son home so his friends and the rest of the family can have a chance to pay their respects. You're not married, are you Mister Helka?" She waited for his head shake while she dug into her necessary for a handkerchief to dab her eyes, staining it black with her mascara. "It's hard enough outliving one's spouse. My darling George had been a good husband and a decent enough father. It's only too bad he didn't live long enough to see the kind of man his son grew up to be. Did you ever lose anyone close to you?"

Glenn thought of his mama, picturing her broken body after the fatal accident that changed his father forever. Then of his time in South Vietnam, about what happened at the siege of Huế during the '68 Tet offensive. Closing his eyes, Glenn could still smell the blood mingled with sweat, the way the burnt gunpowder stung your nose, still hear the screams of the wounded and dying combined with the rattle of the M-16s or the AK-47s, the earth-shaking tank cannons that never seemed to stop. They were the kind of sounds a man could never forget, no matter how hard he tried. There wasn't enough liquor in the world to drown out those memories, or those sounds. Yeah, he had lost people, a lot of people.

He jerked upright when Monica shoved the empty glass across the desk. Mentally shaking his head, Glenn added another three fingers worth. She took a big gulp. He could tell she wanted to talk. The least he could do was keep his yap shut and listen. "Losing George like we did, it was hard on both of us, but we had each other to get through it. Now? In this day, it's unnatural for a parent to outlive their children. You know what the worst thing about all this is, Mister Helka?" She closed her eyes and released a shuddering sigh. "It's all those people with good intentions. The ones that tell you it must be a part of God's great plan, or that heaven needed another angel, or that he's in a better place now. Lord help me, but I hate those people, the ones who want me to just accept it and get on with my life. It doesn't make the world a better place, just an emptier one."

"Trust me, Mrs. Hamilton. It does get better. It takes time, but it does."

"That's assuming I want it to get better, Mister Helka. Right now, I'm not sure that's true. I believe the pain helps me keep the memory of Darren alive." She set the empty glass down and opened her purse to pull out an envelope, which she slid across the desk. "That's the rest of the five thousand we agreed upon. I also included my address, so when you complete your expense report, you can send it along. I'm sure that will complete our business. I have a car waiting downstairs to take us home. I know it's a long drive, but I couldn't bear to be apart from Darren any longer. Thank you, once again."

Monica stood with her gloved hand extended. Glenn got to his feet and swallowed it with his own, giving her an encouraging squeeze.

"It was my privilege, Mrs. Hamilton. I hope you have a safe trip home, both of you. I know Darren would appreciate everything you've done for him."

"Thank you." She replaced her hat, then gently lowered her veil. She hesitated, almost as if she didn't want the conversation to end. "Would you mind escorting me down the stairs to my car?"

"My pleasure." Glenn tossed back the last finger of whiskey and circled his desk to offer Monica his arm. Linked together, he led her down the stairs until they reached the sidewalk. A large black Cadillac hearse sat idling at the curb, covered with dust from the long drive. The capped driver, blonde hair sticking out like straw, opened his door to get out. But Glenn waved him back, stepping forward to open the passenger door himself.

"I had my doubts about you. I mean hiring you to bring my son home."

Glenn laughed. "You think you're the first woman to think that? You should talk to my ex-wife sometime. She had so many doubts, she packed up and left me flat."

"Maybe she was wrong."

"Maybe, but I quit trying to second guess what a woman thinks. Given a fifty-fifty chance, I'm usually wrong ninety percent of the time."

Before climbing in, Monica spun around, flipped up her veil, and stood on tiptoe so she could plant a kiss on his grizzled cheek, a lingering touch where he could smell the whiskey on her soft breath. Blushing, she stepped into the car, then waited for him to close the door. Glenn stood back on the curb, watching as the vehicle pulled away until it vanished. Sighing, he moved toward his Ford. For now, all he wanted was a hot shower. He needed to wash away the road dust and grit that had worked its way into all his intimate places, making his life damned uncomfortable, on top of having to deal with that pair of Mick bodies to save Seamus' ass. Glenn figured a shave followed by ten hours of hard sleep wouldn't do him any harm, either.

thirty

TWO DAYS after returning from Mexico, Glenn sat behind his desk with both his Chesty and Smedley stripped down, the parts spread across an oil-stained towel while he cleaned and inspected each piece. Behind him, the radio blared out a local country station. He hummed along with a Johnny Cash song. While holding one of the barrels up, he pointed it at the window to check the bore in the bright sunlight. Satisfied, he pistoned an oil-soaked cloth attached to the cleaning rod through it while muttering off-key about a ring of fire.

He stretched out to pick up the next barrel when a hard knock echoed off his door frame. Spinning his chair around, he saw Charlie Gaines standing there, wearing a grim look. Glenn dropped the cleaning rod, grabbed a dry rag to wipe his hands, and motioned for the sheriff to come in.

"You making house calls now?"

"Where's Paloma?"

"Out fetching us some lunch, probably at the Woolworths."

"Paco?"

"He had a family to do for one of his nieces, her quinceañera. I don't expect to see him back here for a couple more days."

Charlie tossed his Stetson onto Glenn's desk before he took a seat with a weary grunt. "Good, want to talk to you alone, anyway. I just got back from paying a visit to the Department of Public Safety's crime lab. You'll never guess what I found."

Glenn spun around to turn off the radio in the middle of a Lefty Frizzell song. "Look, Charlie. I just got back from a hard trip across the border, playing nursemaid to a rich Dallas matron's dead son and dealing with a couple of Ortega's goons he sent to chase me down. I left one dying in the desert, not that I'm admitting I left one dying in the desert, while the other took off for parts unknown. I'm in no mood for playing guessing games."

Charlie ducked his head, scratched his gray kinks. "Maybe you're right. Maybe I'm just getting gun-shy in my old age. You know those East Coast boys you asked me to keep an eye on while you were gone? They just upped and disappeared a few days back. Vanished one night, leaving their luggage behind at the Paraíso."

"Do tell? Maybe they went across the border to have a little fun. Nuevo Prado is just full of places offering illegal, immoral, and downright illicit entertainment to entice the people on this side of the border. Wouldn't surprise me one bit if those boys got itchy feet. Could be they decided to wander over there for a little taste of that entertainment."

Standing, Glenn moseyed over to the refrigerator to fetch a couple of beers, passing one to Charlie. The sheriff took it with a look of gratitude and tilted his head back for a healthy swig, then smacked his lips in appreciation.

"That tastes mighty good. I considered that, too, until we got an anonymous call a couple of days ago, saying we should check out that wash on the west side of town. That's where we found the bodies, both of them plumb full of bullet holes. The rats out there didn't help matters. Those boys were gnawed on like a pup with a soup bone until there wasn't all that much left. Luckily, they still had their wallets on them with their IDs, or we would have played hell figuring out who they were. Happened to be the day after you got back."

"Owen and Patrick?"

Charlie nodded. Reaching into his shirt pocket, he pulled a slip of paper he laid out on the desk. He waited for Glenn to pick it up, to gauge his reaction. "Funny thing about those two. They were traveling across the country with this list. Notice anything peculiar about it?"

Glenn scanned the piece of paper, then stabbed it in the center with an oily finger. "You mean that they have Seamus O'Rourke's name on it?"

"Yeah, but he never mentioned he knew these men."

"Maybe he didn't. Maybe they knew him, but not the other way around."

"Could be." Charlie took the list back. "These other names here, the ones crossed out. I made some calls, talked to the local police. Seems those men are all dead, murdered. Every one of them originally from the Boston area. I found some receipts in those boy's bags that show they happened to be in those particular cities about the same time those murders took place."

Glenn leaned back in his chair and rubbed his face, thinking. "You considering they might be a couple of hitmen?"

"That's the way I figure it, but what were they doing in McHenry? Why did they have Seamus O'Rourke's name on their list? He's lived here for more than twenty years with never a lick of trouble."

"Can't say, but whatever kind of life they were leading, it seemed to have caught up with them."

"Yeah, but the bodies aren't all we found. It took some considerable digging through all the trash, but we came up with a Colt Python along with a .45 revolver. The revolver proved to be clean, couldn't even find a partial print anywhere. It's like someone went to a lot of trouble to make sure we wouldn't find anything. Thought the Python would be just as clean, but when they stripped it down, they managed to find a couple of prints on the shell casings. Turns out they matched our suspected local drug dealer, Alonzo Ortega. When we picked him up, he claimed he sold the gun to you."

"I thought you would have busted him while I was out of town for using those kids to sell his drugs."

Charlie dropped his head and scratched his scalp. "About that. We, uh, were waiting for Judge Halper to give us the warrant. Seems he wanted to think on it a bit, to make sure we had enough evidence to justify a raid."

Glenn laughed as he made a sweeping gesture that took in his desk. "Sounds like the old bastard, but what the hell would I want with a cannon like a Python? I track down bond jumpers. I only get paid if I bring them back alive so they can go to court, get convicted, and be hung all legal like. The caliber might not be all that big, but they pack a damned big load. With something like that, I might as well be Dirty Harry blowing the shit out of people just for the hell of it."

"That's what I thought." Charlie finished his beer. Rising, he grabbed his hat and headed for the door. He paused there but didn't look back. "If I find out he's right and you're using me for a patsy to take him down, I'll be on your white ass like black on a cat, friendship be damned."

"I wouldn't expect anything less."

"There is one odd thing about the situation, though."

"What's that?"

"All the prints came from Ortega's right hand."

"What's so odd about that?"

"His right hand is in a cast. Claims it has been since you broke it. I talked to the clinic. They verified they put the cast on the same day you left town. That was before the two men disappeared. Just so you know."

"He could have handled those loads at any time. The pistol could have been lying around for weeks before he used it."

"I considered that, too. That's why his ass is sitting in jail right now. One more thing before you go. Sylvia still has that friend she wants you to meet. I told her you would be over for dinner next Saturday. Bring your own damn liquor—I'll be fucked if you're going to drink all of mine."

"Charlie." Glenn's voice had a pleading edge to it.

"No arguments, now. I'm tired as hell of making excuses for you. Just do it so she'll stop nagging me about it. Then if things get screwed up between you and her friend, it's all on you. That means I'll be in the clear. If it goes good, it will keep you away from Lilly's whorehouse for a change." Charlie slapped his Stetson on while he marched for the door, closing it before he vanished down the stairs.

Glenn dropped the empty beer bottles into the trash before he sat back, wondering if Charlie would figure it out. If he did, what would he do about it?

A moment later Paloma came in, carrying a grease-stained sack she plopped on his desk. She pulled out his burger and a bag of Fritos. "I saw Charlie leaving. What did he want?"

"He said Sylvia wants me to come over next weekend to meet one of her girlfriends."

"Aw, *jefe*, that's sweet. You need somebody to take care of you."

"You don't mind?"

She arched an eyebrow with a grin. "Why would I mind? You're just my boss, and nearly old enough to be *mi papi*. Besides, I have my hands full with Miguel, so I don't need a man in my life to complicate things. Especially not a broken-down private detective. You probably have flat feet, too."

"Now that hurts." Glenn stared at her hard for a minute, but Paloma refused to budge until he cleared his throat. "Charlie also found a couple of bodies dumped in the arroyo west of here. He told me that he arrested Alonzo Ortega for the murders."

"Truly? *Gracias a Dios.*" She made the sign of the cross over her chest, circling his desk before she plopped down in his lap to plant a wet one on his cheek. "Now I won't have to worry about Miguel getting involved with his drugs. How did you do it?"

His arms snaked around her waist; she lay her head on his shoulder. "Me? Do you forget we were both down in Mexico when this happened? I think we just lucked out."

"No. Your luck is too lousy for something like this. If you didn't do it, it had to be the hand of God."

Looking through the window, he watched the flashing neon lights of O'Rourke's pub and said with a chuckle, "Might be right. But I doubt it. That old man and I haven't been on speaking terms for years."

"You're too much of a pessimist. You always expect things to go bad."

"True, but it's a pessimistic world out there."

"Says who?"

"Says Murphy."

"Who's Murphy?"

"The guy who wrote the law."

"What law?"

"You know. The one that says anything that can go wrong, will go wrong." He slapped her on the thigh, then gave her a push until she stood beside him. With his lap empty, Glenn opened the bottom drawer, removing his bottle and two glasses. Splashing a few fingers of whiskey in each, he passed one to Paloma.

Holding hers, she stared into the glass, her brow wrinkled in thought. Then she asked, "What should we drink to?"

Glenn sat silently for a couple of minutes. "Hell, I don't know. Life, love, family?" He pointed to the greasy wrapper. "Maybe Woolworths' hamburgers? Let's just drink."

acknowledgments

The old saying that it takes a village to raise an idiot is true. Well, this idiot had more villagers helping me get to this point than I can count. First in line is my lovely bride, Rosemary Gouger, who allowed me to lock myself away like a troll terrified of the sun so I could tell lies all day while she occasionally slid a tray of food under the door to keep me going.

Second is the Dallas Fort Worth Writer's Workshop, a like-minded collection of sun-fearing trolls who found me wandering in the wilderness and took me in. A group who nurtured and taught me, before allowing me to be unleashed on an unwary world. They listened to my weekly reads, then would come the critiques without mercy, until the tears and blood would flow. I'm looking at you, A. Lee Martinez. I also have to give thanks to Brooke Fossey, carpooler without peer, for the many discussions on writing we've had over the years while driving to and from the workshop.

Third is the Wednesday night pancake posse at IHOP, where we would sit and solve the world's problems. It was there the germ of an idea that would become *Mexicanos Hustle* was hatched, with the help of Brian Tracey and Daryle McGinnis. I have to thank the Beta readers, Larry Enmon, Brian Tracey, John Bartell, and Leslie Lutz. Anyone I failed to mention, I apologize, the fault lies with me.

Lastly, I think, I want to thank Fawkes Press and Jodi Thompson for taking a chance on me. I never understood those writers who would thank their editors until I was given the chance to work with the marvelous TwylaBeth Lambert, and I cannot say enough nice things about her. Her guidance and patience got *Mexicanos Hustle* across the goal line to where it is today.

If you enjoyed this book, please do one or more of the following:

- Leave a review on your favorite book review site
- Tell a friend about *Mexicanos Hustle*
- Ask your local library to put J Benjamin Sanders Jr's work on the shelf
- Recommend Fawkes Press books to your local bookstore

Visit us online

www.FawkesPress.com

www.ingramcontent.com/pod-product-compliance
Lightning Source LLC
Chambersburg PA
CBHW020751190726
48285CB00006B/1981